WEB OF TRUTH

By Amy DuBoff

To Connor
Amy DuBoff

WEB OF TRUTH
Copyright © 2016 Amy DuBoff

This is a work of fiction. Names, characters, organizations, places,
events, and incidents are either the products of the author's imagination
or are used fictitiously. Any resemblance to actual persons, living or
dead, business establishments, events or locales is entirely coincidental.

Published by BDL Press
Editor: Nicholas Bubb
Cover Illustration: Tom Edwards

ISBN: 0692648410
ISBN-13: 978-0692648414

0 9 8 7 6 5 4 3 2 1

Produced in the United States of America

To Annie,
for her encouragement and guidance

CONTENTS

PART 1: DISCOVERY

‹ CHAPTER 1 ›

Wil put the prototype IT-1 jet through its paces—each movement a natural extension of himself. The neural interface bonding him telepathically to the ship made each command effortless and instantaneous as he navigated the ship through the obstacle course in open space. But, combat maneuvers were only the beginning. The interface with the new independent rift drive was the real test.

"Everything checks out. I'm going to jump," Wil informed the observers over the comm embedded in his flight suit.

"Nothing too fancy," cautioned Deena Laecy, the Chief Engineer on the project.

Wil grinned. "You know I have to do everything with style."

He swung the jet around to face the obstacle course he had just traversed. It was the primary training ground for new recruits to the Jotun division of the TSS inside the rift, simulating battle conditions with the Bakzen. Set against an eerie backdrop of the echoed starscape in the rift, the obstacle course was the only solid form from Wil's current vantage. Remote controlled decoy jets stood in for enemy crafts, and electronic mines could mimic the effects of an assault without causing permanent damage. If the new independent rift drive functioned as planned, Wil would be able to bypass all of the obstacles and hit his mark.

With one last check of the system readings on the heads up

display, Wil cleared his mind in preparation for the jump. He eyed his destination at the center of the course and pictured approaching it from the right, just within his cone of fire before darting out of range.

As the action solidified in his consciousness, a subtle vibration spread throughout the jet. Space distorted as an iridescent subspace bubble formed around the craft.

A pulse of blue light flashed across Wil's vision, an indication through the neural link in his nav console that a jump point was locked in. With a low rumble, the jet initiated the jump.

The blue-green hue consumed the ship in one gulping wave. Time seemed to stand still as the jet slipped between subspace and reality.

The jet emerged from subspace with fluid forward momentum, taking Wil directly toward his target. He quickly reoriented and fired at the sensor. It lit up red; a clean hit.

And now for the second part of the test. Wil envisioned the point of his departure jump. Except, rather than a simple forward trajectory from his current location, he pictured an exact return to the original jump point—a one-hundred-eighty degree reorientation from his present position.

The blue indicator light pulsed in his vision to confirm, then the jet initiated the return jump.

A blue-green subspace cloud consumed the jet again. Wil barely had time to blink before the surreal view of echoed stars once again filled the windows. He looked ahead at the obstacle course. He was right where he started.

Cheers erupted in Wil's ear as the crew observing the test flight celebrated back at the nearby TSS Headquarters—H2— within the dimensional rift. Wil had visited with them on several occasions since he'd graduated to Agent three years prior, but this was by far the most exciting trip. All of their work on applying his model for the independent jump drive was finally paying off.

He grinned. "All right! Now we're in business."

"Do you want to try a dimensional jump?" Laecy asked.

"That's the next step." Wil scanned over the system status readouts. Everything was within optimal performance ranges. "I'll try it."

Wil once again cleared his mind to picture his destination point, but this time he felt his way through the dimensional fabric, reading the energy signatures for normal space outside of the rift. Years of practice had attuned his senses to differentiate between the planes. Extending himself to read the electromagnetic composition of the surrounding space was second nature.

With a calming breath, he identified a fixed point in normal space corresponding to the middle of the obstacle course within the center of the rift. If the jump drive worked properly, he would be able to instantaneously pass through subspace and arrive in normal space in a different relative physical location than where he started.

A blue light flashed in Wil's vision and the jet rumbled as it initiated the jump. For an instant, the view changed to the ethereal shifting blue-green of subspace, and then solid stars came into focus in the distance. He had made it to normal space.

Wil smiled. "Everything looks good," he said over the comm. "I'm coming back."

"See you soon," Laecy acknowledged.

Wil envisioned his destination at the center of the obstacle course inside the rift, next to the central target he struck on the first test run. The jet confirmed the destination with a blue flash and initiated the jump. The blue-green swirling light enveloped the craft.

As soon as the jet passed fully into subspace, a red warning flashed across Wil's vision. The nav system was unable to confirm a lock to complete the jump.

Shite! He tried to reinitiate the command. Another red flash. The jet shuddered as it was pulled helplessly through subspace. There were only moments to act before he'd be swept away.

Fok, I have to get out of here! Wil felt around himself, extending his consciousness to identify his position within the dimensional planes.

Normal space was only a vague place barely within his grasp, but the extra energetic charge of the rift called to him. He latched onto it with his consciousness and extended a subspace distortion around his body. He'd be safe in the flight suit, so long as he didn't exit subspace directly into an obstacle on the test course. There was no other choice. He began to slip between the planes, but— *The jet.* He couldn't leave it in subspace. If the Bakzen found it…

Wil panicked, his breath ragged and heart racing. He couldn't give up. Saera was waiting for him back home, the TSS was counting on him, Tararia was counting on him.

He refocused on generating a spatial distortion around himself, extending it beyond his body to encompass the entire jet. Nerves clouded his mind at first, but his fear soon grew into a sense of control. The jet was enveloped in a soft glow. Keeping the forms in his mind, he pulled himself and the craft toward the rift.

As he pierced the shroud of subspace, the physical objects within the rift began to take form. Wil quickly scanned for an open area, unsure how long he'd be able to hold the jet in the suspended state. He strained to make the necessary adjustments—avoiding a simulated mine directly in his path. Once clear of the hazard, he brought the jet back fully from subspace into the rift with a shudder.

The blue-green cloud lifted and all was still.

"Beautiful!" Laecy exclaimed over the comm.

Wil took an unsteady breath, his heart pounding in his ears.

I did it… He shook his head and swallowed. *Anyone else would have been trapped.* "I'm coming in."

"Is everything okay?"

"We'll talk inside." Still shaking, Wil directed the jet toward H2.

The massive space station was a bright spec in the distance. As he neared, the structure of tapered rings and surrounding space docks took shape. It was no more elaborate than his home Headquarters inside Earth's moon, but it was impressive to be able to observe such a structure as a whole. However, it was engineered for war, and seeing it was a reminder of why it had been constructed.

His stomach knotted. *They were counting on the IT-1 jets being brought into battle next month. Can they take another setback?*

Wil directed the jet toward the bottom level of H2. It glided through the nearly invisible force field across the entryway to the hangar. With a gentle bump, the craft came to rest on the floor.

Wil powered down the engine and released the top hatch as half a dozen crew members ran up to secure the jet. He released the helmet on his flight suit, savoring the rush of cool air. His pulse began to normalize.

"What happened?" Laecy called out as she approached with the other crew members.

Wil climbed out of the cockpit and made his way down the wing. "The guidance system glitched on the calculation for the return jump."

Laecy frowned. "Everything looked fine from our end. The jump was right on target."

"That wasn't the jet."

The engineer's jaw dropped. "You mean, *you* made the jump?"

The other crew members stiffened up with surprise and confusion, but remained silent.

They didn't know anyone other than the Bakzen could do that. "It was that or get stuck in subspace." Wil looked over the jet that had almost been a deathtrap. "Admittedly, it was my first time trying it with anything this large. I wasn't sure I could do it." *And far more dangerous than my previous tests in a spacesuit with an escort ship.*

"Well shite…" Laecy breathed.

"I don't want anyone else in one of the IT-1s until we address the guidance system."

The engineer scowled. "Taelis isn't going to be happy."

When is he ever? "It's too dangerous. Losing Agents on a training run is way worse than another production delay."

Laecy let out a slow breath. "Well, what do we do about the guidance system?"

"I think we need to add a secondary processor to reconcile the moving objects around the destination point. The drive can identify the relative jump points across the plains, but I underestimated the demands of navigating through a battle zone."

"Two ateron cores in each jet? Are you crazy?"

Wil looked down. "I don't see another way to make the system reliable enough."

"Well fok! We can barely get enough cores for the test fleet. How are we supposed to double the number?"

The crew glanced between Wil and Laecy, clearly uncomfortable with the exchange.

"I don't know yet, but I'll figure something out," Wil told her, keeping his voice low and calm.

Laecy groaned. "Can we never get a break?"

"It's a setback, not a dead end." Wil gestured Laecy toward the nearest engineering lab room divided from the open hangar area. She followed him away from the other crew members with a huff.

Once inside the lab, Wil set his helmet on a table. He turned to face Laecy and telekinetically closed all the doors in a single pass.

The engineer jumped with surprise as the door closed behind her.

Wil stared her in the eye. "You can't talk like that around them."

"Oh, they're used to my outbursts—"

"Maybe so, but I can't afford to have them doubt me. This drive was my design, and if it doesn't work yet, they need to be confident that it still will. Jumping to a 'we're doomed' attitude will only lead to dissent."

Laecy squirmed under Wil's intense gaze. "I hadn't looked at it that way, sir. It won't happen again."

Wil leaned against the edge of the table. "You know you never have to be formal with me like that. I didn't mean to lecture."

The engineer relaxed, but her scowl remained.

Wil examined her. "You can't be the only one to have expressed doubts."

"I don't doubt you," Laecy insisted.

"Well, I don't fault you for it," Wil said. "I haven't exactly delivered on everyone's expectations." *I still hope I can.*

Laecy set her jaw. "We do believe in you."

"So morale is completely fine. Really?" Wil asked the engineer.

She nodded. "Yeah, everything's—"

"I don't buy it," Wil cut in.

Laecy looked at the floor then back up at Wil. "Okay, yes. It's been tough," she admitted at last.

Wil ran his hand through his short chestnut hair with his gloved hand. "I wish I could give you all the solutions we need right now. But it's a process."

"I know that."

"But what can I do in the meantime? I don't want them losing faith in me."

"They won't, Wil." She shook her head. "What we're feeling now—it's not doubt in you. It's just that we've been at this for way too long. We're all tired."

Wil nodded. *I can't even imagine what this is like for them. It's been five years since I learned about the war and I'm already burned out. After a whole career...* "Soon. Only a few more years and it'll be over."

"That doesn't seem possible. The war has become a way of life."

"Once you retire, you'll forget all about it," Wil said, trying to assure her with a lighthearted smile.

"On Militia pension? Shite..."

Wil wasn't sure if she was joking or not. "Don't worry about that. I'll see to it everyone is rewarded for their years of sacrifice."

"Oh, it's not about money, Wil." Laecy tugged on the end of her braided light brown hair. "This bomaxed war has messed with our heads. When you've lived in fear for long enough, I don't think you ever can feel secure again."

I can relate to that. "Well, we'll deal with that when the time comes." He looked out the window in the broad, sliding door to the lab. The crew was busy running diagnostics on the jet. "In the meantime, I need to know if morale gets too low."

Laecy shrugged. "I don't have a very broad perspective."

"You interact with the crew. That's way more valuable than whatever filtered answer I'd get from the officers."

"You don't trust Command to be straight with you?"

Considering the High Commanders communicate directly with the Priesthood, I can't fully trust either of them—not even Banks. "I always like to have more than one viewpoint."

"Okay," Laecy acquiesced. "I'll let you know if I hear anything beyond the usual gripes."

"I appreciate it, thank you."

"Now, don't you have a meeting with Taelis?"

Wil frowned, recalling the appointment. "Yes, and he's no doubt heard by now that the test flight was cut short and is probably waiting for me to explain." He took off the gloves to the flight suit and started releasing the other seals.

"Good luck telling him you want two ateron cores per jet."

"Yeah…" Wil shed the flight suit and folded it up on the table. He took a deep breath and turned to Lacey. "We'll figure it out."

She nodded. "Yes we will."

Wil said his goodbyes to the crew on his way to the central elevator, hoping to set them at ease. They gave him wary smiles on his way out of the hangar, but he had become used to being regarded with caution long before. It was impossible to have such abilities and not stand out.

He took a few minutes to gather his thoughts on the ride up to High Commander Taelis' office. Aside from a general check-in and update on the most recent application of the independent jump drive in the IT-1 jets, there hadn't been any specific talking points for the discussion. However, the failed test flight would undoubtedly become the main topic.

Wil arrived at the upper level of H2 after several minutes. He made his way around the curved, windowless hall to the High Commander's office, inclining his head to the Agents he passed going about their duties. Militia guards stationed outside the door saluted to Wil as he approached, and one of the guards hit a buzzer next to the door. A moment later, the guard opened the door and gestured for Wil to step through.

Inside, High Commander Taelis was examining a holographic map projected above his desktop. A single window along the back wall looked out over one of the expansive space docks surrounding H2, though it presently berthed only a handful of ships since so much of the fleet was deployed in the combat zones along the outskirts of the rift.

Taelis looked up from the map as Wil entered. "That was a

short flight."

"The IT-1s aren't ready to roll out yet," Wil replied, keeping with Taelis' style to forgo pleasantries. "The current guidance system can't account for other ships and variable hazards."

The High Commander scoffed. "So it's useless."

"No, it just needs some refining."

"And how long is that going to take?"

As long as it takes to make it safe. "I don't know."

Taelis scoffed and shook his head. "We need the IT-1s."

"Well, they're not ready," Wil maintained.

"You see this?" Taelis pointed to the map above his desktop. Red points surrounded several larger blue objects scattered throughout the field. "The Bakzen have us pinned down. How are we supposed to make any headway without the ability to make precision strikes?"

Wil eyed him. "Do you want a genuine answer? Because you've repeatedly requested that I stay out of command decisions for now."

Taelis shook his head. "That's because you aren't prepared yet."

Wil held in an exasperated sigh. "Then I'm not sure what you want from me."

Taelis minimized the holographic map with an irritated swipe of his hand. "What, exactly, have you been doing for the last three years since you graduated?"

"Aside from redesigning your whole fleet?"

"If that's been your only endeavor, where has it gotten us?" the High Commander countered. "I think you have unnecessary distractions."

He's undoubtedly referring to Saera. Shows how little he knows about me. "Well, now you actually have warships that can jump into Bakzen space, for one."

Taelis shook his head. "You've been wasting time on schematics when you should have been training a set of officers."

Wil crossed his arms. "What good are new officers if they have no fleet to command?"

"The fleet can be constructed in short order. But I've been at this for long enough to know that trust is built over time. You need your own people in the key positions to maximize the effectiveness of your command."

"Trust? I wasn't the one lying to trainees for years. At least now they're mentally prepared before being pulled into the Jotun division."

The High Commander scowled. "So you're just as impulsive as always—exactly why you aren't ready to step into a true command position yet."

If I had my way, the disclosure wouldn't be limited to just within the TSS. How the Priesthood was able to keep it contained is still astounding. "I'm only doing what's necessary to rally support."

"Support will come from your officers."

"And where am I supposed to find those officers?"

"Banks has a list of candidates prepared for you," Taelis said.

Wil faltered. *He does?* "So why are you the one telling me now?"

"Because he's foolishly insisted on leaving you alone to work on design specs for a fleet. Since even that sole focus wasn't enough to make the designs work, it's time to reprioritize."

I work around the clock to practically rewrite the accepted laws of space travel, and it's still not enough to satisfy him. "That kind of thinking isn't going to get you the IT-1s any faster."

"Let Laecy deal with that."

"While she's perfectly capable of making the engineering revisions, I don't think she has remotely the right connections to double the TSS' access to ateron cores."

The High Commander's eyes narrowed behind his tinted glasses. "What for?"

"To make any of this new tech work properly! You claim I've been wasting my time, but I'd like to see you make any of this function. Most of what I've been doing is just sourcing materials for construction. All of the resources are tapped out. I've had to go through three or more design iterations on most of the processing components in every new ship design just to accommodate alternate materials since production can't keep up with the demand for the standard parts. The IT-1 prototype might not be perfect, but at least it exists."

Taelis took in Wil's words before replying, "One of the most important traits of leadership is effective delegation. Pick your officers. The rest will follow."

Oh... So this isn't about any one issue. He doesn't want to me to get caught up in the details and lose sight of the bigger picture. Realizing what Taelis was doing, Wil let down his defense. "I may not have overseen battles like you, but I know what's at stake."

The High Commander nodded, giving the hint of a smile. "Good. So you know why I have to be tough on you."

"Yes, sir."

Taelis took a deep breath. "Given the current circumstances, I think perhaps it's best you focus on the rest of your preparations back home."

Wil was caught off-guard. "No longer visit here, you mean?"

"I had hoped for you to become comfortable at H2, but I think maybe it's more valuable for you to be able to step in with fresh eyes when the time comes," Taelis explained. "I'm confident that the relationships you've forged so far with my officers will carry through until then."

It was possible the change was a demotion, but Wil couldn't help but feel relieved. "If you think that's best."

"I do."

Wil nodded. *At least I'll have Laecy keeping a lookout for me.* "All right. I guess I'll see you in a few years, then."

"Take care. We'll be waiting for you."

‹ CHAPTER 2 ›

There are so many strong candidates. How do I choose?

Wil had spent the last several days since he had returned home from H2 scanning through thousands of prospective Trainee files. He needed to find twenty men to train as his officers under the Primus Elite designation—while there were plenty of qualified women like Saera, he couldn't risk potential complications in the interpersonal dynamics from a mixed group.

The decision of who to choose was all too daunting. The men needed to be bright and strong, but also ready to take direction. It was a delicate balance, and tough to find. He had narrowed the applications down to fifty candidates, but each cut was more difficult than the last.

"How's it going?" Saera gave Wil a hug from behind as he sat at the desk in his Agent quarters.

"Making some progress, finally," Wil replied.

Saera adjusted her newly acquired tinted glasses. She had just completed her fourth year of training with the TSS and had remained at the top of her class even after moving up to Junior Agent. Any doubts about Wil's recommendation to have her follow the Primus Command track had been long forgotten. "Do you have a short list?"

Wil sighed. "More or less. The problem is, they've given me so many good options. Banks told me they intentionally held back a few prospective Trainees from previous application cycles so I'd have my pick of the best candidates from the last few years. The biggest challenge is figuring out the right distribution of skills—I need to make it a diverse group."

Saera rubbed his shoulders. "Well, come on. I grabbed us some dinner from the mess hall. Why don't you take a break?"

"All right, thanks." Wil rose from the desk and joined Saera at the dining table in the living area.

Saera had a well portioned plate of food waiting on the table for each of them.

Wil immediately dug in. "Thank you," he said after a few mouthfuls. "I didn't even realize how late it'd gotten."

"That's why you have me to look after you," Saera replied with a smirk.

I don't know what I'd do without her. Wil ate a few more bites. "So, you have a short leave coming up."

Saera lit up. "Yes, I do! Finally."

Wil took a breath. "I thought it might be a good time to take you to Tararia."

The proposition seemed to catch Saera by surprise. She looked at Wil warily. "Why now?"

"As my intended, you need to be properly presented to Tararian high society. It's an important part of the Advancement Act."

Saera looked down at her half-eaten dinner. "I thought it didn't matter if I was formally accepted under the Act?"

"It doesn't to me, but it would protect you in the event anything happened to me." *She's given me reason to live through what lies ahead, but there are no guarantees.*

Saera nodded. "Of course I'll go with you, if that's what you want."

Wil bent his head down to catch her eye. "Oh come on, you're not even a little excited?" He gave her a wry grin.

His playful response had the intended effect. Saera cracked a smile and straightened in her chair. "Okay, maybe a little," she admitted. "It's just… intimidating, I guess. I adore your parents, but they've made it sound like the rest of their families are different."

"They aren't nearly as bad as my dad has made them out to be," Wil assured her. "I really would love for you to go with me."

Saera relaxed. "I'm happy to."

"Excellent." *Besides, I have other reasons of my own.*

Saera gathered herself. "Now, can I help you out at all with the application reviews?"

Wil smiled. "Yes, that would be great. I could really use a fresh perspective."

They finished eating and then went back to Wil's work desk. He pulled up the files for his top fifty candidates and spread them out on the holographic display with their name, age, estimated telekinetic potential, and primary aptitudes displayed in front of each picture.

Saera scanned over the group. "I can see why this is so difficult for you. I don't see anyone here with an estimated CR potential below an 8."

Wil sighed. "And I know that telekinetic strength is just one part of the necessary skills, but it's critical for so many things. I keep running through the scenarios for how I'll need to use this team, and I keep coming back to precision strikes. I'll need several pilots with the intelligence to quickly calculate inter-dimensional jumps in their heads, but who also have the telekinetic ability to be one with their craft and maneuver through seemingly impossible scenarios."

"So you're looking for people just like you?" She cocked her head.

I guess I am. "That's my problem, isn't it?"

"You will never find others with your level of ability," Saera reminded him. "The potential of some of these guys is astounding by most measures, but anyone will pale in comparison to you. However, even if others aren't gifted in as many areas, you can still find individuals with specific areas of exceptional brilliance."

Wil thought for a moment. "So, I should look at it in terms of teams."

Saera nodded. "That's certainly one approach. Several specialists can accomplish a lot when grouped together."

"Okay, let's see." Wil began sorting people on the display. "I need Pilots, Commanders and a handful of Seconds. The pilots need to be capable navigators—I don't see a way around that. I can't tie up resources by relying on a tandem craft with a pilot and navigator for each."

"That's reasonable," Saera said. "Look, these five here have CR potential marks around 8.5 for telekinesis and also have the highest marks for piloting aptitude." She tapped on the pictures and slid them over into a group at the side of the display.

"Yes, I've been eyeing those five for a while now." *At least some of the selections are easy.*

"But that's still following the same basic approach. I think you need to take a bigger step back," Saera urged. "When it comes down to it, couldn't any one of these men do any of those functions if you trained them?"

"Yes, I suppose they could."

"You're so caught up on strengths and aptitudes that you're not thinking about who you want to work with. You're going to be with these guys almost constantly for years—you'll be family. Maybe you should be paying more attention to personality?"

She's absolutely right. "People who I can trust. Friends."

Saera nodded.

"But that's so difficult to quantify."

"So don't quantify it directly," she said. "What specific traits do you find most difficult to work with? You have the complete psychological profiles for every candidate at your disposal."

Wil thought for a moment. "Arrogance. It leads to

boastfulness and unhealthy competition."

"I totally agree. So let's screen out anyone with narcissistic tendencies." Saera made the adjustment on the computer. Twelve pictures dropped off the list. "What else?"

"I can't have anyone with a short temper," Wil continued. "I need people who are calm and collected under pressure."

"Okay, screening out anyone with a volatile temperament," Saera said as she made the adjustments. Another seven pictures faded from the display. "Any other deal-breakers?"

I can't have anyone who'll second-guess what needs to be done. "Compassion. I hate to say it, but I can't have anyone who would hesitate about taking a life if it came to it."

Saera swallowed. "You're right. But it can't be too far to the other end, either." She adjusted several attributes on the computer to filter for individuals who fell into the middle ranges of the scales. Six more pictures were removed. "That leaves you with twenty-five."

Wil looked them over. "Just five more to go." He felt some relief at getting the list down to a manageable number, but then apprehension about making a poor final selection started to set in.

"Now, what do you absolutely *need* in everyone?" Saera asked him.

He took several seconds to reflect. "They need to be inquisitive. They need to trust me, but also be willing to challenge me when necessary," he responded at last.

Saera looked pensive. "Hmm, I guess that comes down to high openness and mid-range agreeableness." She made some adjustments. Four more pictures faded from the display.

Wil's heart sank. "How do I pick who gets cut now?" *And what if I make the wrong choice?*

"I think it's more a matter of who you want on your team," Saera replied. "Whoever is last-picked just wasn't meant to be."

"Well, those five prospective pilots made all the cuts, so

they're definitely in." Wil moved them to the top of the screen. He studied the remaining sixteen faces. *Who among you will be my greatest friends?*

"And you should probably keep these ten with the highest CR potential." Saera paused. "Wait…" She was caught by one of the faces on the display. Her brow wrinkled as she wracked her memory. Then, there was a spark of recognition in her eyes.

"What is it?" Wil asked.

"I know him," Saera said with bewilderment, pointing at one of the candidates.

"Michael Andres?" Wil read his name aloud. He was 18-years-old, had medium-brown hair and light blue eyes, and his aptitude scores and CR potential were all unusually high. *One of my top picks.*

"Yes. Wow, that really is him. Crazy."

"Who is he?"

Saera shook her head with disbelief. "Remember, years ago, when I told you that there was only one guy in school who was ever genuinely good to me? Well, that's him."

Wil let the statement settle for a moment. *Never mind being a top pick!* "Well, there's our final cut."

Saera laughed. "No, quite the opposite."

"Pardon?" *She can't be okay with this. I'm certainly not.*

Saera took Wil's hand. "Michael is brilliant, kind, and loyal. He's the sort of guy who could be your second in command and you would never have to worry."

Wil was skeptical. "That wouldn't be weird for you?" *It's weird for me.*

"No, that was so long ago," Saera said with a dismissive flip of her wrist. "He may be a part of my past, but you're my future." Her gaze showed nothing by adoration for Wil.

Can I really turn away someone with so much potential because of a fling from years ago? Wil took a deep breath. *I trust her opinion more than anything. If she says he's a good choice, then he must be.* "Okay." Wil placed Michael at the top of his list.

Saera looked him in the eye. "He's the sort of person you need. I know it."

Wil nodded, hoping she was right.

"It's kind of crazy, though. Finding anyone with telekinetic ability on Earth is rare, let alone two in the same neighborhood."

"Too rare for coincidence," Wil agreed. He brought up Michael's detailed file and scanned through it. "Oh, right. That's why I flagged him. His father was an Agent."

Saera's jaw dropped. "No way!"

"Retired about twenty years ago and decided to settle down on Earth."

She thought it over. "Mr. Andres… Huh. Come to think of it, I guess there was always something about him that seemed unusual."

"People with abilities do tend to be drawn to each other, but ending up in the same neighborhood is still…" *Nothing is mere coincidence in my life.*

"Well, we need all the friends we can get, right?"

"That's true." *But sometimes it's difficult to tell who are the right friends.*

Saera returned her focus to the display. "There's still the matter of the final cut."

Wil let out a slow breath. "Yes."

"These six are the lowest on most measures," Saera stated. "That is, if you can call a CR potential of 8.3 'low.'"

Wil zoomed in on the six files on the holographic display, seeking any differentiating traits. He brought up the details and noticed that one of the men was raised on a freighter, but all of the others were from planets or moon colonies. "Him. He's the last cut. I need men who have a sense of home—something tangible to fight for." He removed the final candidate and arranged the twenty remaining profiles on the display.

"So there's your twenty."

Wil looked them over. "It's a good group. I hope they're up for the challenge."

Banks read over the report from Taelis. "These delays to the IT-1s put the entire production schedule in jeopardy." He eyed the other High Commander through the viewscreen.

"I know." Taelis sighed. "It's not something we'll be able to overcome in a timely manner.

At this rate, we'll never have the fleet ready in time. I don't want to know how Wil would react if he found out about the true extent of this deficit. "We need to do something."

"Clearly." Taelis looked down. "You know I wouldn't normally ask it, but I need your help. See if there are any strings you can pull to get additional capacity at any of the shipyards in your jurisdiction."

"Our TSS shipyards are already working overtime, same as yours."

Taelis looked pensive. "Civilian?"

We may not have another choice. "I'll look into it."

Wil entered Banks' office to find his father already waiting in one of the guest chairs.

"You wanted to see me?" Wil asked.

"Yes," Banks replied. "Have a seat."

Wil sat down in the chair next to Cris.

"I hear you're planning a trip to Tararia," Banks stated once Wil was settled.

"Yes. It's past time I took Saera. This is the first leave she's had that's long enough." *Plus, we need a vacation.*

"Yes of course." Banks pursed his lips in thought.

"I assume it would be okay if Kate and I accompanied them,"

Cris added.

Banks nodded. "I figured that would be the case." He steepled his fingers. "In fact, I was counting on it. I was hoping you could conduct some business on behalf of the TSS while you're there."

"What kind of business?" Cris asked.

"I've been talking with Taelis, and it's become clear that the TSS shipyards are no longer able to keep up with production demands, especially not with the recent delays to the IT-1s. We need additional capacity," Banks explained.

I was afraid that might happen. It's obvious where he's going with this. "So you want us to strike a deal with SiNavTech?" Wil asked.

Banks smirked. "I was going to ease into it a little more slowly than that, but yes."

Cris shook his head. "I'm not sure that's a good idea. We've always been intentional about keeping the military and civilian vessel manufacturing separate, especially if the Priesthood insists on knowledge of the war staying within the TSS."

"Yes," Banks replied. "But, I'm asking now because I have recently learned of a shipyard near Prisaris that has been shut down. My hope is that we can acquire the facility for our exclusive use."

"Prisaris… That's one of the outer colonies near Bakzen Territory, isn't it?" Wil asked. *It makes strategic sense. We could construct a rift gate and easily get the new ships to H2.*

"Precisely," Banks confirmed. "So you understand my rationale."

Cris took a deep breath. "I don't know if they'll go for it, but we can try."

‹ CHAPTER 3 ›

Saera stared with wonder out the window of the shuttle. The landscape of Tararia below was lush and mature, carefully preserved through stewardship and technology. Vibrant green trees and a rainbow of decorative foliage stood out between historical structures and along grand parkways dotting the developed land. Her home back on Earth seemed tainted and abused by comparison.

The shuttle descended at a shallow angle over a vast lake and passed the sprawling city of Sieten on the way to the Sietinen estate atop a terraced hill. Ornate stone buildings filled the city, with a unique mixture of old-world charm and modern elegance that contrasted against architectural accents of gleaming glass and metal.

A white stone wall five meters tall surrounded the enormous Sietinen estate, and within its confines the gardens bloomed across the full spectrum, arranged to create dazzling geometric patterns. Beds with exotic flowers lined white stone pathways, and vast lawns of luxurious grass surrounded the main mansion and annex buildings. Behind the estate, an evergreen forest rose up the hill and stretched into the mountain range beyond. The mansion itself was constructed of the same gleaming white stone as the perimeter wall and pathways through the gardens. Expansive windows overlooked the grounds, tinted for privacy and to minimize the sun's afternoon glare. Terraces and balconies protruded from each of the mansion's three levels, adorned by potted plants in bright colors that stood out against the white facade.

The shuttle set down on a paved port at the southern end of the estate grounds. Saera's chest tightened as the shuttle depressurized and the main door opened. She looked over at Wil, who had been calmly staring out the window on the other side of the aisle as they made their approach.

Seeing her apprehension, he gave her a reassuring smile. "Come on."

Taking Wil's hand, Saera felt calmed by his presence but the knot in her chest persisted. She followed him out the side door. *Relax. There's no reason to be nervous. You're just meeting the extended family.*

Saera descended the steps from the shuttle, immediately struck by the freshness of the air. She squinted behind her tinted glasses in the afternoon sunlight; after so many years in space, it was an assault on her senses. As her eyes adjusted, she saw a man and a woman approaching, accompanied by several people in dark gray a few paces back. After a moment, she realized that it was Cris and Kate coming to meet them.

"Welcome!" Cris greeted once they were within acceptable range.

Saera and Wil returned the pleasantries.

Though she'd had plenty of dinners with Wil and his parents, it was strange to see Cris and Kate outside the context of TSS Headquarters. They both wore their tinted glasses in the bright sun, but otherwise their identity as Agents was muted. Cris wore only the black t-shirt and pants from his most casual Agent uniform, and Kate had donned a flowing light blue dress that suited her so perfectly it would make anyone question her position within the TSS. While Kate seemed completely at home, Cris had a tightness in his lips that suggested an inner tension.

"Did you have a smooth trip?" Kate asked.

"Yes, uneventful," Wil answered. "Sorry we were delayed getting out of Headquarters, but it looks like you've taken the extra time to get settled in." He looked around the nearly empty port. "Not that I mind, but I'm surprised there isn't more of a welcoming committee."

Cris let out an aggravated grunt and shook his head.

Kate collected herself. "It was decided to have our family reunion be a more formal affair."

"What your mother is trying to say is that my father is making our lives difficult, as usual," Cris interjected with more than a touch of bitterness in his tone.

Oh dear. Saera looked to Wil for help. "Should I not be here?"

"Of course you should be here," Wil insisted.

"They're just honoring tradition," Kate assured.

Cris looked like he had more to say on the matter, but he kept it to himself. He turned and led the way along the main path toward the mansion.

The path was wide enough for the four of them to comfortably walk abreast—Cris to the outside right, Wil to the left, with their partners next to them in the middle.

"What does this formal meeting entail?" Saera asked as they walked.

"We'll have dinner with my parents tonight," Cris informed her. "And then there's supposed to be some sort of reception with delegates from the other Dynasties tomorrow night."

"A reception?" Wil muttered with a hint of disdain.

"It should be relatively painless. I'll instruct you on everything you need to know for tonight," Kate told Saera.

"Thank you." *This trip is already taking on a life of its own. I was worried this would happen.*

A light breeze caught a strand of Kate's hair, and she tucked it back behind her ear with her left hand. The light caught a ring on her finger, sending a fractured rainbow in a flash across her face.

Saera had never seen Kate wear the distinctive ring before; it had a large round center stone that resembled a diamond and several smaller stones set into the band amid delicate swirls in the white metal.

When Kate lowered her hand, she noticed that Saera was admiring her accessory. "I don't get to break this out of the vault too often," she said with a smile.

"It's beautiful," Saera breathed.

"He did pretty well with the design." Kate flashed a knowing smile at Cris. "It's made from a Starstone. There are only ten such gem veins known anywhere in the galaxy. The High Dynasties each have claim to one. Only enough material for one set of wedding rings is produced by each vein every generation." She took Cris' left hand and held their rings close together. It was then that Saera noticed Cris had on a different ring, as well—inset with stones rather than the plain white metal band he usually wore. The stones in the two rings glowed slightly in a shifting rainbow when they came into close proximity. "The Starstones from each vein all carry memory of their kind and resonate when they come close to other gems cut from the same vein."

"Don't even ask about the price," Cris added. "I'll just say that each High Dynasty may have first right of refusal, but even if the claim was turned down it'd be next to impossible to find another buyer."

"That's incredible. I've never seen anything like it." *Will I have one eventually?*

"You'll see a lot more tomorrow night," Cris said.

They approached a side door of the mansion. Once indoors, Cris, Kate and Wil removed their tinted glasses.

Saera followed their example. Even though she'd only had the glasses for a few months, already she felt exposed without them.

"Since dinner isn't until later tonight, I figured I may as well give you the grand tour this afternoon," Cris said. The glow in his cobalt eyes was visible even in the well-lit hall.

"Sure." Saera looked around in awe at the interior hallway of the mansion. It was even more grand inside than out. The stone walls were carved with abstract patterns reminiscent of flowers and vines, and accents of gold and silver adorned even more detailed molding along the ceiling and floor. On the outer wall, arched windows spanned nearly floor to ceiling, overlooking the gardens. On the interior wall, tapestries and paintings of mountains and other natural landscapes covered much of the space between decorated doorways.

Saera shook her head. *It hardly seems real.* "I can't believe you grew up here," she said to Cris.

"Neither can I," he replied. "It feels like another lifetime."

The group spent the next hour following Cris on a tour around the property. The grounds and mansion were even more breathtaking up close, each area displaying the finest craftsmanship and materials. They wove through the halls—passing sitting areas and training rooms—and into gardens and several outbuildings that contained pools, recreation facilities and gazebos for lounging.

Saera tried to take it all in, but it was overwhelming. *I came from so little. I don't belong in a place like this.* "You always talked about the family's wealth, but I guess I could never really picture it before now," she commented as they strolled through a particularly exquisite hall with striking sculptures of animals displayed on pedestals along one wall.

Cris shook his head. "Honestly, this is just evidence of the old wealth. Transport and colonization have been on the upswing over the last few generations, and the balance in the central bank account makes all of this seem modest."

I can't even fathom that kind of lifestyle. "Where does all of that money go?" Saera asked.

"Most of it just sits in various accounts collecting interest," Cris replied. "But we do take care of our people. You won't find a single homeless, hungry, or uneducated person on Tararia."

"We just send anyone who doesn't pull their weight off-world," Wil added flippantly.

Saera's eyes narrowed. "Why charge for services at all if there's that much to go around?"

"Why not? It keeps all of us Dynastic types feeling so great about ourselves," Wil said.

Kate gave Wil a stern look with her glowing hazel-green eyes. "Not here."

"That's just the way it is," Cris answered Saera more seriously. "It always has been, and so it persists. Things are much better than they used to be, though."

"There's a reason we don't come here often," Wil continued. "Once you've been in the TSS long enough, where status is earned rather than assigned at birth, it's tough to be back in a place with such clear distinctions."

It was this way in so many places on Earth, too. Things may look better on the surface here, but it's an illusion. "I know what you mean."

"Don't worry," Cris said in a low voice, "we're working on it."

They finished the tour in the gardens, and then Kate gave Saera a quick tutorial on how to properly greet the Heads of the Sietinen Dynasty. It seemed straightforward enough. They practiced a few times until Saera felt comfortable with the routine. When they were finished, Wil and Cris left to meet with Wil's grandfather on some TSS business.

A servant showed Saera to the guest suite she would share with Wil, which consisted of a sitting room, a lavish bathroom, and a bedroom with a terrace. Saera was about to go onto the terrace when she noticed two ornate evening gowns hanging from hooks on the wall in the bedroom. *This is no casual family get-together.*

Cris led Wil toward his father's office on the other side of the estate. He was reluctant to discuss business with Reinen, but they may as well get it out of the way.

When they reached the large outer office, an attendant directed them back to Reinen's private study.

Reinen stood when they entered. "Cris, Wil, it's good to see you. It's been too long."

Too long for you, maybe. "Hello, father."

"Grandfather." Wil inclined his head.

"You're looking well," Reinen continued, venturing a smile. His hair had turned predominantly gray, but there were very few lines on his face to show that he was in his mid-eighties. He still carried himself with shoulders square and a straight back, and he looked quite regal in his dark blue suit that more closely resembled a robe. "Has it really been almost five years? You've grown up, Wil."

"Has it? The last few years have been a blur," Wil replied.

Reinen looked him over. "It appears you recovered well."

"Yes, I got right back on track as soon as we returned," Wil said without missing a beat. "I've been much more careful in practice since then."

Except there never was a training accident—only an assassination attempt by a traitor. Cris eyed the guest seating in the office. "Should we sit down?"

"Yes, forgive me. Please, make yourselves comfortable." Reinen gestured to the chairs in front of his desk. "I understand you wanted to discuss some business with me before dinner tonight?"

"Yes, thank you," Cris said, taking a seat in the left chair.

"It's a somewhat sensitive matter," Wil explained. "I'm afraid we can't get into the specifics."

Even the High Dynasties don't know about the war. "The TSS is seeking additional ship production capacity. We would like to negotiate for SiNavTech to provide use of a facility."

Reinen examined them. "The TSS has always tended to its own affairs. Why the change of heart?"

Cris glanced at his son. "We're making some preparations. There are time constraints." *More than we've wanted to admit, apparently. Banks would never have asked for this if there weren't a dire need.*

Reinen folded his hands on the desktop. "What did you have in mind?"

"We'd like to acquire the Prisaris shipyard," Wil stated. "The TSS is prepared to pay a fair price for the facility."

The Head of the Sietinen Dynasty leaned back in his chair. "Business isn't always about the money. There is a significant amount of proprietary technology at that facility." He shook his head. "Besides, that shipyard is shared among several Dynasties. I can't make a sales decision for everyone."

Cris let out a slow breath. The ship manufacturing division of SiNavTech was one of the more complicated, since it was taken over from the fallen Dainetris Dynasty several generations before. "What kind of compensation would make it worth your while?"

"Well, I understand that the exclusivity on the independent jump drive has expired. We'd like to license the technology for civilian use," Reinen replied without hesitation.

They've been gunning for that technology for years. It was a smart business move, after all—an independent jump drive put the entire SiNavTech beacon infrastructure in jeopardy. Cris looked to Wil. *I can't speak for him on this.*

Wil frowned. "That isn't something I ever intended to commercialize."

"You personally hold the license. You can do whatever you

want with it," Reinen said.

"Still, I developed it for a specific military application." Wil shifted in his chair.

Reinen leaned forward. "Wil, you have the opportunity to change the face of space travel. Since you have resisted working with SiNavTech directly, the least you can do for this family is license your work to us."

Wil laughed with disbelief. "Resisted? You have no idea how busy I am with the TSS. I have no time to work with SiNavTech."

"Both of you have given your lives to the TSS. It's time to start thinking about your duties to Tararia." Reinen rested his gaze on Cris.

He shouldn't try guilting me. I'm above that now. "Wil, it's your decision about what to do with your work. We have other manufacturing options if SiNavTech isn't agreeable to working with us." *I'm not sure what those options are, but there has to be something... right?*

"I'll need to think about it," Wil said.

Reinen evaluated Cris and Wil. "You came all this way but weren't prepared to negotiate final terms? Surely you had another reason for coming all the way here to Tararia."

Wil shook his head. "This business was just coincidental timing. The purpose of this visit was always to introduce you to Saera and begin the process of getting her enrolled under the Advancement Act."

"And it sounds like a reception has already been arranged, thank you," Cris added.

Reinen's eyes widened with surprise. "What are you talking about? She could never be accepted under the Taran Social Advancement Act."

Cris and Wil exchanged glances. "What do you mean?" Cris asked his father. "It exists for this very purpose of elevating the standing of someone with superior genetics to Dynastic status."

"It only applies to Taran citizens," Reinen stated. "Earth is not a recognized Taran colony. Our relationship with the planet is in the distant past."

It doesn't count?

"There has to be an exception. She's a far better candidate than most who are accepted," Wil insisted.

"I can attest to it." *Did I lead Wil astray? I told him there would be no issues for him to be with her.*

"That doesn't matter," Reinen said. "Candidates must be at least half Taran. It's a requirement."

"But the reception—" Wil began.

"The reception is for *you*," Reinen replied. "We need to find you a suitable wife. That's become even more important knowing we'll need to make arrangements to buy out the shareholders in the shipyard."

"What!" Wil exclaimed

Stars, no! "I think there's been some miscommunication here," Cris said, trying to stay calm. "Wil and Saera are together. They're bonded."

"You never should have let that teenage romance persist," Reinen said with a flick of his hand. "I know the culture in the TSS is different, but in Dynasties on Tararia such as ours, we must think about bloodlines."

Wil shot Cris a look of desperation. "She's a perfect genetic match for me. It doesn't get any better!"

"But she's not Taran," Reinen stated. "You didn't honestly think you would be permitted to *marry* her, did you?"

"How can you be so dismissive? You haven't even met her." *He can't be doing this...*

"I don't need to meet her to make a decision. We have extended the courtesy of a dinner and will grant her attendance at the reception tomorrow because we want to be gracious hosts, but it is nothing more. I don't know why you bothered to bring her here, because that little fling of yours is far past its expiration."

"No, I'm never giving her up." Wil jumped to his feet.

This can't be happening. "Father, there's more at stake here than you know. Wil's relationship with Saera is much more than anything concerning this Dynasty. I know she might not offer the same sort of strategic alliance as my partnership with Kate, but it's something you'll have to accept."

"You're in no position to make such a declaration. As long as I'm Head of this Dynasty, I will never permit a marriage of any heir to someone that isn't of pure Taran blood."

Wil glared down at his grandfather. "Don't try to forbid this. There's nothing you can do to stop it."

Reinen stared back, resolute. "Regardless of my personal feelings on the matter, a marriage license wouldn't be valid. Any child between you would be viewed as a bastard and could never be a rightful heir. If you won't find someone suitable for yourself, we will. We'll turn to the Archive if it comes to it."

"You wouldn't!" *I've never heard of using the Genetic Archive for such a perverse purpose.*

"If you don't want it to come to that, then I suggest you find someone at the reception tomorrow. There are plenty of suitable daughters that would help expedite procurement of the Prisaris shipyard you're so keen to acquire." Reinen folded his hands on his desk. "It's up to you."

"You have no idea who you're messing with." Wil stormed out.

Cris rose. "Wil will be with Saera whether you approve or not. He needs her for reasons that are far beyond your comprehension."

"The affairs of the TSS don't concern me."

"Well, I must straddle both worlds. If you stand in between Wil and Saera, you'll have to answer to me."

Reinen narrowed his eyes. "Are you threatening me?"

"Just advising."

‹ CHAPTER 4 ›

Shite! I can't tell Saera about any of that. She's nervous enough already. Wil let out an unsteady breath. *I have to figure something out.*

He went to meet Saera in their suite and managed to change into his TSS dress uniform without giving her any indication that something was wrong. Normally she'd see right through his mask, but she was too distracted by nerves.

Saera set about fixing her hair into a braided bun and applying some minimal makeup around her eyes. When she finished, she turned her attention to the two evening gowns. "Which one should I wear tonight?"

Wil looked them over. "The green one," he suggested, opting for the more modest design.

Saera took down the dress from its hanger and slipped it on.

Wil's breath caught as she began to secure the clasps on the side of the dress. The sequined strapless bodice flowed into a straight skirt with a slit to her left thigh, accentuating every curve. A sheer dark green scarf draped from the front of the bodice over her left shoulder and hung to the back of her knee like a single ethereal wing.

"Saera, you look incredible!" he breathed. *It's so rare I see her dressed up I forget she can be even more stunning than how she is every day.*

"Thanks." She blushed. "This fabric is unreal. I thought that dress for the TSS party was nice, but this…"

Wil took her hand. "It's beautiful, but no one else could wear it as well as you."

She smiled, momentarily forgetting her nerves. "You're quite the charmer."

"You make it easy."

Saera rolled her eyes, but her cheeks flushed deeper and the corners of her mouth turned up. She glanced toward the door. "Are we heading out now?"

"My dad said he'd come by to get us," Wil replied.

With a faint nod of acknowledgement, Saera wandered toward the window, wringing her hands with anxious anticipation.

"Don't worry, I'll be with you the whole time." Wil wished he could offer Saera more assurance. *She's everything to me. I need to know she'll be safe if I can't be there for her.*

Saera's brow knit as she placed her hand on her stomach. "What if they don't like me?"

"Then that's their problem." *I already chose you as my life partner. I don't need their approval.*

The queasy look didn't entirely leave Saera's face, but some of the tension in her stance diminished. She smoothed the green gown hugging her hourglass figure. "This feels way too formal."

Wil smiled. "All part of blending in." He adjusted his TSS formal uniform, which displayed ribbons for his numerous commendations—already more than most retiring Agents. The entire affair did feel too formal, but he was in no position to argue about dinner attire when there were bigger issues to address.

A buzz sounded at the door. "Come in," Wil assented.

Cris popped his head through the doorway from the hall. He was also wearing his TSS formal uniform, decorated with a multitude of his own professional accomplishments. "Ready?"

Wil looked to Saera. She nodded. "Let's go," Wil replied. *I have no idea how we're going to get through this dinner.*

Cris and Kate—dressed in a modest midnight blue evening gown—led Wil and Saera out of the guest hall toward the formal dining room. The entire wing was designed for entertaining, and many of the decorations were a particularly ostentatious presentation of wealth. Wil found himself trying to calculate how many small planets could be acquired for the value of the materials; he felt pretty confident that the answer was three.

Eventually, they came to a grand set of double doors off of a giant foyer.

"Our Lord and Lady will receive you now," a servant stated.

Two servants swung open the doors. Inside, a long table was adorned with flowers, candles, and silver serving dishes. At the far head of the table, Reinen Sietinen stood behind his chair, and his wife, Alana, stood behind her chair to his right.

"Welcome." Reinen smiled pleasantly at Saera, but he shot a contentious glare toward Cris.

Unphased, Cris led the way into the room with the others following close behind. "Father, Mother, I'd like to present Saera Alexander to you." He beckoned for Saera to come forward.

Reinen and Alana rounded the table to greet them. Alana gracefully maneuvered the full skirt of her long-sleeve, ocean-colored dress to avoid the chairs. Her hair was grayed from its former blonde, but her face was still surprisingly youthful. Only her wise, sky-blue eyes betrayed her years.

Saera dropped into a polite curtsy next to Cris. "It is my honor," she said, keeping her luminescent green eyes downcast.

"It is you who do us honor," Reinen replied, though Wil knew the statement wasn't genuine.

Saera rose from her curtsy and met Reinen's gaze. "Thank you for welcoming me into your home." She looked to Alana. "I feel privileged to be among you."

"Please, dine with us," Alana responded, gesturing toward the table.

At least they have the decency to feign politeness.

Reinen and Alana returned to their seats, and Cris sat down to his father's left with Kate to his other side. Wil and Saera were about to sit next to his parents when Alana stopped them.

"Come sit next to me," Alana said to Saera.

"Yes, my lady," Saera affirmed with a bow of her head.

Oh, no. What is she up to? Wil followed Saera to the far side of the table and helped her into her chair before sitting down next to her. As they were getting situated, several of the Sietinen senior staff members entered and took their seats around the table, but one empty chair remained in the middle.

"Now," Alana began, "how did you two meet?" She included Wil in the question.

"Well, we sort of met on my first day with the TSS during orientation," Saera replied. "But, we weren't officially introduced until a few months later when Wil barged into my study room."

"I wouldn't say I barged in," Wil clarified. "You did forget to lock the door, after all."

"I see," said Alana. "It would seem that random hallway encounters at TSS Headquarters have replaced our more traditional matchmaking practices."

I can't tell if that was an insult or a joke. Wil glanced at Saera. "Space is quite romantic. Past generations were missing out."

His grandmother gave a subtle smile in response.

They're judging Saera without even giving her a chance. This isn't fair. "I was her mentor for most of our early time together. Though I was already a Junior Agent, everyone close to my age was just entering the training program."

Alana nodded thoughtfully. "That must have been difficult for you."

"It was at times, but I made it through with Saera's help," Wil responded.

"And, in time, you forgot the boundaries that were set for

you," Alana said.

Can this get any worse? Wil glanced at Saera, but she was putting on a brave face. *How can I change their mind about her?*

A servant glided over and hovered at Alana's shoulder. She beckoned him, and he bent down to speak to her. "Shall we wait for your final guest?" he whispered, glancing at the empty chair in the middle of the table.

"No, proceed," Alana instructed.

"Yes, my lady." The servant bowed and left through the back door.

"Where was I?" Alana mused. "Oh yes, I've heard so much about your work with the independent jump drive."

Great, they're working me from both sides. But business... this could be a safer topic. "Yes. Is there something you wanted to know?"

"I'm curious about the technology's use of the existing SiNavTech infrastructure," Alana said. "What would it take to roll out the drives on a large scale?"

"The drive can operate on its own, but a level of integration is possible." As Wil began explaining the details to her, a bowl of vegetable soup was brought out to each of the guests. Wil and Saera sipped it as they continued their conversation with Alana about the potential commercialization of independent jump drive navigation technology. When the soup was finished, a main course of fish and risotto was served.

The dinner plates were nearly empty when the missing attendee appeared. Wil came to attention when he heard the back door open. Across the table, Cris visibly tensed as they simultaneously caught sight of Marina Alexri entering the room. As one of Reinen's Court Advisors, she had been a longtime adversary of Cris despite her brief stint as his telepathy instructor before he left Tararia.

Marina gave a slight curtsy to Reinen. "I apologize for my tardiness." She was about to take the open chair when she was stopped in her tracks.

"Mom?"

Wil gaped at Saera, who was transfixed by Marina. *Wait...*

The two women stared at each other as the other dinner guests looked on with bewilderment. Wil waited for Marina to denounce Saera's comment, say that she must be mistaken and that she had no daughter. But, Marina stood calm and poised, meeting Saera's piercing gaze. Then, she turned and fled the room through the back door where she'd entered.

Saera leaped from her chair, nearly tripped on her long gown as she ran after Marina.

If Marina is Saera's mother, that means... Wil dashed after Saera. He found her frozen just outside the door, and sounds of running footfall in the distance echoed through the corridor.

A shudder wracked Saera and she fell to her knees on the marble floor, sobbing. "She—she was here all along?"

Wil knelt down next to Saera, putting an arm around her hunched shoulders. *I didn't see that coming.*

"Everyone out!" Cris bellowed. The advisors darted out of the room through the main door at the front of the room, but Kate and his parents lingered. As soon as the room was cleared and the doors were closed, Cris rounded on his father. "You were intentionally keeping Wil and Saera apart! No wonder you didn't want her to come here, you knew we'd find out about her true lineage. How could you do this?"

Kate tried to reach out to calm Cris, but he would have none of it.

Reinen was completely taken by surprise. He took a step back. "Cris, I had no idea."

The rage mounted, the hum of a telekinetic echo filling the air. "Oh, right! She's on your senior staff—of course you would have known. She was gone for five years!" *Of course! That's why she left Saera when she was four.*

Reinen shook his head. "She was on personal leave. I didn't know where. I swear it."

Cris lashed out to his father's mind, searching. Anger and confusion swirled on the surface above cold calculations for the ramifications of the discovery. Beneath it was a deep hurt—something Cris had never sensed in his father's stoic demeanor before. Reinen was vulnerable and open. No deceit, no lies. Cris recoiled, feeling ashamed for the violation. He took a deep breath. "Well, if Marina really is her mother, then you can't stop a wedding between Wil and Saera. She'll qualify under the Advancement Act."

Reinen hung his head. "That's true, she would, but—"

But nothing. "I won't let you stand in the way of this. I won't allow you do to him what you did to me."

Reinen's brow furrowed. "What do you mean?"

"All you ever do is try to force people into your vision for who they should be, no matter the personal cost. You wanted me to pretend I didn't have my abilities—wouldn't even allow talking about the TSS even though it was the one organization that could bring me into my full self. And now you would forbid Wil from a partnership with Saera, even though he needs her to help him fulfill a purpose far greater than anything you can see from your narrow vantage."

"Cris, don't mistake my concern over this family's future for trying to suppress either of your desires."

Desires? You would have us deny part of our very beings. "The 'family' is all you think about."

"It's all I have."

Cris shook his head. "I was always just a pawn to you. Just like you're trying to use Wil now."

Reinen looked pained. "Is that what you think?"

"When did you ever make me feel any differently?" *When you weren't ignoring me, you were trying to control me.*

Reinen cast his eyes down. "Son, I realize now just how much I must have failed you if you truly feel that way."

Cris' anger receded, replaced by a hollow sadness. "I know you're ashamed of me."

Alana came around the table and looked Cris in the eye. "Never! You're our son."

Hah! "Don't even try to say otherwise now. As a kid, I never saw you. You never took an interest in me."

"It wasn't because of you—" Reinen tried to explain.

"Shite!" Cris exclaimed, cutting him off. "If you hadn't turned down that meeting with the Priesthood right before I left, I would have thought you were behind their attempt on my life a year later."

Reinen and Alana looked appalled. "Wait… the Priesthood attacked you?" The blood drained from Reinen's face, making him look his age.

Alana shrank back, not wanting to believe. "Why would—" Her face twisted in anguish. "If they came after you, does that mean…?"

"Tristen's death wasn't an accident," Cris confirmed.

Reinen staggered backwards to steady himself against one of the chairs.

"But why?" Alana cried.

"He was too focused on the Dynasty to suit their militaristic needs. The Priesthood was dissatisfied with me, too, but by then they were out of time and were stuck with me. They were desperate to have their tools to end the war." Cris caught himself a moment too late. *Fok, I shouldn't have said that.*

Reinen tensed, digging his fingers into the back of the chair. "A war? And the Priesthood is involved?"

"I mean, there's always one fight or another in society," Cris hastily replied, hoping his statement would be forgotten. It was not the time or place to divulge the war, even though he was eager to expose the Priesthood's covert manipulations.

His father hesitated. "Everything changed when Tristen was killed."

I never would have come into being. Thankful his slip about the war had gone unheeded, Cris took a slow breath. "We're all being guided, whether you want to acknowledge it or not."

"Like Marina having a child that's now involved with Wil?" Reinen asked

"Just the latest thread binding us together." *Marina's tie to Saera is the answer to our problems, but it means the manipulations run far deeper than I ever imagined.*

"I never wanted this life for you," Reinen murmured.

Kate cleared her throat, eyeing the back door.

"Right." Cris took a moment to quiet his thoughts. Reaching any level of understanding with his parents would take time he didn't have at the present. He turned his attention to the more pressing matter. *Why did Marina have a child on Earth?*

Wil brought Saera to her feet. He held her close as she trembled, staring into space. *How can I even begin to comfort her? How can I even process this myself?*

"There has to be an explanation. It'll all be okay," Wil tried to sooth. "I can't believe you recognized her."

"I... felt it," Saera stammered. "She barely looks like the old pictures I have of her, but there was a bond—like a faint form of what I feel with you. I just knew."

Wil nodded. "I have something like that with my parents, too."

"Let me go after her," Saera said, pulling out of Wil's arms.

"Maybe we should let this settle—"

Cris barged out from the dining room, with Kate following close behind.

"Which way did Marina go?" Cris demanded.

"Dad—"

"Which way?" Cris repeated.

There's no stopping him. "Down that hall." Wil pointed to the left.

Cris and Kate took off in the direction he indicated.

"Are you sure you're up for this?" Wil asked Saera.

She nodded. "I have to."

Wil took Saera's hand and they jogged to catch up to his parents.

They spotted Marina through a window, standing on a nearby terrace with her back to the glass doors.

Cris stormed outside. "Marina, you owe us all an explanation."

Marina withered. "I do. I almost ran back to my room, but I've already spent enough time hiding."

Saera slipped through the door next to Wil and approached her mother. "Mom, what happened? Why did you leave me?"

Marina closed her eyes and shook her head. "I'm so sorry, Saera."

"Mom…"

"I had to!" Marina finally met Saera's gaze, distraught. "They didn't give me any choice."

"Who?" Cris asked.

"Who else? The Priesthood," Marina replied.

Cris clenched his jaw, silently fuming.

Wil took a deep breath. *It all comes back to them. It always does.* He wrapped his arm around Saera and she slumped against him, hugging herself.

"Just over twenty years ago, they approached me one night as I was returning to my home here on Tararia," Marina explained. "They said there was something important I must do for them— that the fate of Tararia was at stake. I tried to resist, but they insisted. I was forced to put in a request for extended leave the following morning."

"Doesn't sound like you resisted much—" Cris began, but

Kate stopped him with a debilitating stare that Wil had only seen her use on rare occasions.

"It seemed like my only choice at the time," Marina continued. "The Priesthood gave me a new identity of 'Mary Alexander.' They instructed me to go to Earth and seduce a specific man to bear a child with him—a girl. I was given his name, picture and location, and then I was sent on my way. It wasn't until later that I found out he was married and already had other children."

With a retired Agent watching to make sure she followed through—Michael's father, Wil realized. *Fok!*

"Why him?" Kate asked.

"I don't know. I tried looking into him afterward, and there didn't seem to be anything of note. His grandfather was Taran and immigrated to Earth, as people occasionally do. The bloodline doesn't trace to any Dynasties. I think they just searched far and wide, and he and I were the right genetic match," she looked at Wil, "to produce someone complementary to the Cadicle."

Wil felt like he had been stabbed in the stomach, but he was careful to not show any outward emotion. *They made her for me.*

Cris startled. "What makes you think Wil is the Cadicle?"

Wil came to attention, realizing his father had picked up on a key detail. *Only a handful of people know me by that title.*

"It's the only explanation that fits," Marina replied. "You three Agents are more powerful than most, and add in the clear manipulation of genetic lines… The Priesthood was seeking their namesake. And for whatever reason, they want that new line to continue through another intentional pairing."

Saera looked even more ill. "And knowing that, you just left me?"

Marina shook her head. "Saera, I tried to fight them, but they took me away. They told me I had to leave you. I couldn't even begin to comprehend what it was all about until now."

"I don't understand why you couldn't have stayed with me," Saera murmured. "Been my mother and raised me."

"Probably because of me," Cris cut in. "Because when I was a hot-headed teenager I had a stupid grudge against one of my teachers. And because of those lingering feelings, however ill-placed, once I was Lead Agent I may not have given her daughter an honest chance with the TSS—let alone allow her to get close to my son."

"They watch everything," Marina whispered.

Why does the Priesthood want us together? Wil could barely maintain composure, crushed by the realization that the single most important person in his life was yet another piece in the plan directing his fate. *I would have fought for her to the end, but it turns out we've been forced together this whole time.*

"No organization should have this much control," Cris muttered.

Marina ignored him. "I'm so sorry I wasn't there for you," Marina said, trying to reach out to her daughter, but Saera pulled away.

"But you *weren't* there!" Saera cried. "You have no idea what it was like for me after you left!"

"I'm sorry…" Marina hung her head.

Tears streamed down Saera's cheeks, her breath ragged.

Wil watched the exchange unfold, too shocked to intervene. *I didn't even choose my own love.* He caught himself. *No… I did choose her. They may have made her for me, but I still chose to be with her. And I still choose her, despite everything.*

With renewed vigor, Wil put his arm around Saera. "Come on," he urged. *"Take some time to process this. It's too much to take in at once,"* he added telepathically.

Saera nodded and followed his lead.

They departed without another word. Kate brushed Wil's arm as he passed by, but she couldn't meet his gaze.

Wil silently escorted Saera back to their suite. Her eyes were red and swollen, but eventually the tears subsided.

When they made it to the privacy of their room, Saera's shoulders rounded. "So it's all a lie? Just one big setup?"

What I feel for you isn't a lie. Wil smoothed her hair. "Our meeting may have been contrived, but that doesn't mean what we have together is any less real."

Saera searched Wil's face, perplexed. "How can you be so calm about this?"

"Because this is my life, Saera. Everything about my entire existence has been manufactured and manipulated. My very genetic code was part of a master design." He took her hands and eased her down onto the edge of the bed. "What I came to realize a long time ago was that I can't control everything around me, but I still have freewill. So, rather than be upset about everything that's out of my hands, I've made a conscious choice to focus on what I *can* do. Being with you is something I chose to do because you make me happy. Frankly, I don't care how we came to be together, because I wouldn't want it any other way."

Saera thought for a moment. "You're right."

They changed out of the formal attire, and Wil tucked Saera into bed. She tossed and turned at first, but eventually her breathing settled into the slow, deep rhythm of slumber.

Wil lay in bed next to her, staring at the ceiling. He had to put on a strong front for Saera's sake, but he was more unnerved by the Priesthood's actions than he would readily admit. *My grandparents may not want us together, but the Priesthood does. They made the Cadicle—me—but why go to such lengths for Saera? What do they want out of our partnership?*

◄ CHAPTER 5 ►

Saera awoke in the morning to a sore throat and itchy eyes. *What a miserable night.*

Wil rolled over to wrap an arm around her when she stirred. "How did you sleep?" he asked.

"Apparently not well. I still feel exhausted."

Wil hugged her close. "We'll have a mellow day and relax. I think we could all use a break from reality."

"I just want to go home," Saera moaned and buried her face in a pillow.

"No moping allowed," Wil said in an upbeat tone as he removed the pillow from over her face. "Think about it this way: things can't possibly get any worse than last night. It has to be on the upswing now."

Saera groaned and tried to roll away from Wil.

"Nope! Time to get up." He threw back the covers and gently began dragging her toward the edge of the bed.

She made an exaggerated frown but let Wil direct her. At the side of the bed, he pulled her to her feet.

"See? Not so bad." Wil gave her a kiss.

"I still want to go home." *But I guess there's no escape no matter where I go.*

"Not an option. So, we may as well try to enjoy ourselves. How does a pool day sound?"

Saera pondered the proposition. "I suppose that's

acceptable."

"All right. Let's get ready for breakfast."

They showered and dressed in the spacious bathroom—well equipped to accommodate two people. With a little more encouragement, Wil coaxed Saera down to the patio on the lower level of the residential wing for their morning meal.

When they arrived, Wil's parents were lounging at the outdoor table. Kate was gazing out over the gardens with a cup of tea in her hands, and Cris was reading through what looked to be a report projected from his handheld resting on the table.

"Good morning," Cris greeted. "I was afraid you might run off in the middle of the night." He minimized the report.

"The thought did cross my mind," Saera replied, only half-joking. She and Wil sat down in the cushioned chairs at the wooden table. An enticing spread of sliced fruit, juice, and pastries was arranged at the center amid vases of fresh-cut flowers.

"It's a new day now," Kate said. "We adjust, like always."

Cris glanced at his wife. "Things are what they are."

The Priesthood bred me for Wil. To be a complement to the Cadicle. Saera's stomach turned over.

Wil let out a slow breath. "Last night was just another 'that figures' moment after everything I've been through in the last few years."

"I can't believe those sorts of revelations are starting to feel normal," Kate admitted.

"I really thought I was getting used to taking things in stride, too, but that… Stars!" Cris shook his head.

Kate nodded. "Somehow it was easier when it was just us. But knowing there have been others…"

Saera wilted. *What does the Priesthood want with me?* "None of this feels real."

Cris ducked his head to catch Saera's downcast gaze. "I know it's not a lot of consolation right now, but we know how you feel. We'll get through this together."

Saera fought to keep from tearing up again. "I always wanted to see my mom again. I ran through what I'd say to her countless times in my head. But now…"

"Everything was out of your control. You can't get caught up in 'what if' hypotheticals," Kate said. "We went through this a few years ago ourselves. You have to accept the fate you were dealt, but you don't have to let it define you."

Wil took Saera's hand. "We know what we have. That's all that matters."

Kate smiled, caressing Cris' forearm. "Exactly."

Saera tried to take comfort in the words. She squeezed Wil's hand and gave an assured nod, but inside the emotion was still too raw.

Wil eyed the basket of golden pastries at the center of the table and grabbed one. "I honestly did have hopes that this would be a relaxing, uneventful vacation."

Cris chuckled. "Around here? Impossible."

Saera grabbed a pastry for herself. It was still warm and had a delightfully airy texture.

"Though I don't expect any more life-changing announcements, the drama might not be completely over. The party is still on for this evening," Cris stated.

"Is that really such a good idea?" Wil asked.

Cris shook his head. "It wouldn't look good to cancel last-minute. Appearances."

Wil slumped back in his chair. "But of course. We are the perfect family, after all."

Kate set down her empty tea mug. "Let's try to keep the sarcasm to a minimum. The circumstances could be far worse."

"Easy for you to say," Wil countered. "You won't be the one on display."

"What do you mean?" Saera asked.

Wil faltered—only for an instant, but she knew him well

enough to recognize that he was keeping something from her. "Nothing. These events are just an excuse for the absurdly rich to show off."

"Sounds lovely." Saera took a bite of her pastry. It was the perfect balance of sweet and savory that left her mouth watering for more.

Wil grinned. "It'll be great."

Saera and Wil finished eating, and then went back to their room to change into swimming attire. Wil led her down to one of the infinity pools carved into the hillside of the estate overlooking the city and lake below.

It felt strange, at first, to wear a bikini outdoors after years of TSS uniforms, but the warm sun on her skin soon set her at ease. She selected one of the lounge chairs facing the sun head-on and got comfortable.

Wil stripped down to his swim shorts and dove into the water. He slicked back the hair from his forehead when he surfaced. "I miss swimming. The ocean on Orino was frigid, but there's something freeing about the water."

"You just like it because it reminds you of freefall."

"Now that's probably true." He laid back in the water and floated with his eyes closed.

Saera admired the view, starting to feel more like herself again.

In time, she closed her eyes and soaked up the sun. After several minutes, she felt a cool shadow pass over her leg.

She cracked open one eye to see if a cloud had manifested in the clear sky, but instead saw an orb of water approaching overhead. Wil was floating in the pool watching her with a mischievous grin.

"You wouldn't!" Saera exclaimed. She raised a telekinetic shield just in time to deflect the water as the orb burst above her. The water splashed down around her protective dome.

"Now you're asking for it!" Saera leaped to her feet and

raised a retaliatory wave in the pool toward Wil.

He parted the wave to either side of him with the slightest raise of his hand, causing water to splash over the lip of the pool onto the pavement.

Before Saera had time to plan her next move, she felt herself lifting off of the ground, her skin tingling with electrical energy. "That's not fair!" She could have tried to fight against Wil, but she knew there was no way she'd win if he didn't want her to.

Slowly, Wil levitated her above the center of the pool. Saera scowled down at him.

He laughed. "I'm sorry, I couldn't resist."

"There's still time to put me back and pretend like this never happened."

Wil tilted his head. "What's the fun in that?"

Saera plunged into the water with a scream of surprise. She surfaced with a gasp from the warm water, pure as a mountain spring.

Wil took a couple strokes over to her. "Forgive me?"

Saera gave him a playful glare. "I guess—this time." She splashed at him with her hand.

Wil splashed her back. "You know, I think this is the most time we've ever spent together in a row."

"I guess it is," Saera realized. She hadn't been able to stay overnight with Wil since he graduated, due to the unwanted questions it would raise with her roommates. "And you're trying to drown me already?"

"Oh, hardly!" Wil swam to Saera and pulled her in for a kiss.

She kissed him back. "Uh huh."

They played around in the water for a while longer before returning to the poolside lounge chairs. As they dried off in the sun, Saera traced the outline of the dragon tattooed on Wil's left shoulder blade.

"I'm glad you brought me here," she said.

"So far it hasn't gone quite how I pictured."

"Me either."

Wil turned to face her, his glowing cerulean eyes fixed on her. "My new trainees will arrive as soon as we get back. We won't get many more moments like this for a long time."

Saera took his hand. "So let's enjoy it while we can."

They spent the rest of the day lazing around the pool and gardens. So much had happened the previous evening, Saera was happy for some quiet time to process. Servants brought out a picnic lunch to them and refreshed their glasses of iced lemonade.

When the day turned to late-afternoon, they made their way inside to begin dressing for the party.

Wil again donned his TSS dress uniform, and Saera put on the second gown she had been given—this one light silver in color. It had a wide V-cut at the bust and two straps secured behind her neck. The back of the dress was almost completely open, and the rest of the metallic fabric formed around her in a tight sheath to the floor, with a slit to mid-thigh on either side.

"This feels a little… risqué," she commented after twirling a few times in front of the mirror with her auburn hair still loose around her shoulders.

"It's the current fashion for people our age. You look stunning," Wil said, the awe apparent on his face. "You'll be the center of attention."

"I guess I wouldn't mind turning a few heads."

Wil smiled. "You definitely will."

A knock sounded at the door.

Saera's heart jumped. "Is it time to go? I'm not ready yet." Wil went to answer the door while Saera looked around for her hair clips. *What did I do with that bag?* She felt someone watching her and looked up to see her mother standing in the doorway, fully dressed and with her hair done in her signature twist-and-braid style.

"Will you be okay?" Wil asked Saera telepathically from the

adjacent lounge room.

"*I think so.*"

"I'll be right outside," Wil said aloud and left.

Marina watched Wil go and then turned her attention to Saera. "I thought you might like some help getting ready."

Saera fought the urge to scream at her. *No. Though I can't easily forgive her, I shouldn't turn her away now when she's trying to reach out to me.* "Sure, thanks."

Marina came forward. "Why don't you sit? I'll do your hair, just like old times."

Saera sat down at the vanity in the bedroom. She looked at Marina in the mirror, weighing her intentions.

"I never imagined a reunion like what happened last night," Marina went on, her voice quavering slightly. "I'm so sorry for what I put you through." She set down a small clutch on the vanity and began extracting various clips and pins.

"Last night was nothing," Saera replied. *I can get over that shock. The years of abuse she left me to are harder to forget.*

Marina took some pins in her hand and began sectioning out Saera's hair. "I know it isn't any consolation, but I've thought about you every day since I left Earth. I was never much of the nurturing sort, but you brought out a side of me I never knew I had. I tried to suppress it, but it's been there all these years with nothing to fill the void."

She's right, that isn't any consolation at all. "We can't just pick up where we left off. You've missed most of my life."

Marina paused the hair styling for a moment, the muscles around her eyes and mouth twitched. She took a breath and then continued arranging the strands of Saera's hair. "I know we can't. But I hope things can be different going forward."

"I've already had a fresh start. Joining the TSS was an escape. I don't think you understand how awful things were living with dad's other family."

"Maybe in time you can forgive me," Marina murmured.

That's easier said than done. "I'll try."

They made small-talk for a while, starting the process of rebuilding the foundation of their relationship. It felt forced to Saera, but she owed it to herself to make a genuine attempt at reconnecting with her mother, so she pushed through the awkward silences.

Eventually, Marina took a step back and looked at Saera from several angles. "There. How's that?"

The hairstyle was sleek and sophisticated, with braided sections folding over each other and twisted up into a looping bun. Saera tilted her head to either side and admired the up-do. *She made it suit me now—not the child I was.* "I love it. Thank you."

"You're going to make a lot of girls very envious tonight," Marina said with a smile.

"What do you mean?"

Marina seemed surprised by the question. "You're about to show up to a party with the most eligible bachelor in all the Taran worlds."

"Wil?"

"Of course. He *is* the son of Sietinen and Vaenetri."

The nerves that Saera had tried so hard to settle came flooding back. "I guess I just never think about him that way. Our entire time together has been within the TSS."

Marina shook her head. "I don't believe he thinks of himself that way, either. You're fortunate to have someone so thoroughly taken with you."

He does love me. I've never questioned it. That's one part of my life that I'll never regret. "I am lucky."

"Well, I'll let you gather yourself," Marina said and glided to the door.

Am I about to walk into another trap? Saera's chest knotted. "Thank you for coming by."

Marina bowed her head. "I hope we can spend more time

together in the future."

"Me too."

◆ ◇ ◇

"Well, she may have failed you as a mother, but she makes a pretty good hair stylist," joked Wil.

"Very funny," Saera replied, not sounding amused at all. She was pacing the room as Wil sat on the edge of the bed in their suite.

"Seriously, though, you look incredible," Wil said, a swell of love in his chest as he admired her.

Saera continued to pace in front of him, her fists clenched with nervous energy.

I need to set her at ease. We just have to get through the next few hours... "I'm glad you're at least on speaking terms. It's a start."

"Yes, it is."

How can I distract her? "We should get going. We have a ball to attend! I may even make you dance." He grinned at her.

"Oh, like you're the dancer in this relationship," retorted Saera, stopping in front of Wil.

"Hey, I can dance. I think. I figure all that hand-to-hand combat training has to have yielded some transferable skills."

"Like flying kicks?"

Wil smirked. "I was thinking more like back-flips, but that would be fun, too."

"Sounds dangerous."

Wil shrugged. "It would keep things interesting."

A smile finally broke through on Saera's face, lighting up her eyes. "Let's just stick to the finger-food and mingling."

And she's back! "Very well, if you insist." Wil rose from the bed. He held out his hand. "Shall we?"

With a deep breath, Saera took his hand, entwining her fingers in his. She had her jaw set with determination to get through whatever Wil's grandparents had planned.

Wil admired how she was taking everything in stride. The visit had already unveiled more surprises than he could have ever anticipated.

He escorted her through the labyrinth of halls to the largest ballroom on the other side of the manor. As they approached, orchestral music swelled, interwoven with the buzz of conversation.

"It sounds like quite the party," Saera commented.

"Undoubtedly. Sietinens don't mess around when it comes to event planning."

Before them was a massive set of double doors, more than three meters tall. The wood was painted white to match the marble walls and floor, and it was carved into a delicate geometric pattern accented with gold and silver. Attendants standing to either side of the door bowed.

The attendant on the left straightened his back but kept his head down. "My lord. Our guests await you."

"Thank you," Wil said, unsure if there was some formal protocol he was missing.

The attendant paused for a moment, as if waiting for something else, and then proceeded to swing open the double doors with his colleague.

Wil's breath caught when he saw the ballroom, and he heard a gasp from Saera next to him. The doors opened onto a marble staircase that descended half a story to the main level. Crystal chandeliers hung from the ceiling, set with tiny lights that sent cascading sparkles across the ceiling and walls. Three walls of the room were almost entirely glass, shaped into a sweeping curve that overlooked Lake Tiadon below. An elaborate buffet was arranged along the left wall, and to the right was a twenty-piece orchestra providing the festive music. In the center of the room, at least four hundred guests were talking amongst themselves. Seeing Wil and Saera standing at the top of the stairs, the conversation halted and everyone turned toward them.

Wil gulped. *"I'm sorry, I didn't expect this,"* he said to Saera telepathically.

Saera smiled at the crowd despite her nerves and took Wil by the upper arm.

They were about to walk down the stairs when Reinen emerged from the sea of people with Alana close behind. He climbed the staircase to stand next to Wil.

"Esteemed guests," he addressed the crowd, "thank you for joining us. I am pleased to present to you Williame Sietinen-Vaenetri."

So he's still making this all about me? Wil gave a little bow, and Saera dropped into a curtsy when he started to move. They rose and Wil looked to Reinen for guidance.

Reinen came alive in the crowd's presence. "Our family has experienced so much good fortune, but so rarely can we share it with each other. All of us being here together is a special occasion indeed. We are honored for all of you to share in this joyous time with us. Have a wonderful evening!"

There was light applause from the audience as Wil and Saera descended the stairs with Reinen. Wil felt the hundreds of eyes on him, and many people leaned over to whisper to their neighbor. Saera's grip tightened on his arm, but she kept her face composed. When they reached the bottom of the stairs, Reinen clapped Wil on the shoulder and then went back to hosting with Alana.

"That should be the worst of it," Wil said to Saera.

Saera looked around. *"Everyone is watching us."*

In particular, the younger members of the crowd were paying special attention. The women were all staring daggers at Saera while checking out Wil, and even the men were subtly distancing themselves from their dates. Wil decided to just make matters easier for everyone and put his arm around Saera.

We won't have to deal with this for much longer…

To Wil's relief, he saw his parents approaching. "I can't imagine attending these things all the time," he commented as they walked up.

"You're telling me," Cris replied.

"Oh, you get used it," said Kate. "Come with me, my brother is here and wants to meet you." She beckoned Wil and Saera to follow her.

Wil sighed but complied. He took Saera's hand.

Kate led them around a few groups to a man in his late-sixties and his wife. They both wore Starstone rings. "Wil, this is my brother Kaiden, heir to the First Region."

Kaiden had the same hazel-green eyes as Kate and dark hair with touches of gray. He held out his hand, which Wil took. "Wil! I've heard so much about you. It's a pleasure to finally meet you."

"And you, as well," Wil replied. "This is Saera."

"Yes, of course." Kaiden held out his hand to Saera. "You make a striking couple."

At least some people aren't as dead-set against us being together as my grandparents.

Saera blushed and took Kaiden's hand. "Pleased to meet you."

"And this is my wife, Renae," Kaiden said, presenting a graceful fair-skinned woman with graying brown hair. Everyone greeted her.

Kaiden looked over Wil's TSS uniform. "I'm interested to see that the family is trending toward life in the TSS. We were all surprised when my little sister asked to join, and now you have continued in her footsteps."

"And my father's," Wil pointed out.

"Yes, very true. There's always been some consternation over the Sietinen heir being Lead Agent of the TSS."

"But think of all that delightful 'real world' experience I'm getting," Cris chimed in.

"Fair enough," Kaiden conceded. "I suppose I just wasn't cut out for such a rigorous life. I don't know how you all do it."

"You certainly had it in you. I'm just your little sister—as you were so quick to say—but look at what I've done," Kate said.

"You have me there. I should make my retreat now before I misspeak again. I applaud you all for your service." Kaiden looked to his wife. "Now, if you'll excuse us, I need to keep making the rounds. Business, you know." He inclined his head to them and departed.

"Is being in the TSS really so strange?" Wil asked his parents.

"They're coming from a different perspective," Kate replied.

"They'll be in for quite a shock when they learn the extent of the power it's granted us," Cris added. "Then they'll wish they were alongside us the whole time."

And aligned with me, most of all, Wil thought as he surveyed the room. But, there was little time for reflection. Kate eyed another relative, a cousin from the Fourth Region, and quickly dragged Wil and Saera along. Wil was content to follow his mother, knowing it diminished his chances of being pulled aside by any of the young women and their fathers who were eyeing him from a distance.

Wil was introduced to—and, in some cases, reacquainted with—various other family members over the next hour before he and Saera were finally able to extract themselves so they could get some food. They helped themselves to the buffet, while trying to not appear too gluttonous, and then washed it down with sparkling wine.

With his hunger satiated and feeling slightly buzzed, Wil couldn't take the predatory stares any longer. "Are you okay leaving here for a little while?" he asked Saera.

"Sure."

"Great, I need a break." He took her hand and led her out a side door in the ballroom directly into one of the gardens surrounding the Sietinen estate.

The air was a perfect temperature and they strolled through the garden hand-in-hand. After some time, they arrived at a bench along the walkway in front of a large lawn overlooking the lower gardens and the lake—one of the most spectacular views on the entire estate.

"Let's sit down here for a while," Wil suggested.

Saera smiled. "Okay."

This is your time to finally do something for yourself. Don't rush it. Wil gave Saera a moment to take in the view. "This is a special place to me. It's where my parents got married, and it's always been one of my favorite spots on all of Tararia."

"I can see why. It's beautiful." Saera looked out at the moonlight dancing on the surface of the lake in the distance.

Wil swallowed. "There's no one else I'd rather have here with me. I'm so thankful to have you in my life."

"Me too, Wil." She met his gaze, and there was nothing but love in her eyes.

She has no idea what's coming. "Times haven't always been easy for us and there will be even more trials going forward, but you give me the strength to make me feel like I can get through anything. I can't imagine a life without you." In one motion, Wil dropped to his knee and reached into his inner jacket pocket. "And as we go through that life together, I want you to be by my side as my wife." He pulled his hand out from his pocket, holding a Starstone ring.

Saera took in a sharp breath of surprise.

Wil looked into Saera's eyes. "Will you marry me?"

Saera teared up. "Yes!" She pulled him in for a kiss. "I'm yours forever."

And I'm yours. Wil held her close. He couldn't keep the grin off of his face.

Saera trembled slightly in his arms, but he could feel the joy radiating from her. She pulled back and looked at the ring in

Wil's hand. "It's stunning."

"Oh, right!" Wil took Saera's left hand and slipped the engagement ring on her finger. A perfect fit.

She admired her new accessory, awe in her gaze. The round center Starstone was complemented by delicate swirling metalwork accented by smaller Starstones. "So this is why you brought me here."

"It was the main reason, yes. Even with everything that's happened, I wanted to make things official with us."

Saera couldn't take her eyes off the ring on her hand. "What happens when we get back home?"

"We'll need to keep the engagement quiet for a while. We can have the wedding after you graduate."

She brought her gaze up to meet Wil's eyes. "Here?"

"Probably. But there's plenty of time to figure that out." He leaned forward for a kiss and she relaxed into him.

They took some time to revel in the moment before returning to the party. As they strolled back, Wil was overcome with a sense of elation. *I don't know how this will go over with everyone, but nothing could take away this feeling.*

Wil led Saera back into the ballroom through the same side door. Cris and Kate came over as soon as they entered.

"Where did you—" Kate began, but then she noticed the ring on Saera's finger. "Stars! Congratulations." She gave Wil and Saera hugs, beaming. Cris did likewise.

"We have your back, don't worry," Cris said.

"What does he mean?" Saera asked Wil.

Wil took her hand. "I didn't exactly have my grandparents blessing to propose to you, but I would never let that stand in the way."

Saera's face drained. "You never said anything. I thought they were fine with this."

Wil glanced over his shoulder and saw his grandparents approaching to see what all the commotion was about. "It'll be okay," he said to Saera. He put his arm around her protectively and turned to confront his grandfather.

Reinen's eyes narrowed. "How dare you so openly defy me?"

Wil stared down Reinen. "It isn't your right to decide who I can be with. Especially now that we know she's from a well-respected lower Dynasty."

Reinen hung his head, his disappointment evident. "That discovery doesn't change the fact that you've gone against me. There are so many who would be a better match."

"No. You might not see it, but there is no one else." *Not everything is about what happens here on Tararia.*

"I just can't abide this." Reinen looked away.

Alana stepped in. "Reinen, let the boy be happy."

"Oh, this is about much more than happiness," Cris said, forcing himself between his son and father.

Reinen examined Wil and Saera. "Whatever is so important about them being together?"

Cris looked around at all the party-goers watching the conversation. "Let's go outside." He led the group into the gardens.

Wil examined the place his father had selected. It was a private enough setting. *We need them on our side.* He took Saera's hand and met Reinen's eye. "I know you wanted a different path for me and my father, but we had another fate. I'm sorry if it's made you feel betrayed or abandoned. However, I have been handed so much responsibility, there are times when I must act in seemingly selfish ways to look out for myself. Choosing to be with Saera is one of those instances. I need her, because she's the one person who can fully support me in what I need to face."

"That's all the more reason for your partner to be someone with more meaningful connections," Reinen protested.

Wil met Reinen's steely gaze. "The kind of support she offers to me has nothing to do with assets or politics. I bonded with

Saera years ago because it was the one thing that could keep me sane. Asking me to walk away from her is the same as condemning me to failure."

"Failure in what?" Alana asked.

They can't be trusted with the truth. Not yet. "Performing my duty within the TSS. The specifics are irrelevant."

Reinen scoffed. "What do you expect from me? Sympathy?" He shook his head. "I see the anger in your eyes, but I'm not to blame for whatever troubles you're facing. If you want to be upset with anyone, it should be your father. He was the one to run off and join to the TSS, raise you there and get you wrapped up in this madness. I was trying to keep us all from such a life."

Wil let out a little laugh. "I assure you, we all would have ended up with the TSS whether we chose to or not." *It was part of the master plan we can't escape.*

"None of this changes that you have a responsibility to Tararia. To this family," Reinen said. "All I ever wanted was to keep us together."

Cris stared down his father. "Then why do you insist on pushing us away?"

Reinen shook his head. "I've only tried to grasp onto what I can—doing right by this family, ensuring the prosperity of SiNavTech. When your brother died, we lost the future we'd envisioned. I needed something, anything, to keep me going. So, I latched onto the one constant I had: my duty to the Dynasty. I've been alone with that responsibility for almost three decades now, since you never took an interest. Every time I've tried to pull you in, you've run further away. I can't bear that the family's continued well-being is at stake."

Wil took in his grandfather's pained expression. *I'd feel alone and betrayed in his position, too. I need to give a peace offering in terms he can understand.* "Look, I may have responsibilities to the TSS that take priority, but I'm not abandoning this family. As a gesture of good faith, I will license a civilian version of the independent jump drive to you, as you requested—and without royalties. However, I must insist that we install some navigation safeguards to minimize the chance for operator error. I can't have people getting lost in subspace on my conscience."

"On the condition that I agree to you marrying Saera?" Reinen questioned.

"That's happening with or without your blessing—I don't need your permission," Wil countered. "This offer is only to demonstrate that I do respect the Dynasty's interests."

"Technology is hardly a substitute for your involvement in the family's interests," his grandfather replied.

"Well, it's all I can offer at the present," Wil said. "If you want us involved in your life, finding common ground is the first step."

Reinen eyed him. "Does this offer come with any additional conditions?"

Wil glanced at his father. "There's still the issue of construction capacity for the TSS fleet. But I'll ask you now as your grandson, not as a TSS officer. I am facing a nearly impossible task, and I need all the help I can get. It would make all the difference for the TSS to have the retired Prisaris shipyard."

Reinen hesitated. "There are many political considerations with that sort of arrangement."

"Getting the independent jump drive should be more than enough to buy the support of SiNavTech's board members," Wil pointed out.

Reinen took a moment to think through the proposition. "If that's what it will take to get us working together toward a common goal, then I suppose I have no choice. I'll make sure the other Dynasties won't stand in the way of the TSS acquiring the shipyard."

"Thank you." Wil shook Reinen's hand to seal the agreement.

Reinen turned his attention to Saera. "I apologize for my behavior. That was no way to treat you."

"It's okay," Saera replied, somehow maintaining her poise. *"What the hell was that?"* she added telepathically to Wil.

"Sorry," he responded. *"Like I said, things are a little complicated around here."*

"I'll say," she replied.

"I hope this can be a new beginning for us." Reinen took Saera by the hands. "Welcome to the family."

◄ CHAPTER 6 ►

Every one of the young men had the same look of bewilderment on their face. They had arrived at TSS Headquarters along with the other Trainees, but had then been immediately pulled from their orientation groups and ushered into the training room on Level 11 where Wil now stood before them. Everyone was looking at him warily, their eyes darting while they shifted on their feet.

Wil evaluated them, studying the stance and expression of each person. He noted those who were taking the situation in stride and those who appeared most uncomfortable. It was apparent through their light gray training uniforms that most were already in decent physical shape, but there would still be a long way to go.

"You're all probably wondering why you're here," Wil said, finally breaking the silence.

The men nodded, with varying levels of distress.

Wil smiled for a moment, trying to set them at ease. "Let's start with an introduction. My name is Wil Sights. I am currently the sole Agent in the Primus Elite class."

The men's glances shifted between each other and Wil.

"I personally selected you twenty men out of thousands of candidates. I am going to train you as Primus Elite Agents." *Let that sink in for a minute.*

The shifting glances changed to murmurs and gawks. "Is he

serious?" "Primus Elite?" "Is that even a thing?"

Wil straightened and looked down the line levelly. "Normally, we'd give Trainees a year before they have to make a long-term training commitment. I need you to make that decision today."

"Why?" asked a seventeen-year-old with light brown hair named Ian Mandren, his amber eyes narrowed with suspicion.

"Because the TSS is at war," Wil replied. He pulled out his handheld and activated a holographic projection containing footage from the war in the rift. Ships under fire, planets burning in the aftermath of Bakzen attacks. Brutal and uncensored—the same images the Priesthood always took such lengths to hide. Wil stopped the video after two minutes.

The young men took it in with confusion and horror.

"Where is that?" Ian questioned.

"It can't be real," protested Tom Aldric, the youngest of the group. "Why are you showing us this?"

"It's very real," Wil stated. "A war is underway—just out of sight in a dimensional rift. Our enemy is the Bakzen. They have advanced capabilities to travel within the dimensional planes, and they have torn a rift in space beyond the outer territories. Select members of the TSS are told the truth and are brought into the conflict on the other side of the rift. They have been able to keep the enemy from reaching too far into normal space, but they will not be able to hold out for much longer.

"The Bakzen have been building their forces for centuries, preparing for an all-out onslaught against the entire Taran race. The nature of the conflict doesn't matter—only that our complete and utter destruction is their singular goal. There is no longer hope for a diplomatic solution. It is simply our survival or theirs, and I have been charged with leading the Taran people to victory." His gaze passed down the line of shocked faces struggling to make sense of what they'd just been told.

"The Bakzen?" Curtis Jaconis, a dark-haired eighteen-year-old, said. "Never heard of them."

"And the Priesthood would like it to stay that way," Wil replied. "Except, the Bakzen are coming for us. They are vicious and powerful, and if we don't strike back with everything we can, there won't be a world anywhere that's safe from them."

"What does any of that have to do with us?" Ian asked.

Wil clasped his hands behind his back. "Because to win this fight we need a new approach. I stand before you as the future Supreme Commander of the TSS. I have been tasked with training a group of elite commanders and pilots who will be able to do what no one else can. But I don't have time to waste on quitters. Anyone who's with me needs to be all-in from Day One. Today. I know you have next to no information to go on— it's a leap of faith and I'm asking you to take my words at face value. But I picked you because you are the best of the best. You can help me win this fight."

Many of the men took shaky breaths and focused on the metal floor.

All of them are too smart to go along with this. But maybe there's just enough crazy in there to sway them to join me. "I can promise you this: training with me will make you the strongest, best Agent you can possibly be. If you're serious about being in the TSS and making this your career, this group is the place to be. Anyone who joins me will train outside of normal TSS training channels on an accelerated timeline. I'll push you to your limits and beyond. Other groups train together, but ultimately the instructors are looking for the star individuals to emerge. This group will be different. We need to be a team from the beginning. We need to trust each other implicitly—know each person's strengths, weaknesses, and how we fit together as a unit. You all have enormous telekinetic potential, but moreover, you have the brains and heart that will keep me grounded as a leader."

"So you're saying you want us to train as officers to fight in a secret war against a vastly superior enemy?" Curtis asked.

"That's right," Wil said with a grimace. "Some get to choose their role, but mine was assigned. It's a shite job, but someone has to do it. Can I count on you to help me?"

The silence in the room was palpable. The men all stared at the floor or the walls in introspection.

Wil's chest constricted. *Don't make me beg. I can't do this alone.*

Finally, one man raised his head and looked Wil square in the eye. He was close to Wil's height and had medium-brown hair and light blue eyes that shone with insight and comprehension. "I'm in."

Wil instantly recognized the man as Michael Andres. *Saera was right about him.* "Thank you," Wil said with genuine gratitude. "Who else?"

"So am I."

"Me too."

One by one, the other men joined Michael in the resolution to support Wil in his mission. They quivered slightly from restrained nerves, but they set their jaws and stood ready for direction.

Wil smiled, both from relief and gratefulness. *I have a team now. We can do this together.* "Now, it doesn't take a telepath to tell that you're wondering how I came to be in this singularly unique position of being the sole Primus Elite Agent."

Several men nodded confirmation.

"Well, the short answer is that I was born into it. Both of my parents are Agents. My father is Cris Sights, Lead Agent of this TSS Headquarters, and my mother is Kate Sights. I grew up here at Headquarters and entered the training program when I was twelve. I graduated at sixteen with a CR of 13.7 and have been waiting for this day ever since. I'm only nineteen now—barely older than some of you—but I am the only person to have spent time face-to-face with the Bakzen and lived to tell about it."

Someone raised his hand. Wil recognized him as Ethan Samlier, a blonde seventeen-year-old from Tararia's Second Region. He had exceptional piloting ability and an estimated CR of 8.9. When Wil nodded his consent for the question, Ethan said, "Excuse me, sir, did you say 13.7?"

"Yes, I did," Wil replied, unruffled. *But your inexperience means you're latching onto the wrong thing—surviving an encounter with the Bakzen is far more remarkable.*

"I thought the CR scale only went to 10," Ethan added.

"Just because no one ever scored above 10 before doesn't mean that was the cap," countered Wil.

Ethan seemed unsure what to say. "Okay. Well, a 13.7... That's an extremely high limit."

I need to give them some perspective. "I didn't say that was my limit. That's the CR I obtained."

"But I thought the entire purpose of the Course Rank test was to document limits?" Ethan tried to clarify.

"Usually, yes," Wil confirmed. "But I broke the testing sphere, so I guess we won't know what I can really do until we're in battle." *I'm scared to see what I'm capable of.*

"Wait, you *broke* the testing sphere?" Curtis asked incredulously.

Wil nodded. "Yes, it cracked at 13.7, so they stopped the exam."

"So... what's your limit, then?" Ian asked.

"I don't know," Wil confessed. "If I have one, I haven't found it yet. All I can tell you is that my CR exam was three years ago, and I'm stronger now than I was then."

"The Cadicle," Ethan breathed.

"That's what they tell me."

"What does that mean?" Tom asked meekly. He was barely sixteen-years-old and had a thin frame with a dark complexion. Though he appeared frail compared to some of the older Trainees, unlike most others he had the rare potential to score above a CR of 9.

"It means that you should listen to me when I give you instruction because I know what I'm talking about," Wil retorted with a hint of sarcasm, though most of the men seemed too nervous to see it as lighthearted humor.

"We will," affirmed Ethan. "The Priesthood has foretold the coming of the Cadicle for thousands of years. To many, your presence will signal the beginning of a new age for Tarans."

A foretelling the Priesthood was all too eager to help realize through any means necessary. "Please don't misinterpret the title. I'm not a special icon or miraculous incarnation. I'm a mortal man with my own hopes and desires just like you. What I do, I do because I must. I probably wouldn't have chosen this life if I'd had another option, so I'm just trying to make the most of the role I was handed."

Most of the men seemed dumbfounded by Wil's blunt honesty. He had all that power, but he'd give it up if he could? It was easy for them to think that way without knowing the true burden of the responsibility.

Once they see the toll it takes on me, then they'll understand. Wil looked from face to face. They all seemed so young and innocent. *Was there ever a time I lived without the weight that I carry now?* A twinge of sadness struck his heart. *I'm going to ruin them. I'm going to show them the darkest, evil nature of people and they'll be changed forever.*

"Tell us what to do," Michael said at last. "We'll support you in any way we can."

There were murmurs of agreement down the line.

Already they're keeping me on course. "Okay, let's see what all of you can do. Form a straight line a pace out from that far wall." Wil pointed to the wall across the room from him, and the men lined up as he'd instructed. "Good. Take a step forward if you've had any hand-to-hand combat training, even if it was just as a kid."

All but three of the men took a step forward.

"Now, take a step forward if you've ever had any marksmanship training."

Twelve men took a step forward, including one of the three with no combat training.

"Take another step if you've studied navigation or applied mathematics."

Eighteen men took a step forward.

"Take another step if you have any piloting experience—actually behind the controls, not just navigation theory."

Six men took a step.

"Now," Wil instructed, "go back to the starting wall if this is your first day with the TSS."

Everyone returned to their starting place.

"Did you get anything out of that exercise?" He looked down the line of Trainees.

"We all bring things from the outside, but we're all starting from the same place here," Ian answered for the group.

"Very good. Now, break into teams of four." While they sorted out their teams, Wil went to a door on the wall behind him, which concealed a storage compartment that contained five identical boxes. The boxes were unlabeled, approximately half a meter cubes. "In each of these boxes is a puzzle. I want each team to work together to assemble it." Wil handed out the boxes.

Each team started pulling out the pieces of their three-dimensional puzzle. The pieces all looked remarkably similar, with no distinguishing color or marks—plastic blocks, matte copper in color. The men eyed him skeptically.

"Oh yeah, and pick someone on your team to blindfold. Only he is allowed to touch the pieces," Wil added.

No one seemed pleased with the order, but each team picked someone to blindfold and the others began giving instructions to lay out the pieces so they could figure out how everything fit together. It took some time, but eventually each team was able to construct a square-based pyramid out of the pieces. Next, Wil split the men into three groups and ordered them to form human pyramids of six people by arranging themselves on their hands and knees, doing so while everyone was blindfolded except for two instructors. It was haphazard and awkward, but they pulled it off. Afterward, Wil had them break into groups of five and he gave them each a tablet from the storage compartment. They had to work together on a specified problem of how to most effectively move some cargo from Point A to Point B while avoiding several pitfalls. Some teams came up with distinctly better solutions than others, but the exercise fulfilled the intended purpose of allowing group dynamics to unfold.

Wil evaluated everyone as they ran through each of the exercises. He knew all of their personality and capability profiles by heart, and he was pleased to see that everyone was performing just as he'd hoped. In the end, four individuals stood out from the others: Ethan Samlier, Michael Andres, Curtis Jaconis, and Ian Mandren. They had some of the highest CR potential, but they also proved to be the most natural leaders; the other men were already looking to them for validation. *They will be my Captains. I'll groom them, and once they've already gained respect from everyone else, I'll make it official.*

"All right. Fall back in line," Wil ordered. They complied. "Now, do any of you have questions for me?" he asked the group.

Ethan raised his hand right away, and Wil called on him. "So, we're an established training group, contracted under the Primus Elite designation. Does that mean we're Trainees or Initiates?"

Wil nodded. "A fair question. You're Trainees for now, but you won't be confined to the same one-year timeline as the others. I'll advance the group when I feel you've met the milestones for Initiates—be that in two weeks or ten months."

"So, where are our quarters?" questioned someone named Kevin Haelis from the main city on one of Tararia's moons, Denae.

Wil smiled. "I was able to pull some strings to get you placed directly in Initiate housing. You're in Primus I-06, and you'll find your bed assignments waiting for you on the screens." Wil had arranged the rooms while the men went through the exercises so each subgroup was housed with their eventual Captain.

Michael raised his hand and Wil called on him. "Will we attend classes with the other Trainees?"

"Yes, some," Wil replied. "I've tailored the class schedule for each of you based on your aptitudes and baseline knowledge. Some classes will be with the other Trainees and Initiates, and some will be with me. As time goes on, we'll focus on more specialized topics in subgroups."

Curtis held up his hand. "Forgive me if this is too much of an intrusion, but if we're going to be your backup, then we should know if there's anything that would impact your decisions," Curtis said after Wil acknowledged him. "Do you have any biases we should know about?"

That's a very astute question. "Yes, there are two things you should know." Wil took a deep breath. "First, Wil Sights is not my birth name. I am Williame Sietinen, second in line to the Sietinen Dynasty of the Third Region of Tararia."

There were gasps around the room. Even Michael, despite being Earth-born, seemed to recognize the significance of the disclosure.

"Secondly," Wil continued. "I recently became engaged. Her life and well-being is more valuable to me than my own. She is everything to me." *My greatest strength, and my greatest vulnerability.*

"Who is she?" Ethan asked.

I can't share that with them yet. "I will tell you that she is a student here at Headquarters. Our relationship is highly confidential. I'll give you her identify in time, but for right now it's not important."

"Is she high-born like you?" Tom questioned.

"No."

They all mulled over the new information.

"So, how should we refer to you?" asked Ian.

"Feel free to call me 'Wil' when it's just us," Wil responded. "'Agent Sights' and all the 'sir' business is best in the more formal settings. As a reminder, no honorifics for Tararian social standing should ever be used within the TSS."

A young-looking sixteen-year-old named Kalin Evari spoke up, asking the question surely everyone was thinking. "If you scored a 13.7, what can you do?"

"A lot," Wil replied. Without knowing his limits, it was the only truthful answer.

"What about a demonstration?" Curtis asked.

"Are you sure you want me to do that?"

There were emphatic nods all around.

"Okay. Everyone form a circle around me." Wil moved to the middle of the ring. "Now, try to run toward me." All of the men tried to run forward, but Wil held them back through a combination of telekinetic manipulation of the air and a subliminal telepathic message telling them they couldn't move. "Satisfied?" he asked them.

"This is basic stuff!" objected Kalin.

"Oh really?" In an instant, Wil shifted the simple restraint into full levitation, fanning the men out into a ring in mid-air two meters off the ground. They strained against the immobilizing hold he had over them, but were helpless. Without letting them down, Wil formed an energy orb in his hand. It shone brightly with white and blue light, hovering on the edge of subspace. He grew the orb until it was the size of his torso, then he tossed it to the floor, where he continued to feed it until it was as tall as himself. Wil paced around the orb, watching the mystified looks on the faces of his men. "If that isn't enough…" Wil cleared his mind and detached from his fixed physical state—creating a spatial dislocation that took him to the edge of subspace. In that state, he passed through the energy orb and came to rest on the other side. To the men in the ring above his head, he appeared to move from one side of the room to the other in less than the blink of an eye.

There were cries of confusion and awe overhead. He looked up, and it was clear from their expressions that it had been a suitable demonstration.

That's enough for today. Wil lowered them to the ground. "Take the rest of the day to get settled into your quarters. Your training contracts will be waiting on your assigned tablets," Wil informed them. "We start group training in the morning. I'll meet you at your quarters at 07:30. Dismissed."

Relieved to be back on the ground, everyone started making their way to the door.

One more order of business. "Michael, hold up a minute," Wil called out.

Michael stayed back as the other men filed out of the room.

"Thank you for voicing the first support earlier," Wil said. "I appreciate your willingness and decisiveness."

The corner of Michael's mouth twitched toward a smile. "Of course."

"And, it's rather fitting that you were the first," Wil continued. "I selected you for this elite group because you were recommended by my fiancée. She told me you were someone I could count on and trust."

Michael's brow furrowed slightly. "How do I know your fiancée?"

"She grew up on Earth," Wil answered. "But I need to know

that if I reveal her identity, you'll keep it to yourself."

"Of course. But why are you telling just me?"

Because I'm worried you're still in love with her. I know I could never let those feelings go. "You two have a... history, as I understand it. I want to make sure there won't be any issues with us working together."

The creases in Michael's brow deepened. He looked down, clearly running through everyone from his past in an attempt to figure out who it could be.

"You knew her as Saera Alexander."

Michael's body went rigid for a moment, his face stoic. Then his shoulders rounded and he slumped forward. "Of course it would be her."

He certainly remembers her better than she remembered him. "So, is that going to be a problem?"

Michael took a deep breath before looking Wil square in the eye. "I won't lie, she made quite an impression on me. But, I knew I would never have her, and I accepted that a long time ago. If I can have her back in my life just as a friend, that's more than I could have hoped for."

The words seemed sincere enough. Wil detected no deceit on the surface, and he couldn't start out the friendship by invading Michael's inner mind. *I need to trust him, as I'm asking him to trust me.* "That's good to hear."

"Is there anything else?"

Wil shook his head. "No, go on. I'll see you in the morning."

"See you then." Michael made his way toward the door. "And give my regards to Saera," he called back over his shoulder.

"I will."

The report was far from conclusive, but if it were true, the implications could be devastating. There was a buzz at the door and Banks minimized the projection on his desk. "Come in."

Wil entered, looking tired, but that was to be expected.

"How did the first day of training go?" Banks asked.

"It went well, sir. I feel confident that I picked the right group," Wil replied.

"I'm glad to hear it. I was hoping to talk through the training timeline—what you have planned."

Wil was pensive. He walked forward and sat down in one of the chairs across from Banks' desk. "Well, sir, I haven't thought through all the specifics yet."

That was no cause for concern, given Wil's adaptiveness. "Do you have any milestones in mind?"

Wil nodded. "I've already selected four Captains. I'll train them as Seconds once they're ready. Each one of those Captains will have a specialized tactical team. I'll start everyone out with a mixture of hand-to-hand and freefall training. Most of them have had at least rudimentary training already, but they're going to need to hone their spatial awareness to a ridiculous level if they're going to be able to do what I have in mind."

"And what is that?"

Wil smiled. "I've been working on a design for a fighter jet that can make near right-angle turns. Pair that with a precise rift jump drive and the Bakzen won't ever be able to see us coming."

That's just crazy enough to work. "And what about telekinesis training?"

Wil shook his head. "I can't push it. But, I'd like to hold all study sessions and classes on the training level so they can practice telepathy and basic object levitation all the time."

"You can have any resources you need—study rooms or otherwise," Banks said.

"Thank you, sir."

And now the toughest question… "How long do you need to raise them to full Agents?"

Wil cracked a faint smile. "How long do I have?"

Banks looked at him levelly. "Five years." *That's all we can spare.*

Wil thought for a moment, running the scenarios. "That will be difficult, but I think we can do it."

"Good. It's imperative that this be a success." *We don't have any other option.*

Wil nodded. "Yes, sir. I know. I'll do everything I can."

"And we'll support you to the best of our ability," Banks stated. "To that end, we just signed the agreement to acquire the Prisarus shipyard."

"Yes, my father let me know," Wil replied. "I'm not surprised you sent him to conduct the negotiations."

Banks smiled. "He does have a knack for it." He paused, reflecting on the report he just read. "There's one other matter."

"Yes, sir?"

Banks swallowed. "Are you familiar with the Aesir?"

"The Ascended?" Wil asked with surprise. "Taelis mentioned them to me once. They live in the furthest depths of space, seeking enlightenment by reading the patterns of the multiverse... Or something like that."

Banks nodded. *The only ones who have always known the truth I guard.* "The Aesir haven't taken much interest in Tararian affairs since they left after the Revolution a thousand years ago. The only time we hear from them is if they have detected someone potentially worthy of ascension. To test them."

Wil nodded slowly, already bracing for the punch line.

"I have reason to believe they may come for you. You need to be prepared, when and if they arrive."

Wil took a breath. "And when might that be?"

"I have no idea. But, their 'test'... no outsider has ever survived."

Wil paused for a moment, then nodded. "I'll be ready."

‹ CHAPTER 7 ›

Deena Laecy awoke to a buzz from her handheld. Good news never came first thing in the morning.

She rolled over and grabbed the device off its charging pad on her nightstand. The message was flagged as Fleet Critical. Nothing urgent.

Earlier in her career she would have been out of bed and dashing down to the main hangar in an instant after getting a message like that. But after twenty-five years with the TSS and more than two decades in an active warzone, she had her priorities. Starting the day off with a proper hot shower was one. *I can at least have that even if the rest of the day is going to be a foking disaster.*

Her quarters were compact and minimally furnished—with little more than her bunk, a work desk, and wardrobe—but at least she had the room to herself. She took her time getting ready in her private bathroom and then grabbed an energy bar from the stash on her desk to eat on the way down to the hangar.

Nothing seemed particularly out of place when she arrived. Her core crew members were gathered around the central holodisplay in the main engineering lab. "I got the alert. What did we lose now?" she asked after swallowing the last of her energy bar.

Becca, the lead navigation tech, frowned. "The encryption on the TX-80s was compromised."

Laecy groaned. "We just updated the sequence."

"It's worse than that," Becca continued, crossing her arms. "All of the primary nav boards are fried."

The day was off to a great start, indeed. "The entire TX-80 line?"

"Every single one," Becca confirmed.

"Shite." Laecy looked at the other faces in the group, all with expressions of defeat. "Were the jets recovered?"

"Yes," Richards jumped in. "Fortunately, the transport cruiser was nearby."

"At least there's that." *Maybe we can salvage something.* Laecy clapped her hands together. "Well, on a somewhat brighter note, I just got the revised IT-1 specs from Wil. We'll be using two ateron cores going forward, but there's a production backlog."

"That's good news how?" Becca asked.

"Because at least we'll have a functioning jet eventually. A delay is better than nothing at all."

"How long of a delay?" Nolan asked. He was one of the newer engineers on her team but showed some promising aptitude. He had a knack for getting into details that many overlooked, making him an exceptional quality assurance inspector on new projects.

"Not sure yet," Laecy replied. "But, we did get the go-ahead to initiate production at the Prisarus shipyard next month. The TSS was able to acquire the whole facility."

Richards relaxed. "So that's where the ateron cores will come from."

Leave it to the bioelectronics expert to piece it together. "You've got it. All those specialized components we could never get will now be produced onsite right alongside the hull plating and washroom fixtures."

"What do we do for the time being?" Nolan asked.

Laecy took a deep breath. "We keep the existing fleet flying, same as always."

"What's left of it, anyway," Richards murmured.

"Hey, we work with what we've got." Laecy glanced at all of the TX-80 jets permanently grounded from the most recent assault. "And I think we can retrofit the directional thrusters and command interface from the remaining TX-80s into the old TX-70 shells."

Richards lit up. "Of course! The TX-70s run on the old encryption protocol."

Laecy grinned back. "Which was never cracked, just retired."

"Roaming the fields of Aderoth," Richards added with a wistful lilt to his tone. An inside joke that only Laecy would get.

She didn't let herself get distracted by thoughts of their after-hours dreaming. "All right, team. You have your challenge. Go."

Saera was surprised to find that she was nervous about seeing Michael again. Though, it wasn't so much him, but that he reminded her of a part of her life that she'd tried to leave behind on Earth.

She had reserved a study room where they could chat. Knowing that Wil had disclosed their relationship to Michael, it was better to have a preemptive conversation than wait for a random encounter in a hallway.

The door to the study room beeped as it slid open. Michael stood framed by the doorway—taller and filled out compared to when Saera had last seen him at fourteen-years-old.

"Hi," Saera greeted, her heart pounding in her ears. *Things are different now. You're in control.*

Michael stepped inside the study room and closed the door. He evaluated Saera. "You look great."

"The TSS has been good to me." She returned to her seat.

Michael hesitated by the door for a moment, then sat down

across the table from Saera. "And a Junior Agent already, huh?"

"Yeah, it's been a whirlwind." *Has it really been almost five years since we last saw each other?*

"I can imagine." Michael wouldn't quite meet her gaze.

Saera shifted in her chair. "I know this is weird."

Michael leaned back and crossed his arms. "You're pretty much the last person I expected to find here."

I hope it wasn't a mistake encouraging Wil to include him on the team. "I've come to understand some things about these abilities over the years. We're drawn to each other."

"So that's the only reason we became friends—because of the latent 'gifts'?"

That, and your father was there to watch over me. Saera made him look her straight in the eye. "No, it was always more than that."

Michael tore his gaze away. "Shit, Saera! What do you want me to say?"

"Nothing. I don't know." She swallowed hard, regretting that she scheduled the reunion, even though finding some sense of closure was necessary if they were ever to move forward.

"It wasn't fair for you to take off without saying goodbye," Michael said after a pause.

"I know it wasn't. I'm sorry."

Michael stared at his hands resting on the tabletop. "I thought that night would change things."

"What, that we'd start dating like normal people and everything would be great? I was way too fucked up back then to have that."

Michael's eyes narrowed and he looked up at her under his brow. "Don't diminish what we felt."

I did feel it. In another life we could have been happy together. But that's not what was meant to be. "I cared about you then, and I always will. I was completely lost and you showed me that maybe things could be different."

"And for that, a follow-up text message was too much to ask?" The venom was thick in Michael's words.

Saera's chest was tight thinking back to that night and everything that followed. She bit her lip to keep it from quavering, thankful that her tinted glasses hid the tears forming in her eyes. "Justin somehow found that you and I… I was walking home from the school when he showed up with his friends and they all took me up to the Pointe, and…" She didn't want to complete the thought. To remember that it really happened.

Michael sat in silence, but Saera could see him fuming under the calm surface.

"I don't remember most of it, fortunately. I think they drugged me. And they must have been careful to make it not look forced, because I wasn't bruised or anything when I woke up on my front lawn in the morning. But I knew what had happened." She swallowed. "The worst part was my parents just figured I had been to one too many parties, and it was time for a change of pace. So they sent me away to boarding school. By then, I didn't care if they believed the truth—I just wanted to get away and leave everything behind. I know I should have said goodbye to you, but I knew you'd ask why I was leaving, and I didn't want to have to say it. So I left for the new school and started to rediscover myself. I'd been there for a month when the TSS found me."

Michael took a slow breath. "Oh."

"I wanted to forget everything that happened. Like it was a nightmare and I'd finally woken up."

"I can't believe those fuckers—"

"And that's the other reason I didn't want to tell you. I didn't know what you'd do."

Michael took a shaky breath, his face flushed.

"We all needed to move on. And now we're here." She paused. "But I did think about you. And I always wanted the best for you. When I saw your picture in Wil's list of candidates, I thought about what the TSS had done for me. What it could do for you."

Michael thought for a moment. "This is a welcome change, don't get me wrong. Even a dream come true. But..." he shook his head. "Fuck. I never stopped loving you."

"It was—"

"It was just dumb kids mistaking our latent telekinetic abilities for genuine attraction, right."

Saera composed herself. "I'm with Wil, and what I have with him has given me a whole new perspective."

"And while you got to meet your prince—literally—things haven't been so great for me. Like you, when I came here I thought it was an escape. Except, the only girl I ever loved is now engaged to my commanding officer. Classic."

If I knew he still felt that way about me, I never would have suggested he come here. But how could I have known? That was years ago. "I'll tell Wil you want out on your behalf, if you want."

"No."

Saera nodded. "He'd rather hear it from you, anyway."

"No. I'm not going anywhere," Michael said, resolute. "Ever since my abilities emerged and my dad told me about the TSS, I've wanted to come here."

"Even knowing that they could have saved your mom but they didn't?"

Michael's face twisted. "That's precisely why it's so important people like us are also part of the TSS. Ambassadors for Earth. Maybe we can help make Taran science available so others won't have to suffer."

As long as the Priesthood is around, I wouldn't count on it. "You did always try to fight for the greater good."

"Even so, I've spent too much of my life on the sidelines. Being here is my chance to finally make a real difference. I'm here to stay."

"And what about us?" Saera asked.

"There is no 'us.' You're with Wil."

Saera eyed him. "With what you've said, I can't trust that your feelings for me won't interfere with your relationship with Wil."

Michael shrugged. "What other choice do I have?"

"There are other trainers—"

"Give up the Primus Elite opportunity because of you?" He shook his head. "No, I already gave up enough of my life to you."

"You'll see me with him, you know. It won't be a secret forever."

"So I'll be a good friend. To both of you. Just like you always wanted and needed me to be." Michael stood and headed for the door. "I'm sure you'll have a very happy life together."

Saera stared at the closed door and gnawed on her bottom lip after he left. She had no illusions that there wouldn't be drama, but at least Michael cared. That would make him committed to the cause, even if it was just displaced affection toward her. He might resent the circumstances, but there was time to adjust. At least, she hoped so.

It'll only be awkward if you make it that way. Saera took a deep breath and departed. Only time would tell.

Michael shook his head with disbelief. *Why does everything in my life always lead back to her?*

Finding out about the TSS and the ancient culture his dad had left behind when he moved to Earth had changed Michael's perspective—or so he had thought. But when it came down to it, he couldn't grasp the galactic scale of his new reality. Interpersonal bonds always came to the forefront, and his childhood friendship with Saera was one of the most impactful.

She had been there for him when his mom got sick and slowly wasted away. She had defended him when others mistook his hurt for a flawed personality unfit for friendship. She had been so many of his "firsts" that he'd lost count, but it had given her an enduring place in his heart.

He wanted to feel bitter that she had so easily moved on, yet he couldn't. After only a couple of days training with Wil, Michael could already see how there must be a perfect complement between Wil and Saera. He was no competition for their connection—but moreover, he didn't want to come between them. He had his own life to live, even though it intersected with theirs.

On the rest of the walk back to his room, Michael concentrated on moving past the meeting with Saera. Whatever feelings still lingered for her needed to be boxed away.

The Primus Elite quarters were in the middle of the Primus Initiate residential wing on the third floor of Level 2. Michael passed through the hall lined with plants in transparent canisters mounted to the walls, and little nooks with padded benches made impromptu social areas between the private study rooms. He had felt instantly at home.

Michael unlocked the door to his quarters with the palm of his hand. The door slid open, revealing the common room at the center of the four bedrooms that each contained five beds. The spacious common area included several couches. A round table surrounded by twenty-one chairs was the main fixture at the back of the room.

More than half the Primus Elite trainees were gathered around the table, and profiles of several young women were displayed on the holoprojector. A few of the students glanced up when Michael entered.

"Time to weigh in," Ian said.

"On what?" Michael asked as he walked over.

"We're trying to narrow down the list of who Wil's fiancée

could be," explained Ian.

"I don't think Wil would want you doing that." Michael scanned over the profiles up on screen, but Saera didn't appear to be among them.

"Oh come on, you're not even a little curious?" Kevin asked with a mischievous glint in his eye.

"That's not the point." *I know exactly who she is.*

"We already have a list of definite contenders," Ethan continued. "But there's some debate over anyone we may have overlooked."

Michael's stomach sank. "Who are the others?"

Kevin grinned. "Ah ha! So you *are* interested." He minimized the current set of profiles and brought up another file with five women—two initiates and three Junior Agents. Summary notes were displayed next to each profile with a rationalization for why each was a potential match.

Of course, Saera was at the top of that list. Michael tensed. *How couldn't she be?* It was on the record that Wil had provided her midterm evaluation, she was at the top of her class, beautiful—

"So who's your pick?" Ian prompted.

Michael shook his head. "I'm not taking any bets. And you shouldn't, either."

Ian rolled his eyes. "Oh, come on."

"We're here to learn and are preparing to go to war," Michael shot back. "This is—"

"An amusing diversion," Curtis interrupted from the other side of the table. "Don't be so uptight."

Michael looked at the faces of the young men around the table. They were completely absorbed in the exercise. Nothing he could say would change their mind. "Let it go," he said one more time and headed for his room. There were bigger battles to fight.

◆ ▶   ◆ ▶   ◆ ▶

Wil led the Primus Elites to breakfast in the mess hall, feeling pleased with how the group was coming together. *We survived our first week. That has to count for something.*

The team was in good spirits—laughing and joking around as they entered the buffet line. Already he could see the friendships forming. There was true camaraderie—exactly what he had hoped to see, and what they would need to make it through the trials to come.

They helped themselves to food, then took a seat at one of the large tables in the center of the room. As they sat down together, Wil glimpsed Saera having breakfast with her roommate Elise on the other side of the mess hall.

"Good morning," he greeted her telepathically from afar.

"Good morning!" she replied. *"Any time for me to come by tonight?"*

"Please do—any time after dinner is fine. I miss you."

"I know you've been busy with them." Saera snuck a glance over at Wil and the Primus Elites as she took a sip of tea.

"It's making me miss our old study dates."

"Ah, the good ol' days—"

"What's on the agenda today?" Ian asked, interrupting Wil's private conversation.

"Love you. See you soon," Wil said to Saera before turning his attention to the trainees around his table. "The agenda for today is more of the same. Physical and mental conditioning until you're ready to start the real work."

A collective groan passed around the table.

"Hey, this is the easy part. Enjoy the laps and basic freefall maneuvers while you can." Wil dug into his meal. After a few bites, he noticed Ian and Curtis whispering to each other at the other end of the table.

"But she's right there. It would just take a minute," said Curtis.

Ian shook his head. "It's a violation."

"There was nothing in the rules about interrogation," Curtis insisted.

"Regardless, it's an unfair advantage," countered Ian.

"You're just upset you didn't think of it first."

"I—"

"What are you two scheming about?" Wil asked them.

Ian and Curtis tensed. "Nothing, sir," Curtis responded too quickly.

"You sure about that?" Wil pressed.

"It was just some silly speculation about your fiancée," Ian admitted after a moment.

That's all we need. "Whatever you're planning, stop it."

"We were just going to talk to a few of the girls it might be—" Curtis started to explain.

"No," Wil cut him off, firm. "Don't make me regret telling you anything."

Ian gave Curtis a shove.

It was difficult to believe that the same individuals who demonstrated focus and leadership could engage in such trivial undertakings as speculating about his love life. "Clearly you've had too much idle time." Wil stood. "Let's get to it."

The men hurriedly finished up their remaining bites of food and followed Wil out of the mess hall.

Wil led the group down to Level 11 and lined them up in their usual training room. They were all poised with anxious anticipation, eager to learn. Even knowing the burden that Wil carried—that they would all carry—they stood ready to face the challenge.

Wil met the gaze of each one of his men. *They have no idea what they're in for. And I'll be training right alongside them.*

At the end of the line, Michael gave him a resolute nod.

Wil nodded back. "Let's get started. We have a lot of work to do."

PART 2: PARTNERSHIP

‹ CHAPTER 8 ›

Cris ended the video projection of a recent training session from the Primus Elites in freefall. "I can't believe how far they've come in just a year and a half."

Banks nodded from behind his desk. "It's all exceeded my expectations."

The maneuvers Wil was running with his group were quite advanced—the sort of exercises performed by Junior Agents. It helped that the Primus Elites were already manifesting telekinetic abilities. Wil's request to have them spend the majority of their time outside of the subspace bubble seemed to be paying off. That, or just being around Wil made a difference. Their progress wasn't as marked as Saera's had been after Wil bonded with her, but it was evident that exposure to his profound ability level did have a measurable impact on others.

"At this rate, they'll make it to Agent on your insane timeline," Cris said as he rose from the guest chair.

"They're still a long way off from being Agents."

"True," Cris conceded, "but they're already on pace to exceed their CR estimates."

Banks steepled his fingers. "It would be unprecedented for all of them to exceed 9."

"I could see it happening." *And I don't want to think what they could all do when combined with Wil.*

The High Commander sat in quiet contemplation, his mind

guarded as usual.

"What are you thinking?" Cris asked.

"I'm concerned about them becoming too distanced from the other trainees. They train, eat, sleep, and go to class together, but how much interaction is there with others?"

"Many of their classes are with the rest of the population. I made sure of that."

Banks tapped his fingertips together. "I've talked to some of the instructors. Even though the Primus Elites are in classes with the other students, they don't really talk to them. The three or four Primus Elites in each class will form a subgroup and work ahead of the rest of the class."

"They're a smart bunch."

"But they're not winning favor with the others. They need to be viewed as trusted leaders, not genius outsiders."

Cris shrugged. "What do you suggest?"

"I think Wil needs to instruct them to be mentors. Have each of the Primus Elites step up as an instructor in some way."

"The other students might resist."

"We've seen time and time again that every trainee wants to improve" Banks responded. "They'll take an opportunity to grow if it's handed to them, even if it's begrudgingly at first."

"I'd say it's unusual for Initiates to take on mentees, but 'usual' lost its meaning a decade ago."

Banks cracked a smile. "Talk to Wil. Let's see what kind of leadership potential these future officers of his really have."

"No, no, no!" Wil ended the simulation. "Are you trying to get us all killed?"

Ian cursed into the comm. "It seemed like a better idea in my head."

"You can't defy physics." Wil rubbed his eyes. "Maybe we need to go back to the spatial awareness chamber."

"We'll get it," Michael interjected. "These controls are new. We just need some more practice."

"A *lot* more." Wil knew it was unfair to expect much from his men after only two days of practice in the flight simulators. Flying a combat jet was quite different from freefall training, regardless of what instructors told their students. And he was pushing the timeline. Under other circumstances, he would have waited several more months—or even a year—before moving onto the next phase of training. However, given the deteriorating conditions in the rift, the uncomfortably brisk pace was a necessity.

"Let's run it one more time," Wil instructed. He restored the holographic interface around him that provided a simultaneous view of each of his trainee's flight simulators.

Wil's command post was at the center of the twenty pods, each equipped with a set of flight controls for a TX-70 jet. The pods could simulate heavy G-forces and be retrofitted with controls for any craft in the TSS fleet. Ultimately, Wil needed to train his group on the IT-1 jets, but the controls were far too complicated for the newer pilots. One step at a time.

The holographic screens around Wil illuminated with the vantage of each simulated jet in his fleet. Four squadrons of five jets were situated in a mock battlefield amid drifting asteroids. The environment was ideal for testing both maneuvering and tactics.

"All right, you know the drill. Take out the bad guys." He activated the AI enemy. The group had been through so many tactical drills in freefall that Wil was eager to see how autonomous they could be when carrying out his general orders. His Captains needed to take charge of tactics so Wil could focus on overall strategy, but based on how things were going so far, they weren't quite ready for Wil to step back.

"Form up on me," Ethan said. He flew his jet forward from the starting point of the simulation, heading toward the enemy base hidden behind one of the larger asteroids.

They had run through the same scenario multiple times already and the map was familiar. The target was an enemy base on the back side of the asteroid, but it was guarded by a fleet of jets equipped with rift drives. Wil had considered modifying the layout, but considering they had yet to make it past the first wave of enemy defenses, there was no point.

The TX-70 jets piloted by the Primus Elites arranged in four triangular formations behind Ethan's jet.

"The scout will be here any moment," Ethan said. After four prior iterations, they knew the opening of the scenario by heart.

Ethan flew toward the mammoth asteroid and waited behind ones of the smaller rocks drifting through the debris field. He spotted the enemy scout—a single jet slightly larger than his own, built for speed. "I'll take him out."

Wil sighed inwardly. He couldn't figure out how the men had got it in their minds that attacking the scout was a good opening move to the engagement. Yet, they took that approach every time. *Staying hidden until the scout has given the all-clear would be so much more effective.* He decided to let them try one more time before stepping in with specific instruction. Failure was an important part of the process so they didn't feel invincible.

The scout passed by Ethan's hiding place, and he darted out in pursuit.

With Ethan's first shot, the scout took a sharp dive down toward the asteroid.

"I've almost got him…" Ethan gave chase. He opened fire again, concentrating on his opponent.

Shite! He's not even watching where he's going. Wil was fixated on the monitor as Ethan closed in on the scout. He could already see how the scenario would play out.

"There!" Ethan exclaimed as he fired a well-aimed shot. The enemy ship executed a dimensional jump just in time to avoid the blast. His own jet was left on a collision course.

"Boma—" Ethan's jet clipped the asteroid, and his monitor instantly went black.

Wil shook his head with exasperation. "Primus Team Leader is down."

Low curses sounded across the comms.

"Reorganize," Wil instructed.

"All right, regroup at my location," Michael jumped in. "Spread out."

The jets reformed near Michael, fanning out to face the approaching enemy vessels.

"Hold the line," Michael instructed. "Distract them while Trion Squad slips through."

Wil let out a slow breath. It was a similar strategy to others they had already tried, but at least they had spread out rather than clumping together like previous attempts.

The enemy wave approached—six squads of five jets, greatly outnumbering the Primus Elites.

"Only fire when you have a clean shot," Ian cautioned.

"Ready to go," Tom said.

Wil crossed his arms and watched his men engage in battle.

"Evasive maneuvers." Michael broke from the formation and began a series of gentle, random rolls. The other Primus Elites followed his example, dodging the enemy fire.

Suddenly, the enemy jets broke from formation and darted forward. Half of the jets reformed in a staggered line while the others targeted the TSS jets.

"Make an opening for Trion!" Michael ordered. He spun around to focus his fire in a midsection of the barrier separating them from the target. The rest of his squad assisted with the assault, destroying three of the Bakzen jets. It wasn't much of an opening, but it would have to do.

Without hesitation, the Trion Squad dashed through the wall of enemy crafts. They all made it through—barely.

"Now that's how it's done!" Curtis, the Trion Squad Leader, cheered. But the celebration was short-lived.

A second wave of enemy jets rounded the asteroid, heading straight for the Trion Squad.

"Shite," Tom breathed, and he rolled his key away from the squad. "I'm going for the target."

"We'll cover you," Curtis affirmed.

Tom rounded the asteroid just as the main fleet received the first blasts from the full-on enemy assault. As each jet was disabled, its corresponding monitor went black.

Within moments, only half the Primus Elite jets remained.

The Trion Squad put up a good fight, but they, too, were soon disabled under the relentless enemy fire.

The fleet was decimated, leaving only a scattered few survivors, who were also eliminated.

Though it started out better, the scenario ended like all of the previous simulations: defeat.

"You're making some progress, but it looks like you aren't ready to fend for yourselves yet," Wil said into the comm. "For starters, you attacked the scout every time. Sometimes a more covert approach is warranted. This scenario requires patience and stealth. Wait for the scout to pass, then launch a small party for a precision stealth strike before the enemy can mobilize their units."

"I was going to try that next," Michael grumbled.

"Even so, there's a bigger issue," Wil continued. "When we do get into combat—which is inevitable—we need to be able to react faster and work together seamlessly. That's going to take a different approach entirely." With the reliance on comms and verbal commands, the enemy had already moved by the time Wil's men could act. The orders and reactions needed to be near-instantaneous, like their opponents. *A telepathic connection...*

Wil tabled the thought as the training pods swung open and

his men climbed out, frowns on all their faces. They lined up in front of him.

"What did you do wrong?" Wil asked them.

The men stared down at their feet.

"We were focusing on the moment and lost sight of the big picture," Ian replied.

"Yes. And?" Wil prompted.

"We underestimated the enemy," Michael said, finally looking up toward Wil.

Wil nodded. "They're fast and ruthless. The parameters I set for this training AI are generous compared to the real thing."

"I didn't blow up myself this time," Tom jested. "So at least there's that."

Wil cracked a smile. "Fair point. I'll take incremental improvement over none at all. Next time, I'll walk through the strategy step by step. I'll get you thinking just like me."

Ian snorted. "Yeah right!"

"Well, close enough," Wil replied. "I won't always be there to hold your hands. If I tell you to take out an enemy base, I need to be confident you can do it on your own while I'm planning the next move."

"Teach us and we'll listen," Michael affirmed.

"Absolutely," Ethan concurred. "And could we get access to the simulators without you? Aside from tactics, the flight controls are still a barrier. Some of us more experienced pilots could help out the newbies during study time."

That's not a bad idea. I'm glad they're wanting to step up. "I'll make the arrangements." Wil searched the tired faces. They were disheartened and needed a quick win. "I know it's already been a long day, but how about we run through some freefall formations?"

"Back to remedial class," Kalin jested.

"Just a change of pace," Wil assured him. *And a reminder that was once difficult is now second nature.* "Now, wind sprints on the way to the gravity lock."

The men groaned.

"Move!"

Saera rapped her fingers on the armrest of the couch in Wil's quarters. He was late—again.

Ever since the Primus Elites began training, she was lucky to get a few minutes alone with Wil on a given evening. She knew the training took priority over their relationship, but the frustrating part was they could have more time together—if only they didn't need to meet up in secret. Just being able to sit side-by-side at breakfast would be a significant improvement, or getting to stay together overnight. It was fine at first, but all the sneaking around and the little missed moments of togetherness were adding up.

The front door clicked unlocked and slid to the side.

Saera rose to greet Wil. "Hey."

"Oh, hey." Wil closed the door with a long breath.

"Tough day?" Saera asked and walked over to him.

"I'm exhausted." He slumped on his feet, his face tight with worry.

Saera wrapped her arms around him. "You need to take some time for yourself."

"When? I have three and a half years left to prepare everything."

"It's not like it's tomorrow. You need to make it through those years."

Wil took a deep breath and released Saera. "I'm trying."

Saera grabbed his hand. "Come on, time to relax."

He followed her lead toward the couch, but there was a hint of resistance. "I wish. I still need to go over the simulator logs for the day."

"I'll help."

Wil smiled at her and gave her a light kiss. "I'm sure there are plenty of things you'd rather do than look at stats for reaction times and movement accuracy."

"I want to spend time with you. If this is all I can get, I'll take it."

"I know I've been distant lately, I'm sorry," Wil said, slumping further. "Maybe tomorrow—"

"I'm going to Tararia tomorrow, remember?"

Wil caught himself. "Oh, right. The citizenship hearing."

Saera crossed her arms in subconscious defense against the upcoming event. After her last experience on Tararia, she was reluctant to return, even if the hearing was to confirm her status as an official Taran citizen. There'd been a slew of administrative filings and vouchers over the preceding year to assume the birthrights granted by her mother's dynastic status. The final step was the hearing to confirm her acceptance of governing Taran laws and to receive an imprint of the Alexri Dynasty's crest. Once complete, the administrative barriers of her impending marriage to Wil would be removed, but the politics within the TSS remained another matter.

"I'm sorry I can't go with you," Wil continued.

"I know you're busy." Saera forced a smile. "I'll be fine."

"But still."

Saera gave him a kiss. "I'm just looking forward to the day we don't need to sneak around anymore."

Wil nodded. "I wish it were different."

"Well, why can't it be? Once I'm confirmed—"

"That has nothing to do with the TSS. The concern here has always been that I'm a senior officer and you aren't yet."

"Graduation is still a ways off. Are we really supposed to keep it secret until then?"

"I don't know. Maybe. But this isn't the right time."

"Then when is?"

Wil closed his eyes and shook his head. "Saera, I don't want to argue." He opened his eyes and took her hands. "I love you. I know this is difficult, but it's just the way it has to be for now."

Saera's heart ached, but she released the tension with a slow breath. She leaned forward and laid her head on Wil's chest. "I hate having to hide my love for you from the rest of the universe."

Wil rubbed her back with his hand. "Just for a while longer."

She nodded and swallowed. "All right." There was no sense pining about impossible alternatives. "Now, I think we have some simulator data to review."

Laecy wiped the sweat from her brow with the back of her hand. Working inside an engine was its own distinct brand of uncomfortable.

She slid the dolly out from under the jet and found that Richards was waiting for her.

"How's it going?" he asked.

"I got the secondary ateron core installed. Now we need to test it."

"Is Wil coming back for the testing?"

"I doubt it," Laecy replied. "He has a wedding to plan and has been working around the clock with his group of trainees."

Richards scoffed. "A wedding seems ridiculous with all of this going on."

"He's High Dynasty. Of course they'll take time away from the TSS for it."

"I gave up on having a life outside the TSS years ago. Why should it be different for them?"

I'd given up, too. But maybe all of this will really be over one day. "Regardless, we can't afford the distraction of attachments."

"But Wil can't, most of all."

Laecy removed the anti-static gloves from her hands. "Well, his fiancée is a Second. The kinds of attachments Agents have are something I don't ever expect to understand."

"That, and you're a loner by nature."

More by necessity. "I'm wed to my work."

Richards strolled over and leaned on the table next to Laecy while she put her tools back in the transport case. "I wish I could see you happy, just once."

"I'll leap for joy when this bomaxed jet jumps like it's supposed to!"

"No, I mean *really* happy. Fulfilled."

Laecy met his soft amber eyes. She'd seen that look from him before, and she knew better than to engage. "There's time for that after the war."

He inched closer to her, enough that she felt his heat radiating toward her in the cool room. "You really think there'll be an after?"

"I have to believe that."

"I guess we do. For them."

Laecy nodded.

"Your sister would be proud of you."

"And your parents of you."

Richards grinned. "Let's not go too far. I'm not the Engineering Lead."

"You know more about bioelectronics than any scientist back at Tararia's finest institutions. That buys some serious clout in my book."

Her friend looked down. "But not quite enough."

Laecy let out a slow breath. "You know that's not it."

Richards studied her face. "So you *are* afraid to do something good for yourself."

Maybe I am. But that doesn't change that he's my subordinate. "Jack, we can't keep doing this—"

"That's what you said last time." He reached for her hand.

She stepped back from the table. "If there's ever going to be something between us, I want it to be done right. And that can't happen the way things are now."

Richards bit his lower lip and eventually gave a reluctant nod. "Win the war."

"And then we'll see."

He flashed her the warm, genuine smile that always set Laecy at ease. "All right. Let's check the interface with the new core."

‹ CHAPTER 9 ›

Life among the Bakzen remained a refreshing change from Arron Haersen's former existence as Mission Coordinator with the TSS. After five years of gene therapy from the Bakzen, his transformation was well underway.

He examined himself in the floor-length mirror he'd procured for his modest quarters. His skin had started to darken and was rough to the touch, covering a broader frame with enhanced muscle tone. With his head shaved, he could almost pass for a Bakzen drone from a distance, except for the brown tint to his luminescent eyes.

Haersen gave himself a nod of approval before heading out into the hallway.

His quarters were in a structure reserved for officers within a residential block of the Bakzen's capital city. The Bakzen soldiers were still wary around him, even after years of living side-by-side. They knew his time with the TSS made him a former enemy, and they assumed that meant he had spilt Bakzen blood. Despite numerous attempts to explain his position, the officers continued to think of the TSS as a single entity—not caring that only those in the Jotun division were involved in combat. But, in some ways, it was better that they thought he was a TSS fighter. If they understood he was little more than administrative support, he would gain no favor.

Cautious gazes followed Haersen down the hall as he made

his way to the central elevator for the residential building. In regimented Bakzen fashion, the bulk of the officers were departing for their morning commute at the same time.

Mass transit was most efficient when everyone traveled simultaneously, and daytime was the most practical for working hours because the abundance of solar energy and daylighting ensured practical operating conditions. To maximize the populace's effectiveness, four major cities at equidistant points around the equator of the planet kept the Bakzen functional around the clock—rotating functions with the passing of the sun.

Haersen had been stationed alongside Tek in the capital of the four cities. Being the seat of the Imperial Director, the city held the most critical of the Bakzen's resources and its time zone set the standard for all forces operating outside of the home planet. Haersen had settled into his role as Tek's assistant—running errands and offering an opinion when it was requested. Though he occasionally functioned as a punching bag, he was sure to always project a positive attitude and offer meaningful advice whenever he was able. As long as he remained useful, he would have a place among the Bakzen. And, he wasn't about to go anywhere until his transformation was complete.

The Bakzen officers made way for Haersen as he filed into the elevator. Years ago he'd stopped paying attention to their wrinkled noses and glower expressions. He knew he belonged there with them, regardless of what some might think.

The elevator descended the six stories from Haersen's level in a matter of seconds. He strode out into the corridor on the building's ground floor along with the other officers and boarded a maglev train to the military command complex at the center of the city.

Haersen took a seat on one of the molded plastic benches along the outer wall of the train car. As usual, no one sat next to him. He was content to look out the square window at the magnificent city around him. Despite years of observation, he was still awed by the selfless dedication to the greater good illustrated by the Bakzen drones. Workers making repairs, cleaning staff tending to the robotic helpers, construction laborers erecting new buildings—there was never a need to reprimand or argue. Everyone knew their place and fulfilled their role without question.

Only the officers demonstrated any sense of autonomy, but anyone that got too out of line would quickly be removed by the group. Except, perhaps, for Tek. He forged his own path, certainly, but he had a knack for going about it in a way that made others want to follow his lead. Haersen knew better than to question his tactics, having seen what happened to those who stood in the way of Tek's ambition. Plus, there was no arguing with the results Tek had achieved. Especially not since he was letting Haersen go along for the ride.

The train slowed as it entered the enclosed transit hub beneath the command complex. Officers streamed off of the train toward their designated posts.

Haersen followed the familiar route through the central elevator up to Tek's office on the fifth floor. The level was predominantly for high-ranking Bakzen officials. When Haersen was unfortunate enough to cross paths with one of the other officers, he needed to remain vigilant, never knowing when one might grow tired of Tek's pet project and toss Haersen in a prison cell—or down an elevator shaft.

Tek's office was across from the elevator, situated at the front of the building. It afforded convenient accessibility, making it a position of honor.

Haersen pressed the buzzer next to the door, and a moment later the door swung open.

The back wall of the office was transparent glass, filling the room with natural light. It also afforded an impressive view of the city below, though Haersen had learned that none of the

Bakzen seemed to appreciate that aspect.

Haersen stepped into the office and closed the door. "How may I serve you today, General?" he asked in Bakzeni, having grown comfortable with the language.

General Tek rose from behind his metal desk, his broad shoulders squared and tense beneath his tan uniform. His heavy brow was knit above his glowing red eyes that had narrowed to laser points. "I'm sick of waiting," he snarled.

Haersen paused near the entrance. "I'm sorry, sir. I didn't know I was late."

"No." Tek let out a gruff grunt.

Haersen reached for the door handle. Clearly his presence wasn't wanted. "Sorry to disturb you, sir."

"Where are you going?" Tek's heated gaze froze Haersen in his tracks.

"I thought you—"

Tek clenched his fists. "You assume everything is about you." He took a short breath. "This matter concerns the Imperial Director."

Haersen let his hand drop to his side. "Apologies."

Tek shook his head and sighed. "Stop groveling and pay attention."

"Yes, sir."

The General leaned against his desk. "It's time the Imperial Director retired."

Haersen wet his lips and stepped forward. Knowing Tek, he didn't have a retirement party in mind. Likely, it was something far more treasonous. "What can I do to help?"

"Ah, so you have learned the right question to ask, after all." Tek crossed his arms and looked Haerson over thoughtfully. "Have you ever met the Imperial Director?"

"No, sir. I never had the occasion."

Tek nodded. "Well, I think we might have to think of a reason. I'd like you to do some investigating for me."

Those sorts of investigations ended badly for the party in question, based on Haersen's limited experience. "Into what, sir?"

"I'd like to know about his routine and habits, who he keeps close."

"I'm sure his assistant could tell you, sir," Haersen suggested.

"But that doesn't tell me who's loyal to him, who he trusts—and who trusts him. I know some others are displeased with the direction the Bakzen are headed. The war has dragged on, we haven't gained ground at the rate we should. It's time for new leadership. I need to know who feels the same way."

Haersen swallowed. He'd seen the double-cross coming for years, but he had started to doubt whether Tek would ever make a move. Apparently it was finally about to happen. "Yes, sir. I'll learn everything I can."

‹ CHAPTER 10 ›

Saera was transfixed by the city of Sieten before her. The previous trip to Tararia had been confined to the Sietinen estate, but seeing the city up close gave her a whole new appreciation for Taran culture.

Her shuttle had landed on top of a building in the northwest of the city along a district that wrapped along the northern coast of Lake Tiadon. In the distance above, she could see part of the Sietinen estate on the hill. The midday sun reflected off the white-washed walls of the buildings around her, but her tinted glasses mitigated the glare.

"This way, please," a woman dressed in a lavender dress suit said to Saera, pulling her from her thoughts.

Saera smiled at the attendant and followed her toward the glass door at the entrance to a staircase descending into the building.

The stairwell was structured as an atrium, with planter boxes situated at the switchback to each segment of stairs. Saera followed the clerk down three flights to where the stairwell opened into a marble-lined rectangular room with airy ceilings and intersecting hallways.

"The Committee will see you in ten minutes," the clerk explained. "I'll escort you to the waiting room."

"Thank you." Saera admired the stone carvings and holopaintings along the walls as she traversed the hall leading deeper into the administrative building. The energy of the space exuded ancient authority—monuments from the era before the most recent revolution.

At the end of the hall, padded chairs were oriented around a set of double doors in a small room. Next to the door, a viewscreen on the wall displayed a queue of pending cases. A single woman was seated in one of the chairs along the right wall.

When the woman looked up, Saera was surprised to see it was her mother. Marina smiled at her and stood. "Hello, Saera. How was your trip?"

"Fine." Saera glanced at the clerk with confusion, but she seemed unphased by Marina's presence. "I didn't know you were meeting me here," Saera added. Even though it had been more than a year since their initial reunion, Saera's limited interaction with her mother had not helped heal her feeling of abandonment.

"These matters go so much smoother with a personal voucher for your standing," Marina explained. "And, I figured we could spend time together this way, since you came all this way."

A nice sentiment, but I'm still not sure I'm ready for that. Saera shifted on her feet. "Thanks."

Marina seemed to sense her daughter's discomfort. "Are there any questions I can answer for you before the hearing?"

"I don't think so. Cris went over pretty much everything with me before I left Headquarters."

Her mother tensed at the slightest mention of Cris' name. "You're quite entrenched there now, it seems."

"They took me in when I was lost," Saera said, looking Marina straight on. "I have a real sense of family for the first time in a very long time."

Marina maintained her poise, but Saera sensed her inner struggle. "I'm glad you found that."

Saera knew her position had introduced a serious conflict for her mother, both on personal and professional levels. She was in service to Reinen, and in his conflict with Cris, Marina was obligated to side with the elder Sietinen. The new dynamic with Wil and Saera made it difficult for Marina to continue her duty as a Court Advisor with so many variables in play, and so many personal ties clouding the situation. She could see her mother studying her—trying to glean insight into how Wil might navigate the complex environment. Further, with Wil marrying Saera, it was going to be impossible to keep the Sietinen Dynasty's ties to the TSS hidden for much longer, and the Alexri Dynasty would be exposed along with it.

"I appreciate you coming to support me," Saera said, hoping to diffuse the tension. *We don't need to make today more stressful than it already is.*

"Of course." Marina eased back on the seat. "I have a lot to make up for."

Saera sat down next to her mother. Without having Wil, Cris, and Kate nearby, Saera readily noticed the aura of Marina's abilities. She was a gifted telepath and skilled instructor, but so much of her potential remained untapped—stifled by the limits the Priesthood imposed on telekinesis. Suddenly, everything came into perspective. *I'm now getting what she never got to have—growing to my full potential while she's left on the outside.* "It all worked out okay."

Marina sat in silence for several moments. "We need to find a way to work together. All of us."

"For the enduring good of Tararia," Saera affirmed.

"Exactly."

Saera glanced at the clerk waiting on the other side of the room. "This isn't the place to discuss that."

Marina followed her daughter's gaze. "No, but I don't expect there ever will be, given our positions. However, I want you to know that I'm not blind to what's going on. I have certain responsibilities now, but know that that when there is a change in leadership, the new leader will have my allegiance."

When Cris is in power. "Despite everything?"

"Bygones. There's family to consider now."

Saera nodded. "I'll pass on the message."

"Good."

The viewscreen next to the door fluttered, and Saera's name moved to the top of the queue.

"The Committee will see you now," the clerk stated, stepping toward the door.

Marina rose. "Let's go."

Saera followed the two women toward the double doors, and the right door swung open.

Beyond, a chamber that reminded her of an ornate courtroom met her gaze. The domed ceiling rose six meters tall and was decorated with a painted landscape of hills around the bottom perimeter, topped by blue sky and clouds fading into stars. Five older individuals—two women and three men—were seated behind an elevated wooden podium with a dark stain that brought out the swirling grain of the boards. All had gray hair and faint lines around their wise eyes. They watched Saera intently as she stepped to the center of the room.

"Saera Alexri?" the man in the center said when Saera stopped in front of the podium.

"Yes, sir."

"And you also have a voucher?" the councilman continued.

"Yes, your eminence," Marina stated. "I am her mother, of Alexri Dynasty pedigree. She was born on Earth, so her official paperwork was never filed with Taran authorities. In addition, her paternal great-grandfather was a Taran citizen."

"We see that," the councilman stated. "And he renounced his citizenship. Why do you seek it now?"

"The reason is twofold," Saera replied, reciting what Cris had told her. "I have pledged myself to Taran service through the

TSS, but I am also to wed Williame Sietinen."

"Your record with the TSS has been verified," the councilwoman to the left of the man stated, "and Cristoph Sietinen has attested to the engagement. However, the attestation was not ratified by the central Sietinen administrative office."

It wasn't? Saera panicked.

"I am an official for Sietinen," Marina jumped in. "Pursuant to code 18.207 subsection B, I am authorized to speak in the best interest of the Sietinen Dynasty when no member of the Dynasty is present."

"And you wish the record to show you as a proxy in this matter?" the councilman asked.

Marina gave a single nod. "I do."

"Then the conditions for expedited citizenship are satisfied," the councilman stated.

Saera released a long breath of relief. *What would have happened if she wasn't here?*

"Does the council ratify that this woman be admitted as a Taran citizen with the Dynasties?" the councilman asked his comrades.

The council members murmured agreement.

"Saera Alexri, born of Earth," the councilman continued, "do you commit to abide by the laws governing the Taran civilization and uphold your conduct as a Taran citizen?"

"I do," Saera affirmed.

A moment later, a holographic panel appeared around the curved lip of the podium in front of the council. Each member of the council placed their right hand on the projection, and a ring on each of their middle fingers flashed blue, sending a beam of light up to the ceiling.

"The citizenship is confirmed," the councilman stated. "Step forward to receive your Mark."

As Saera approached the podium, a door hidden in one of

the wood panels slid open and a machine on a polished metal arm extended outward. The contraption reminded Saera of a tattoo gun with a curved half-cylinder of acrylic below.

"Place your left wrist palm up," the councilman instructed.

Saera complied, her heart pounding in her ears.

The cylinder tightened on her wrist to hold it in place. When her arm was secured, the device above descended. Before she had time to question what it was doing, a narrow needle plunged into her wrist, sending a sharp pain up her arm. The needle withdrew almost immediately, leaving only a tiny prick of blood. *That must be the ID chip.*

A purple light illuminated over her skin, and the rest of the contraption sprang to life with a low whir. It rapidly circled her wrist, etching the Alexri Dynasty crest of a broadleaf tree against a starry sky. As the final stroke, her name was inscribed below the crest. The Mark suspended just above the surface of her skin, and it became invisible the moment the light on the machine turned off.

"You are now a recognized citizen of the Taran worlds," the councilman stated.

Saera smiled up at him and placed the palm of her right hand over the new Mark on the wrist, which was beginning to sting. "I will fulfill my duties to Tararia with honor," Saera said, following Cris' recommended phrasing, though she left out his sarcastic laugh at the end.

The holographic projection above the council podium vanished with a shimmer.

"This way, please," the clerk said, gesturing toward a door opposite the entrance.

Saera and Marina followed her out the door into an empty hallway with an illuminated sign pointing toward the building lobby.

"Thank you," Marina said.

The clerk inclined her head and returned to the council

chamber.

Saera turned to her mother as soon as they were alone in the hallway. "Vouching for Sietinen... That's why you were really here?"

Marina nodded with a prim smile. "Your ratification would have gone through anyway—our genetic tie is undeniable. But it would have been an unnecessary delay. You and Wil have been through enough."

"Won't you get in trouble?"

"Any difficulty is well worth helping my daughter."

"Still, you didn't have Reinen's permission," Saera whispered. "Speaking on his behalf—"

"The code I quoted is 'acting in the best interest.' That is precisely what I did, even if he doesn't quite see it that way himself yet."

Maybe I misjudged her. Saera bobbed her head. "Thank you."

Marina brushed Saera's shoulder with her hand. "Now, we have a little while before you need to return. I think it's time we start some official wedding planning."

Saera let out a slow, heavy breath. "I'm going to be pretty useless in the planning department."

"Customs may be a little different on Tararia than Earth, but I know you must have some fantasies in mind. I remember you playing dress-up as a little girl."

Saera laughed. "Yeah, when I was, like, three."

"Well, now you can do it for real. I happen to have an inside connection with a extremely talented seamstress."

"Dress shopping?" Saera asked.

"If you're up for it."

I'm not sure when else I'd get the chance. "Sure, let's do it."

Marina escorted her out of the administrative building, and they took a private car east along the coast toward the downtown core of the city.

When the car stopped, Saera stepped out onto a bustling

street with well-dressed citizens and colorful clothing suited to the temperate climate. Her own dark blue Junior Agent uniform was out of place, but she matched her mother's self-assured posture.

The seamstress' studio was on the seventh floor of a glass-walled high-rise. The receptionist led Saera and Marina to a plush couch in an airy room with windows along the back wall overlooking a park below. A round platform was situated two meters in front of the couch.

They took a seat, and the receptionist brought two cups of a floral tea.

"This is one of the finest dressmakers on Tararia," Marina said as she took a sip of tea. "It's rare to get an appointment."

"I guess you can drop the Sietinen name and get pretty much anything," Saera replied.

"Well, there are some advantages."

The door opened, and a petite woman in her middle years stepped in carrying a tablet. Her hair was pulled into a loose bun on top of her head with several strands hanging down to frame her face.

"Hello, I am Danica," the seamstress greeted. "You are here for a wedding dress, yes?"

"Correct," Marina replied.

Danica looked over Saera. "And is this the bride?"

Saera nodded. "I am."

"Let me have a look at you. Take off your jacket," Danica said as she motioned Saera to her feet. Saera rose and slipped off her jacket while the seamstress eyed her from a distance. "You are athletic," Danica commended.

"I'm in the TSS."

The seamstress' eye paused on Saera's tinted glasses. "And training as an Agent, no doubt."

"Yes," Saera responded.

Danica's widened her eyes with surprise and she consulted

her tablet. "Step onto the platform, please," she instructed.

Saera positioned herself on the center of the platform , and a holographic grid appeared around her.

"What did you have in mind for the dress?" Danica asked.

"I'm not sure," Saera replied. "I don't want anything too poufy, but otherwise I'll follow your recommendations."

Danica placed her hand on her chin, thoughtful. "Where will the wedding be held?"

"In the gardens of the Sietinen estate, I think." *I guess we never really talked about it.*

The seamstress smiled. "Very well." She began to manipulate the grid around Saera, molding it to her body along her torso and then fanning it out from her hips. A dress began to take shape—sculpted in light. When the shape was in place, Danica added a layer of white and began adding in details.

Saera was mesmerized by the movement of the seamstress' hands, manipulating the pleats and folds into an elegant, wearable work of art.

After half an hour, Danica stepped back. "What do you think?"

Saera looked over to the mirror that had been on the wall to her back. Her breath caught when she saw herself from a distance. The tight bodice cascaded into a flowing skirt with an asymmetrical waistline and embroidered silver jewels down the side.

"Wow," was all Saera could manage to say. *This makes it feel real. Marrying Wil...*

"Is there anything you want to change with the design?" Danica asked.

Saera shook her head. "I can't think of a single thing."

The seamstress smiled and bowed her head. "I will record the specifications. The design will remain visible so long as you stay on the platform. I'll give you a few minutes." She made a entries on her tablet and then departed.

Marine rose and stepped toward Saera. "It's gorgeous."

"I hope I get to wear it," Saera mumbled.

"What do you mean?"

Saera's brow knitted. "It just doesn't feel like a wedding is possible with everything that's going on."

Her mother cocked her head. "Come, now. A wedding is a happy occasion."

"It is. And being with Wil is all I want. But it's tough…"

"Life in the TSS?"

"That, and seeing what it's doing to him. He gives the TSS everything and doesn't leave anything for himself."

"You mean, for you."

Her mother's observation was astute, but Saera didn't make any indication. "I try to help him remember what we're doing it for." *So we don't have to live in fear. To make a future for those we care about.*

Marina rose and stepped forward to place her hands on Saera's shoulders. "Well, seeing you in that dress—he'll definitely remember."

Saera blushed. "I hope so."

"You need to take time for yourselves," Marina continued. "Enjoy those moments, Saera. You never know when it might be over. Don't have regrets you didn't take that time when you could."

Saera took a deep breath and was impressed to see that the digital fabric of the dress flexed around her. "You're right. I will."

"Hey," Wil greeted Saera as she stepped through his door. "How'd it go?"

She smiled. "All official." She exposed her left wrist and projected a light from her handheld over it. The family crest illuminated in purple on her skin.

Wil ran his thumb over the Mark. "I wish I could have been there with you."

Saera leaned up and kissed him. "We're back together now."

"Now you just need to graduate and we can have the wedding."

Saera traced her finger on Wil's chest. "About that... I ordered a dress."

"Oh?"

"My mom came to the hearing with me, and afterward she took me to see a seamstress to design one."

Wil was caught off-guard. *Dress shopping already? I guess this is really happening.* "Okay, great."

"You seem surprised."

"It's just unexpected. But I'm glad to hear you're getting along with your mom."

Saera nodded. "She's making an effort, so I am, too. And, shockingly, it sounds like she's onboard with that plan your parents are preparing."

Wil's eyes widened. "Really?"

"I'll tell your dad when I see him tomorrow."

"It sounds like everything's falling into place." Wil pulled her in for a hug. "I look forward to seeing you in the dress."

Saera grinned. "As you should. I look damn fine."

"I don't know what I'll do. Probably TSS dress uniform, like my dad did." *May as well make a political statement, right?*

"Fancy."

Wil smiled. "Yeah, well, there aren't many occasions for it normally. "

"I'm looking forward to seeing you all dressed up, too. It'll be a fun day."

Probably one of the last before the war consumes our lives. He pushed the thought away and leaned down to kiss Saera.

The handheld in Wil's pocket buzzed, interrupting the moment. With a groan, he retrieved the device. The message was from Laecy: "The IT-1 works. Thanks for the cores." He smiled to himself.

"What is it?" Saera asked.

"Good news from Laecy. The new rift jets are finally working properly."

"That's a relief!"

Wil sighed. "It really is. Things need to start going our way."

"They are. You're doing great."

"It doesn't feel like it." *Without simultaneous observation, we're still missing half the equation to win the war without even greater loss.*

"One day at a time. We'll get there together."

The words warmed Wil's core. It was true—he did have people there to support him. *There's hope. I can't give up.*

Cris' stomach rumbled. At least it was time for dinner.

He shifted the two pre-packaged meals into his left hand as he palmed open the door to his quarters.

Kate emerged from the bedroom when he opened the door, wearing loungewear. "Thanks for picking up dinner."

"Absolutely. I'm starving." Cris slipped off his shoes.

"How was your day?"

"Good. I heard that Saera's back from Tararia. Everything went through." He opened up the meal containers and handed one to Kate.

"Thank the stars that's over!" she replied, collapsing on the couch.

Is it over? Cris joined her on the couch and dug into his meal. He took several bites. *Everyone was played.* "Even after having a year and a half to sink in, I still can't believe that Saera is Marina's daughter."

"I hate to say it, but it did simplify matters in some ways."

Cris frowned and took another bite. "Only because we're

playing directly into the Priesthood's hands."

"They chose to be together, same as us."

"That's true," Cris admitted. "And I wouldn't have wanted anything else for Wil."

"I wish they had some time to just enjoy each other. We got some good years before…" Kate stared down at her half-eaten dinner.

"And I'd give them that if I could." *I wish I had that, myself.*

"There's no way we'll ever be able to replicate the ignorant bliss of our past," Kate continued, "but maybe we can still give them little moments here and there."

"Hopefully, but it's difficult to know what's truly in their interest, and what's part of the Priesthood's hidden objectives."

"We can't think purely in those terms," Kate objected.

How can we think any differently? It's the truth. "After finding out about Saera, and Michael's father being sent to look after her, I wouldn't put anything past the Priesthood."

"They're hiding something, that's for sure."

Cris nodded. "And whatever it is extends far beyond the High Dynasties."

"But we're at the center of it."

"Without a doubt. And Wil most of all."

Kate set aside her empty meal container. "We may never know what's coming, but we can have each other's backs."

Cris took her hand. "We're in this together, no matter what."

‹ CHAPTER 11 ›

Saera pushed back from her classroom desk. "Ugh. Economic Trade Theory doesn't even sound like it should be a real thing. But moreover, why do we have to learn it?"

"Because we're soon-to-be TSS Agents and are supposed to be well-rounded," Elise replied with a sarcastic smirk.

"I'm pretty sure they won't be sending an Earthling like me on diplomatic missions." Saera grabbed her handheld and checked her inbox as a distraction, but there were no new messages. She set it down with a huff.

"Well, you never know when these things might come in handy," Elise countered, tucking her dark hair behind her ear as she returned her attention to the assignment.

Of course, she's actually interested in sociology. Give me a nav system to reprogram any day... Saera looked over the parameters for the essay again and cringed. It was going to be a long night.

She tried to outline her essay during the remainder of the class session. After making almost no progress, she was relieved for the Agent to dismiss the class. At least the essay wasn't due for another week.

Saera grabbed her handheld and headed for the door alongside Elise.

"Are you still free tonight?" Elise asked once they were in the hallway.

"For what?"

"Hanging out with us."

"Oh, right." The women from Saera's initial cohort of Primus trainees liked to get together once or twice a month for a casual escape from current classwork and training. Their early years together had solidified an enduring friendship that made them prioritize the gathering over anything else. Saera would feel the same way if it weren't for Wil. "Let me double-check my calendar."

She sent a quick text to Wil asking if he was busy that night. His response came back almost immediately: "You're welcome to stop by, but I'll be working."

Saera sighed inwardly. "Yep, I'm free. May as well procrastinate on this essay, anyway."

"Great!" Elise exclaimed. "I love it when we're all together. Just like old times."

"Even Leila's coming?"

Elise shrugged. "Well, you know how she is. She'll 'see if she can squeeze it in.'"

Saera smirked. "That phrasing conjures up so many other images…"

"Wow," Elise said, looking appalled at first, but she laughed. "I think we've been hanging out with the guys too much."

"All in an effort to have a well-rounded character, my dear," Saera jested.

They returned to their quarters for some quick study time. Saera's room was in the back left corner, with Elise next to her. Across the common area, a brand new Junior Agent, Lucia, was in the front right room, and Selma, who was a year ahead of Saera and Elise, was in the back right room.

The four of them rarely hung out together, since friendships had already been established in the previous years with the TSS. Saera was thankful to have a good group of friends—for the first time in her life, really. She felt guilty keeping her relationship with Wil from them, but it was necessary. Elise, perhaps, could be trusted, but the others were too prone to gossiping. Saera had no doubt that being able to keep secrets would be a theme with their upcoming internship assignments.

Saera finished up some interplanetary biology homework when she got to her room, and an hour later she accompanied Elise to the mess hall to meet up with their friends.

The other girls were already situated at a booth in the back corner of the mess hall. Leila was seated next to Caryn, and Nadeen was on the inner booth bench across from them.

Saera grabbed a freestanding chair from a nearby table as they walked past to add a fifth seat.

"Hi!" Elise greeted as she slid on the bench next to Nadeen. "Look who I found."

Saera set down the chair at the end of the booth table. "Sorry I missed last time." She meant it, but her citizenship hearing on Tararia was a valid excuse.

"It's good of you to make an appearance," Caryn said to Saera.

"I've had a lot going on," Saera replied, trying to deflect the hostility. She didn't blame the others for considering her a bad friend after her secrecy over the years. She removed her tinted glasses and placed them in her pocket like her friends.

"Including some trips outside of Headquarters, right?" Leila prodded.

"Great to see you, too, Leila," replied Saera with a forced smile. She sat down in the chair. "Still nosey, I see."

"You do like to sneak around," Caryn pointed out. "It's not like we have no grounds for suspicion."

"I'm here now. And if I did go anywhere, trust it was for a good reason," Saera replied.

"And in this hypothetical travel, where might you go?" Nadeen asked, her dark eyes questioning. "Back to Earth?"

"No." Saera ran through some excuses in her head and tried to settle on one.

"Then where?" Leila asked.

"All right! Enough interrogating," Elise cut in. "This is supposed to be a fun evening."

Saera looked around at the faces of her friends. They only asked because they cared about her. It wasn't fair to them to keep lying. "I was on Tararia," she admitted.

Their eyes widened.

"What for?" Caryn asked.

Maybe telling them part of it will be enough of a distraction to keep them from asking about everything else. "I learned some things about my birth mother recently. She's Tararian."

"And you're using that properly?" Leila interjected. "She's from Tararia, not just a Taran?"

Saera groaned. "Yes, I'm not an idiot."

Leila held up her hands in defense. "Hey, sorry."

"Anyway," Saera continued, "since that discovery, I've been going through the process of getting Taran citizenship."

Caryn flushed a little and looked down. "Okay, that's a pretty big thing to have going on."

"Why didn't you say anything?" Nadeen questioned.

Saera rapidly thought of a justification that wouldn't point toward Wil. "Well, I wasn't sure it would go through. I didn't want to say anything until it was final."

Leila eyed her. "And now it is?"

Saera nodded. "I have my Mark and everything."

Her friends' jaws dropped with shock.

Saera realized her mistake a moment too late. *Only dynastic lines have Marks. Shit, why did I say that?*

"Which Dynasty?" Caryn questioned in a low voice, her eyes darting to see if anyone had overheard, but no one was nearby.

Too late to take it back now. "Nothing special," Saera replied. "My mother is from Alexri."

They thought it over, but there was no recognition on their faces.

"I guess that explains how you picked up New Taran so quickly," Elise stated. "Your mom probably spoke it to you as a baby."

Saera shrugged. "All the same, it would be nice to have not been abandoned on Earth."

"Does your mom have abilities?" Nadeen asked.

"She does," Saera replied.

The girls looked at each other. "Was she an Agent?" Caryn asked for the group.

Saera shook her head. "No. She never had the chance to explore her potential." It was a stock response Saera had seen others use—a way of halting a conversation on the topic of telekinesis.

Her friends nodded with understanding.

"You're the lucky one," Elise said after a pause.

"We all are," Saera responded.

The group fell silent.

I didn't mean to kill the mood completely. Saera shifted in her chair, not sure what to say.

"All right, enough of that," Leila announced, to Saera's relief. "Let's eat."

"Yes, excellent plan!" Caryn agreed.

They all stood and headed for the buffet.

Elise hung back next to Saera as they walked over. "Why didn't you at least tell me about your mom?"

Saera's heart felt heavy, wishing she could confide in her friend. "It's complicated."

"It always is with you."

"I'll fill you in later, okay? Let's just enjoy tonight."

Elise nodded. "Okay. But I want details later." She pointed her finger at Saera and narrowed her eyes. "I'll hold you to it."

Saera grinned. "Deal."

Wil stretched and settled into his desk chair. His bed called to him to make it an early night, but he needed to take advantage of every productive moment he could. With Saera preoccupied with her friends for the night, he had a chance to work uninterrupted. Not that he minded her company—it was just easier to think by himself.

Struck by a wave of tiredness, he decided to take a low-level stim to get him through the next few hours. He knew he'd been relying too much on medication rather than getting a proper night's sleep recently. Saera would chastise him if she found out just how far he was pushing himself. Still, he was able to keep a clear head most days. The schedule might catch up with him eventually, but he would keep going for as long as he could. Too many people were relying on him to allow any reprieve.

As the stim took effect, he pulled up his latest design portfolio. He'd been sketching out some new ship specs on those rare evenings he had alone without data to review on the Primus Elites. His work on the IT-1 jets had him thinking about other applications for the neural interface. It occurred to him that there was great potential for scaling up the design.

The document projected in front of him was the schematic skeleton for one of the many components to a warship built around the neural interface. But, the bridges between the pieces were missing.

If I could only find a way to magnify the energy from multiple Agents through a single vessel... Wil hesitated. His power alone was untested. There was no telling what could be accomplished with others through an official magnifier.

It likely would never work. But even if it did, he didn't want to find out what such a weapon could do.

That's not a path I want to go down. He scrapped the whole design and threw it in his archive of discarded ideas. *Onto the next.*

<>   <>   <>

The message was flagged like countless others Laecy had received over the years: confidential and from an untraceable sender. After Wil's initial visit to H2, she'd been able to piece together that the messages were relayed from TSS Command. Someone would mine his personal files looking for design specs or other engineering notes and send them her way. It was a violation of privacy and she hated being a part of it. All the same, any time she received one of the mystery emails, giddy excitement fluttered in her stomach.

She opened the latest message, anxious to see what it contained. There was no body content and only a single attachment.

The attachment file was a series of digital sketches. Laecy flipped through them on the holodisplay of her work desk in the engineering lab. All of the individual notes dealt with a discrete component for a larger design. She thumbed through the workbook searching for the unifying schematic. Nothing.

Laecy sighed. Another puzzle. Normally she'd like a challenge, but she was already overwhelmed with her day-to-day responsibilities.

She flipped back through the notes, and one of the schematics caught her eye on the second pass. "Oh shite."

The sketch looked simple at first—a vertical column topped by a rod to serve as a handhold— but then Laecy noticed the details. Based on the specified materials, it was intended for biofeedback. *A neural link.*

Looking at the rest of the schematics with that concept in mind, she started to see the overall design. It was a full-sized battleship.

"Will it work?"

Laecy jumped at the sound of the voice. She whipped around and saw High Commander Taelis standing in the doorway. "Sir,

I wasn't expecting you."

"Will the design work?" Taelis repeated.

"I have no idea, sir. I barely have a grasp of how it all fits together."

"See what you can do. Wil needs a ship like this, whether he knows it yet or not. I need you to figure it out for him."

Wil is probably the only person who could figure it out. "I'll need to ask Wil about some of these components"

"No, don't say anything to him about your work on this. He already has dismissed the design."

"If he scrapped—" Laecy started to protest.

"We have reason to believe the dismissal was out of principle rather than technical limitation," Taelis countered.

So who are we to question his decision? Laecy remained silent, knowing there was nothing she could say to change the High Commander's mind. Besides, it wasn't her place.

"We need this ship to win the war. Make it work without him." Taelis departed as silently as he'd appeared.

‹ CHAPTER 12 ›

Haersen's assignment to gather intelligence on the Imperial Director was a frustrating challenge. Since the Bakzen were conditioned to fulfill their role in society, breaking from daily routine was highly unusual. For Haersen to insert himself in a novel situation would be like taking out an ad that he was up to no good.

He needed a valid reason to visit the administrative headquarters—something that could only be done in person and would require access to the highest ranking personnel. And, it needed to stand up to the scrutiny of telepaths far stronger than himself. He needed to tell the truth—or a version of it, anyway. But even then, he wouldn't be able to walk in the front door and gain access. However, there might be a way.

The administrative complex was garish by Bakzen standards, with ten stories of white concrete and glass that could almost fit into a traditional Taran city. Extra decorative ledges and geometric engraving in the concrete panels were superfluous details, underscoring the waste in the current administrative regime.

Inside, the lobby of the administrative building bore a close resemblance to structures serving a similar purpose on Tararia. Haersen had only seen the Bakzen building from a distance previously, and the presence of indoor plants caught him by surprise at first. But, he reminded himself that those were for air purification, not decoration.

A wide reception desk was situated four meters inside the lobby across from the rotating entry door. Two Bakzen guards sat behind the desk. Their glowing red eyes narrowed as Haersen approached.

"Who are you?" the guard on the right asked.

Haersen was used to such questions. He didn't pass as a drone upon detailed inspection, and he clearly wasn't an officer. Outsiders were an anomaly warranting the utmost scrutiny. "My name is Arron Haersen. I am an advisor in General Tek's office."

The guard glanced at his identical colleague and then returned his steely gaze to Haersen. "You're not one of us."

"I am now," Haersen replied, "though not by birth."

"Identification," the first guard demanded.

Haersen scanned his wrist over the indicated device on the desktop.

The guards examined his credentials, which supported his claim. "Why are you in this office?" the second guard asked.

"I have information," Haersen replied.

"Relay it to your commander," the first guard stated. "If you're one of us, you know the protocol."

Haersen shook his head. "Tek was unable to come here himself. This is sensitive information. Electronic relay may be intercepted, so he asked me to present the message directly."

"Whom is the message for?" the second guard asked.

"The Imperial Director."

The first guard raised a telekinetic barrier, poised to act. "You're not authorized for a meeting."

"But this information involves the Imperial Director's safety," Haersen insisted.

The first guard unleashed a telekinetic grapple, throwing Haersen to the ground in an instant.

Haersen winced as his face hit the polished concrete floor,

but he remained calm. It was all part of the plan. "I wish to speak with the Imperial Director, on orders of General Tek."

"The General will need to verify your orders," the first guard stated as he telekinetically yanked Haersen to his feet, his hands pinned at his sides.

Two additional guards emerged from beyond the security blockade separating the lobby from the rest of the building. They took over the telekinetic hold and directed Haersen into a cramped room on the first level. He was thrown into a chair, and his wrists secured by a wire behind his back. They left him alone in the room, bolting him inside.

Haersen sighed as soon as he was alone. Having to do everything the Bakzen way was tedious at times.

He waited for what felt like an hour, though without a clock it was difficult to tell. Finally, he heard the door bolt release.

A guard identical to those from the lobby entered. "Tek confirmed your orders, but he would not vouch for your loyalty."

Haersen groaned inwardly. He was on his own. "You may place me under any level of guard. It is imperative that I speak with the Imperial Director in person."

"He has been informed of the situation and is curious about what you have to say."

"Then take me to him," Haersen requested.

"Under the circumstances, I thought it better to come to you," an elderly Bakzen said from the doorway.

Haersen looked up in surprise. The Imperial Director appeared far older and less formidable in person than he did in any of the videos Haersen had seen. No wonder Tek was doubting his leadership. "Sir, thank you for agreeing to speak with me."

"Say what you came to say," the Imperial Director stated.

Haersen wet his thin lips. "I have heard rumors of a plot against you."

"It's Tek, isn't it?" the Imperial Director asked, his face devoid of emotion.

"What makes you ask that, sir?"

The Imperial Director shook his head, as if weary from a recurring issue. "He's never been fully aligned with the rest of us. But I suppose we made him that way."

If Tek was a different genetic line than the others, he'd never mentioned it to Haersen. "Sir, what do you mean?"

"He was raised from a child."

Haersen took a moment to find his voice. "Born to a birth mother?"

"No, of course not!" the Imperial Director responded. "He was aged for three years in a tank like any other. And I wish we'd never thought to pull him out early."

It was the first Haersen has ever heard of a Bakzen clone being extracted prior to full maturity. The aging process typically took seven years, meaning that extraction after three years would equate to roughly an eight-year-old Taran. "Why not age him all the way, sir? Why is he different?"

"We wanted him to be able to learn naturally—through experience rather than imprinting. He's of my same line, I'm sorry to say. The most ancient of the Bakzen lines, tracing back to our earliest leadership. When we heard the coming of the Cadicle was near, we knew the war with Tararia would be coming to an end. It was a moment of weakness to think that following their example of letting a child grow up on their own would produce better results. No... Tek is emotional and unpredictable. That doesn't make for a strong leader."

Haersen did some quick mental math. There was no way Tek had been "born" at the same time as Wil. "What foretold you of the Cadicle's coming?"

The Imperial Director frowned, to the extent his stoic face allowed. "Another misstep by my former colleagues. They were twenty years too soon—thinking that the elder Sietinen brother would be the father. His untimely death upset more than just the Priesthood's plans."

"You intended Tek to face the Cadicle, sir?" Haersen questioned.

"Not directly, no. We only hoped to have someone to think more like our Taran enemies. And perhaps he does… Except, his ambition is not the way of the Bakzen."

Not the way of historical Bakzen, perhaps, but Tek was not alone in his vision for the future. Haersen thought better than to question the Imperial Director, so he remained silent.

"And yet, you aligned yourself with Tek," the Imperial Director mused.

"He was the only one to take me in," Haersen said. "When the Bakzen approached me during my TSS internship, I saw your superiority. I wanted to work with you. But, most Bakzen officers only saw me as a pawn—someone to give inside knowledge of the TSS and the young Cadicle. Tek, though, offered me a chance to be better. To be more like you."

"That was enough to sway you?"

Haersen shook his head. "How could I maintain my allegiance to a people that wished those with my abilities didn't exist?"

"Maybe you do see things as we do." The Imperial Director straightened his uniform and took a step toward the door. "Go back now to report your findings to Tek," the old Bakzen stated. "Tell him this: if he intends to take my position, he will need to take it by force. I will never willingly hand over the future of the Bakzen to him. He will lead us to our end." He paused. "And Haersen—choose your allies carefully."

The Imperial Director exited, leaving Haersen temporarily alone with his thoughts.

Far from the meeting he had envisioned, the conversation was illuminating nonetheless. Tek's unusual upbringing set him apart, and that vision offered the greatest opportunity for the

Bakzen. The Imperial Director had no doubt divulged the information in an attempt to get Haersen to turn against Tek, by citing perceived flaws. Except, Tek's deviations from the norm were his foremost strengths. Regardless of the Imperial Director's feelings, Haersen was confident in his choice of leader. No words could sway him, and he would never disseminate any information to undermine Tek's mission. He owed Tek too much for his new life.

After three minutes, a guard entered the room to remove the binding on Haersen's wrists. "You are free to go," he stated, gesturing toward the door.

Haersen rose and rubbed his wrists, still processing his first encounter with the Imperial Director. The report wouldn't be what Tek wanted. He had learned nothing about the Imperial Director's routine or weaknesses in security. But, the information he gleaned had been valuable nonetheless. The Imperial Director would see Tek coming, but he had made no mention of others. With the right group, they could walk in and take control before anyone knew what was happening.

‹ CHAPTER 13 ›

Wil rolled to his side and pulled a pillow over his head, trying to block out the low, pulsating tone intruding on his consciousness. With a start, he shook off the haze of sleep. The sound was Headquarters' warning alarm.

What the...? Wil bolted upright in bed. In all his years at Headquarters, he'd never heard the alarm outside of a test drill.

He threw back the covers and grabbed his handheld from his nightstand. There was no message or any other indication anything was amiss.

Wil pulled on his pants and ran into the living room, slipping his handheld into his pocket. The normally subtle orange lights along the baseboard were glowing red, and a red light pulsed above the entry door.

It's impossible to break into Headquarters. Except... The Bakzen had made it in once before.

He hurriedly dismissed the thought—too frightening a notion to acknowledge.

Wil palmed open the door to the hallway, which had automatically bolted in the lockdown. He poked his head into the corridor and saw his father jogging toward him.

"What's going on?" Wil asked.

"No idea," Cris replied, the worry evident in his exposed eyes. "CACI can't—or won't—tell us what triggered the alarm."

"That's..."

"Impossible, like a thousand other things. Go to your men. I'll figure it out."

Wil nodded. "I'll get Saera and stay in the Primus Elite's quarters."

Cris looked like he was about to protest but changed his mind. "I'll call once we know more."

Wil took off down the hall toward the Primus Junior Agents' wing. He followed his bond to Saera and relayed a message to her mind. *"I'm coming to you. Get ready to go."* Continuing to keep his relationship with her a secret wasn't worth the risk.

Michael glanced around at the scared faces of the other Primus Elite trainees. When the alarm sounded, they had congregated in the common room connecting the four bedrooms. The red glow in the room made it quite clear something was wrong.

"What do we do?" Ollie, one of the pilots in Ethan's squad, asked.

"We should stay put," Michael advised. "We don't go anywhere without instruction."

"Do you think it's a test?" Ethan pondered.

Maybe, but this doesn't seem like Wil's style. Michael ran back into his room to retrieve his handheld. "I'm calling Wil."

"If it's a test—" Ian started to protest.

"Then he'll want to know we'll look to him for leadership first," Michael replied as he initiated the call. He joined the others back in the common room.

A chime sounded while Michael waited for the call to connect. Wil answered, "Is everyone okay?"

"We're fine. What's—"

"Stay put," Wil ordered. "I need to make a stop and then I'll come there."

"Okay." Michael ended the call. "He's on his way," he told

the group.

"So it's not a drill," Curtis surmised.

"He sounded worried," Michael admitted.

"We're all going to die!" Kalin exclaimed, always needing to provide melodramatic relief.

"Everyone get dressed," Michael instructed. "We may need to leave on short notice."

"You heard him!" Ethan said as he jogged back to his room, turning to meet Michael's gaze with silent understanding.

Anything could happen. They needed to be ready.

Wil dashed down the stairwell to the floor below containing the Junior Agent and Initiate quarters. Saera's room was in the same quadrant on the circular Level 2 as his own quarters, so the stairs brought him close to his destination. He veered to the right once out of the stairwell and ran the rest of the way.

The warning tone had been silenced—probably by his father—but the red lights remained.

Wil reached Saera's door and used his officer's code to override the emergency lock.

The door beeped as it unlocked and slid open. Saera approached the doorway. Behind her were her three roommates, one of which Wil recognized as her friend Elise. The other two Wil had encountered in past assignments as a class instructor. The three sets of eyes were eyeing him with bewilderment, and Saera looked relieved. The secret was out.

"Come on, we need to get to the Elite's," Wil said to Saera, ignoring the others in the room.

"Do you know what the alarm is about?" Saera asked.

"No." Wil took her and urged her into the hall.

"Be careful," Saera called to her roommates, looking specifically at a confused Elise.

The door slid shut as Wil broke into a jog down the hallway, still grasping Saera's hand.

She kept pace with him. "What would cause an automatic lockdown?"

"A breach in security. It's a new protocol initiated after the Bakzen broke in to capture me."

Saera gripped his hand tighter. "Do you think it's them?"

"No," Wil replied. "This isn't how they operate." *But dealing with the unknown might be worse.*

They reached the end of the Junior Agents' wing. Wil paused at the opening to the central elevator lobby. It appeared empty, but an unseen infiltrator might be lurking nearby.

He made a telepathic sweep of the lobby. No one seemed to be around. "This isn't right," he murmured while leading Saera across the lobby at a jog. "My dad said CACI couldn't identify a trigger for the alarm."

Saera frowned. "So it was initiated remotely?"

"Maybe. But that begs the question, 'why?'"

They reached the empty hall on the opposite side of the lobby. Wil ran another telepathic sweep. It was still clear.

"I don't want to worry the others," Wil continued, "but we have no idea what's going on."

"Great."

"I won't let anything happen to you," Wil assured her.

"I'm glad you brought me with you. When the alarm sounded, I wasn't sure what to do."

Wil eyed her playfully despite his tension. "Did you orchestrate all of this just to support the case for moving in with me?"

Saera smiled back. "That would have been brilliant."

The Primus Elites' quarters were in the center block of the residential wing. No one else was in the surrounding corridors, making the red-bathed hall even more ominous.

When they reached their destination, Wil took a deep breath. "Ready?"

Saera nodded.

Wil unlocked and slid open the entry door. Inside, the common room was empty.

Don't tell me they left. Wil stepped inside with Saera and reset the lock. "Guys?"

All of the bedroom doors were sealed, except for the front left bedroom that was open a crack. Ethan peered out through the opening. "It's him," he said, and then noticed Saera, "and he's not alone."

The other bedroom doors slid open and the men stepped out into the common room. All eyes were on Saera.

Wil looked them over. "So, this is my fianceé, Saera. I didn't plan on you meeting quite this way, but—" He cut off when he heard a low whisper from one of the navigation specialists, Kevin, to his neighbors.

"I foking called it."

"Called what?" Wil asked him.

Kevin's face flushed. "Nothing, sir."

Wil noticed that Michael was glaring at Kevin. "What's this about, Michael?"

Michael hesitated, glancing at Saera. "Some of them had a bet going, about who you were with."

Wil scanned over his men. It was obvious by the downcast eyes and red faces who the offenders were. He was disappointed to see Ian among them. "I'm pretty sure we went over this before."

"It was innocent," Ian voiced in the group's defense.

Unbelievable. Wil was about to object when Saera spoke up.

"How did you make the list?" she asked, looking somewhat amused by the whole thing.

Kevin kept his gaze on the floor. "It was a three-component overall attractiveness rating based on looks, academics, and ability level. We each came up with an algorithm—"

"Enough!" Wil cut in. "This isn't the time. We're under

attack, as far as we know, and the first thing that comes to mind is that you won a stupid bet? Shite! Foking children."

He waited several seconds for the offenders to adopt suitably shamed expressions. "Now, Headquarters is in lockdown. The only way in or out is through the central elevator shaft. That means we're protected, but also trapped."

"What are your orders, sir?" Ethan asked.

"I see that you're already dressed, that was good thinking. Pack bags with emergency rations, blankets, or anything you have on hand in case we need to evacuate. There should be provisions in the cabinets along the back wall." Wil stepped around the sectional couch to the round table toward the back of the room. He activated the holographic projector at its center. "Anyone who's interested in watching me hack the Mainframe can stay here."

No one moved.

Wil groaned as he logged into the system. "Pack, *then* observe!"

Saera offered him a sympathetic smile.

"I swear, normally they're competent," he told her silently.

"I'm sure."

Wil blocked out the flurry of activity around him and focused on creating a backdoor into the Mainframe. A web of code suspended in the air above the tabletop—a visual representation of the system architecture.

The main security blockade was represented by a wall of shifting blocks, each one changing position along the wall and morphing through various polyhedron forms. Such visual representations were simply a way of expressing the underlying code, which Wil had devised for his own projects within the Mainframe. The only way to get into the system was to create a mirror of one of the blocks to slip into the wall, but to do so required matching the ever-changing position and morphing. He'd done it before on numerous occasions, but that had been under ideal conditions. Pulling off the feat on half a night's sleep with an audience would test his abilities.

Tom gaped at the display. "How do—"

Saera waved him quiet, to Wil's relief.

Wil focused in on his target polyhedron. The shape morphs were considered random, but it was technically a piece of programmed software. Any software had some underlying operating parameters, even adaptive AI.

He watched the morphing of the cube and tried to discern a pattern. It did seem completely random, but his trained eye caught telltale signs of the hidden programming. Working through the upcoming iterations in his head, he began to craft the mirror that would allow him to gain entry. Entering the code on the surface of the table, the corresponding mirrored polyhedron formed near the security wall. The polyhedron shifted shape like the target object, and as Wil entered the code its shape began to more closely resemble the shifts of its original counterpart. After several minutes of furious entry, the model was complete.

There was no time to thoroughly vet the code. Wil went all-in.

Carefully, he dragged the holographic representation of the target polyhedron to the edge of the wall. He then took his own model and brought it toward the original, placing it on top. The mirror polyhedron kept perfect time with the other. With it in place, he dragged out the original code.

Wil waited for an anxious minute while a full security sweep completed. It didn't flag his mirror. He let out a relieved sigh. "I think that did it."

The men around the table gave quiet cheers of support. Saera nodded and rubbed his back.

"All right. Now let's see who else is in here." Wil quickly entered a scanning routine to plug into his newly created back door into the Mainframe. It would allow him to access the root files and security logs to identify the source of entry for the breach.

Once complete, the scanner only took moments to deploy. Wil brought up a projection to watch the results compile.

Something's not right. The results of the system scans all came back normal. Wil narrowed his eyes and shook his head.

"What is it?" asked Saera.

"These readings are showing typical functionality in the systems. There's no evidence of a security alert," Wil replied.

"But there's clearly an incident in progress," Michael commented.

"Exactly." Wil crossed his arms. "Which means the infiltrator has the ability to overwrite those logs. That's beyond even my capability."

"Or," Saera ventured, "they have authorized clearance."

Wil pondered the suggestion. "A ghost user."

Saera nodded. "Not in any user bank, but a clone of the highest level administrative account."

"I don't know how it'd be possible. I completely rebuilt the system five years ago."

"Using what?" Saera questioned.

Wil shrugged. "Well, it's based on the original architecture for all Taran computer systems."

"The same one used by the Priesthood?" Saera asked telepathically.

"Yes. but they wouldn't break into the system like this."

She raised an eyebrow. *"Why not? There's plenty you might hide here."*

Wil's stomach dropped. *If they don't trust me or the rest of TSS Command...*

"What are you two talking about?" Ian cut in, recognizing the signs of a telepathic conversation.

"Hypothesizing," Wil replied shortly.

Before Ian could protest, there was a buzz at the door.

Wil looked around the table, and there was silent understanding for them to stay put. He approached the door with caution and checked the screen displaying the outside video feed. It was Banks.

Wil opened the door for him. "Sir, what—"

The High Commander stepped forward and Wil moved out of the way to let him through the door.

"I'm lifting the lockdown," Banks stated.

"But we—"

"There's no evidence of a physical threat, and we've regained control of the systems," Banks cut in. "The danger has passed."

"You know what it was," Wil said telepathically to Banks.

The High Commander didn't reply. "All classes and scheduled activities are cancelled for the morning. Regular schedules will resume at noon." He left without another word.

"All right. Well, I guess we're heading back to bed," Wil told his men. Everyone still looked uneasy. "We're safe here, don't worry," he added, hoping it was true.

"But what was it?" Ethan asked.

"A false alarm. I'll meet you here at noon for freefall training. Good night." Wil led Saera into the hall and closed the door behind them.

Saera examined him. "You have a theory."

"The Aesir," Wil replied. "I know next to nothing about them, but Banks' reticence…"

"You've never talked about the Aesir before. Who are they?"

"A group of ancient Tarans, as far as I can tell. Banks said they may come to 'test me' someday."

Saera took an unsteady breath. "Creepy."

"But if it was them, I don't know why they'd mess with Headquarters and then leave."

"So, what—they could come back any day and take you for this 'test'?"

"Your guess is as good as mine."

"Wil," she grabbed his hand.

He looked into her glowing eyes.

"It's okay to be scared."

Even if I can't show it to anyone else. Wil squeezed her hand. "I don't know what I'd do without you."

He walked Saera the rest of the way to her quarters through the empty halls.

"I guess everyone will know about us now," Saera commented as they reached her door.

"It was time, I guess. Though, it would have been nice to do on our own terms."

"Oh well." She took a slow breath. "What should I tell anyone who asks about us?"

No sense hiding anything now. "The truth. We're engaged."

"Are you're sure you want to put that out there?"

Wil nodded and took her face in his hand. "I don't want to have to stay apart anymore." He leaned in for a kiss and she pulled him close.

"We'll face it together tomorrow," she said.

Wil pulled out of the hug and gave her one more kiss. "I'll see you in the morning."

As soon as Saera was inside, Wil let out an unsteady breath. *Can the Aesir really break the security safeguards without leaving any trail?* The implications were terrifying.

He took a slow pace toward the stairway back up to the Agents' residential level. Just when he was about to open the door, a voice inside his head stopped him in his tracks. *"Next time, it won't be just a test."*

Banks didn't need the Priest to respond to know they were in trouble. The Priest's drawn expression said it all.

"I don't know what else it could have been," Banks continued. "The coding was too sophisticated."

"If the Aesir can gain access to Headquarters so easily, there's no hiding," the Priest said at last.

"Why wouldn't they take him?" Banks asked. If it was the Aesir that had been at their doorstep, then there was nothing keeping them from walking in to take Wil, or whatever they had planned for him. No longer was it just idle speculation about their interest in him. To be so close without making a direct move was downright unnerving.

"Perhaps they don't feel he is ready to be tested yet," the Priest speculated.

"He went through the CR exam four years ago. I'd think that would have been the trigger."

"The Aesir work on their own timeline. Just see that he is ready when the time does come." The Priest ended the transmission.

Banks eased on to the couch in his office. He could only think of one reason worthy of delaying the test, and it had nothing to do with letting Wil's abilities mature. He'd either pass their test or he wouldn't based on his innate skills. Additional training was unlikely to change the outcome.

However, meeting with the Aesir would undoubtedly reveal the hidden truths that the Priesthood was so intent on keeping. The night's strange events were just a precursor to gaining access to Wil when they deemed the time right. They must be awaiting the eve of Wil's involvement in the war. But planning to tell him the truth so soon before he must act… It was either sabotage or a calculated move to fuel his motivation. Either way, Banks shuddered to think of what Wil would do when he learned everything that had been kept from him. Such fine lines between adversary and ally were difficult to tread.

‹ CHAPTER 14 ›

Elise had been watching Saera intently all morning, though she had yet to say anything. Saera knew her friend wanted an explanation for why Wil would come to retrieve her during an emergency, and why he would be holding her hand. The answer was obvious, but Saera needed to say the words to make it real. Yet, after years of keeping the secret, she didn't know how to broach the subject.

By breakfast in the mess hall, it was obvious to Saera that she couldn't stay silent forever. Other trainees were eyeing her from the buffet line with the same disbelief as her roommates, indicating that rumors were spreading. If left unchecked, those rumors could turn particularly unfavorable.

"So about last night…" Saera began, pulling Elise aside into the open area near the cases with pre-packaged meals.

The floodgates opened. "Wil Sights. Coming to our room. For you," Elise burst out.

"Yeah, well—" Saera was still searching for the words when she spotted the other women from her Primus cohort heading over from the entry door. *An audience, wonderful.*

"I just heard the strangest thing," Leila stated. "That you're involved with Wil Sights."

The secret is out. I guess I may as well own it. Saera met Leila's suspicious gaze head on. "Yes, we're engaged."

Her friends took a collective gasp.

"No way!" Caryn exclaimed while Leila burst out laughing, Nadeen rolled her eyes, and Elise's jaw dropped.

Saera waited for Leila's giggling to subside. "I'm serious."

Elise, having actually seen Saera with Wil, seemed most willing to believe the proclamation. "When did this happen?"

"We got engaged almost two years ago, but we've been together for about five," Saera replied.

"I don't believe it," Leila maintained.

"No, he did come to our quarters for her last night," Elise said. "I knew he had tutored you for a while, but… now you're engaged?"

"Wait, he tutored you?" Caryn cut in.

Nadeen's eyes were still wide. "How did you keep that a secret all this time?"

"It wasn't easy—" Saera glanced toward the door when she felt the pull of Wil approaching. Their eyes met as he entered the mess hall.

Her friends fell silent, waiting for him to confirm her story.

"Are we doing this now?" Wil asked her.

"We sort of have to," Saera replied.

With that, Wil headed straight for her. "Hi," he said to the group.

Saera gave him a meek smile. "So this is Caryn, Leila, Nadeen, and Elise," she introduced, motioning to each friend in turn.

Wil looked around the semicircle. "It's nice to finally put faces to the names."

Leila eyed him with suspicion. "Are you two really engaged?"

Wil nodded. "Yes, for some time now."

"Stars!" Caryn breathed.

"Saera wanted to tell you all earlier, but, with my position, we needed to keep it confidential," Wil continued.

"No wonder you're top-ranked," Leila muttered.

Wil shot her a stern glare. "And that way of thinking is

precisely why we kept it private. I won't stoop to arguing the issue with you, but take my word that Saera's standings have not been inflated due to our relationship."

"You have my word, too."

Saera startled at the sudden voice behind her. She turned to see that it was High Commander Banks.

The Primus women snapped to attention.

"Their involvement was sanctioned," Banks continued. "Wil is in a unique position that warrants exception."

He may as well have just admitted that Wil is a Sietinen heir. Saera could see her friends thinking through the implications.

"Discovering a secret romance hardly seems like a reason to be late to class. But, carry on," Banks strolled past them to the buffet line and picked up his breakfast.

"I need to get to practice," Wil said, glancing at his men, who were watching the proceedings from their usual table. "See you tonight?" he asked Saera.

She nodded. "I'll come by after my last class." She thought about grappling him in a passionate kiss to really wipe the smug pout off of Leila's face, but settled for brushing her hand against Wil's instead.

Wil flashed her a parting smile and rushed over to have breakfast with the Primus Elites.

"Stars! And to think all this time I felt bad for you for never going on any dates," Caryn breathed as Wil walked away.

"It still feels like a dream." But Saera knew it could turn into a nightmare at any moment. *They may be envious now, but they'll be thankful they're not with him when we're at the center of the war.*

<>   <>   <>

"That was quite an eventful night," Cris commented as he sat down across from Banks.

More than you realize. "An anomaly. Nothing to warrant

ongoing concern."

Cris crossed his arms. "The alarm goes off in the middle of the night with no explanation and there's no cause for concern? Right!"

There was no way to explain the Aesir to Cris without raising more questions. Dodging and distraction was Banks' best option. "The system was tested, and everyone reacted the way we'd hope during such an event."

"Except *we* didn't initiate that test. What aren't you telling me?"

Banks sighed. Cris always was too perceptive for his own good. "I don't have enough information to make any solid claims, so I will remain silent on the matter."

Cris glared at him from across the desk. "You'd tell me if it was a matter of general TSS security. That means it's about Wil."

Isn't everything these days? "In a sense."

"Is he in danger?" Cris asked after a moment.

"Of course. We all are."

"I mean immediately. Does whatever happened last night change anything?"

Banks shook his head. "No. Wil already knows what's coming. If he hasn't said anything to you, it's because he doesn't want you to worry."

"Wait, what?"

"Let it go, Cris." Banks folded his hands on the desktop. "There's nothing we can do about it, so let's focus on what we can manage. Like how to handle the communication about Wil and Saera's relationship."

Cris silently fumed in protest for several seconds, but ultimately nodded his assent.

Still, Banks knew Cris well enough to recognize that the topic had not been fully put to rest. The best Banks could do was continue differing. "So," he continued, "even though everyone knows Wil is young, it still looks unfavorable for an Agent to be involved with a student."

Cris leaned back in his chair. "Yes, I'm already hearing whispers in the halls about them."

Banks steepled his fingers. *Whispers that could undermine everything we've built.*

"I'm more concerned with her reputation than his," Cris went on. "Ever since his stunt at the graduation ceremony, I don't think anyone would question his ethics—openness and honesty for the common good. But Saera..."

Banks nodded. "She's a relatively unknown commodity. Top ranked, and now known to be involved with the TSS' golden child. No doubt her standing will be questioned."

"We both know she earned it."

"Absolutely. But convincing others isn't as easy. I've considered sending a formal announcement, but I'm not sure that would help."

"Just draw attention to the issue and look like excuses," Cris murmured. "My recommendation is to let them handle it themselves."

Banks nodded. "That's where I landed, too. I'm glad we're in agreement."

"On this subject, maybe," Cris said with a hint of playfulness in his tone, but the words still had bite.

Determined not to get baited, Banks pressed on. "And in the interest of not making a bigger show out of the relationship than it already is, I would strongly prefer for the wedding to take place after Saera graduates."

"That was already the plan," Cris replied. "She's getting close to graduation, anyway. Most of her required courses are already complete."

"I suppose we should discuss an internship assignment soon."

"Stars, that's right!" Cris frowned. "It's not ideal for her to leave for a year right now. Or ever, really. With the relationship out in the open, she can finally start training alongside the Primus Elites."

Banks nodded. "We need her as a Second for Wil, without a doubt."

"So what do we do for her internship?" Cris asked.

"Let's see if Wil has any ideas. If she has any weak points to address, he'd know."

Dinnertime. Normally that wouldn't elicit a stress response, but Wil's day hadn't exactly been typical. After the events of the previous night, he wished he could block out the world for awhile. But, he needed to be there for Saera.

He was still shaken from his first contact with the Aesir. The voice had only spoken the one line to him as the lockdown lifted, but he could still feel the echo of the words in his mind. He had elected to keep the encounter to himself, knowing the words were meant solely for him. Whatever the Aesir had planned, all he could do was wait.

The remainder of the day had helped distract him from worry about what was to come with the Aesir by focusing his attention on the recent domestic developments. Since the showdown with Saera's friends at breakfast, he'd been getting sidelong glances from students at every turn. First it was the Junior Agents, but now even Trainees seemed to know a big secret was out. *It's stupid. Why does anyone care if I'm engaged to someone?*

Wil suppressed the impulse to hide in his quarters for a few days until everyone moved onto the next great piece of gossip, but he couldn't leave Saera to face it alone. With his chest tight, he headed to the mess hall.

When he entered the room, conversations quieted and eyes shifted in his direction. He immediately noticed that their eyes were darting between him and the other side of the room. Following their glances, he noticed that Saera was seated with Elise in one of the booths.

No more hiding. Wil grabbed a tray of food from the buffet and headed for Saera's table.

She looked over her shoulder at the sense of him approaching. Wil gave her an assured nod, and she slid over to make room for him in the both. Across from her, Elise looked petrified.

"Mind if I join you?" Wil asked when he neared the table, directing the inquiry to Elise.

"Sure," she stammered. "I mean, I don't mind." Her face flushed.

"What's going on with everyone?" Wil asked Saera.

"You were always the unattainable crush, but someone actually got you," Saera replied.

I miss being the kid around here. Wil smiled at Elise, hoping to set her at ease. "So, hi. We've met in passing, but I don't think we've been properly introduced."

"Elise, Wil. Wil, Elise," Saera said with a little hand flourish.

Wil beamed. "There. Now, you two have been roommates pretty much since the beginning of time, right?"

Saera nodded and let out a slow breath between her teeth. "Yeah… Now that you two have been acquainted I really need to stay on Elise's good side. She knows all my bad habits."

"Oh, do tell!" Wil urged. "We've known each other for quite a while, but living with someone gives an entirely different perspective."

"Well, she does have this habit of—" Elise began, but Saera nearly leaped across the table.

"All right! I think maybe we've had enough conversation for one night," Saera stated, settled back into her seat.

"Oh, come now. We're just getting started," Wil countered with a grin. "Now, what you were about to say, Elise?"

Saera's stern glare through her tinted glasses kept Elise quiet.

"She was just going to comment on how perfectly normal I am in every way," Saera cut in.

"I recognize that swearing friends to secrecy is a time-honored tradition, but I will remind you, Elise, that you have been asked a direct question by an Agent."

"So I have to answer?" Elise asked, the conflict audible in her voice.

Saera shook her head with an exasperated sigh. "He's joking."

Wil raised an eyebrow. "Am I?"

"Pulling rank is an unfair way to conduct yourself in a discussion."

"But it's so effective!"

Saera scoffed. "Only to the weak-minded."

"Stars! You two really are a couple," Elise exclaimed through a chuckle.

"Well yeah." Saera eyed her friend. "Did you think this was all a gag?"

"No," Elise replied. "but it is strange seeing you together like this."

"It's strange being together," Saera admitted, looking up at Wil.

He took her hand. "But it's such a relief. No more having to sneak through the halls at night or sending coded messages."

Saera scrunched up her nose. "I don't know. I might kind of miss it."

"In any case, it's great to see you happy," Elise said.

I'm glad Saera has had her as a friend. "Thank you for taking all of this in stride. I hope you'll help quell any of the suspicions that Saera is only in Primus Command because of me."

"Absolutely," Elise responded. "I've seen what she can do—anyone who has wouldn't have those doubts."

Saera lit up. "That's right! I'll finally get to practice with you."

Wil tilted his head. "Maybe reserve some of that excitement. They can be a bit challenging to work with at times."

"Then we have to whip them into shape," Saera said.

"You're talking about the Primus Elites, right?" Elise asked.

Wil nodded. "And the fun with them never ends."

"Well, you two enjoy that." Elise slid out from the bench. "Wil, it was a pleasure to finally make your acquaintance. I imagine we'll be seeing much more of each other in the future."

Wil looked to Saera and she nodded. "Definitely. I look forward to it."

‹ CHAPTER 15 ›

Haersen took his seat in the corner of the conference room. He had observed many staff meetings between Tek and his officers, but this one would be different.

Tek sat in silence at the head of the table as the officers entered. Most were young and had yet to witness any real battle—their skin still smooth and unscarred. Among them was Colonel Komatra, whom Tek had taken on as a mentee. Komatra had little patience for Haersen and made no effort to mask his displeasure with Tek's choice to keep Haersen as a pseudo-advisor.

When the eight officers were seated, they noted their companions across the table, using name badges on the uniforms to differentiate where the faces failed. There were some noticeable absences from the usual attendee list.

"You are my most trusted officers," Tek began. "I have gathered you here today to propose a change."

The officers glanced at each other, then returned their attention to Tek.

"For years now the Bakzen have been on a declining path," the General continued. "Our genetic lines are being weighed down by antiquated traits. It all traces back to our leadership. The Imperial Director doesn't want to change, and yet the Bakzeni Empire is transforming around him. It is time we take the future into our own hands."

A murmur of surprise passed around the table.

"A coup?" Komatra asked.

"An overdue transition in leadership," Tek replied.

"I won't have any part of this," a colonel named Felak declared and rose from the table. "It's traitorous—" He gripped his throat, gasping for air.

Tek glared at him from the other end of the table, eyes glowing and vicious. "Then we don't need you."

Felak's neck snapped and he fell to the floor.

"Are there any other opposers?" Tek asked the stunned officers.

No one protested.

"We have an incredible resource at our disposal," Tek continued without missing a beat, "yet the Imperial Director is preoccupied with 'preservation of life'—no better than Carzen's idealistic vision that cost us use of the Cadicle. We need to begin using our drones for their intended purpose, to complete the pathways to extend the rift to our targets. We can't rely on solely subspace travel once the TSS achieves an independent jump drive." Tek gazed at the stoic faces around him. "We need to sacrifice now, for the advancement of the Bakzen."

The officers nodded their agreement.

"How do we proceed?" Komatra asked.

Tek folded his hands on the metal tabletop. "The Imperial Director already suspects I am conspiring against him. I can only anticipate that he will make a move against me. But, he doesn't know that any of you share my intents. Our best course is for you to gain entry to the Imperial Director's office to subdue him."

"It would take at least three of us to hold him," Komatra mused. "His line is especially strong."

Haersen shifted in his chair, knowing that Tek came from that same genetic line. He wondered if the others knew—and if they would be so quick to follow if they did. Or, perhaps that was why they followed without question, since he could overpower them with ease. Superior strength was the mark of a great Bakzen leader, after all.

"So, we must find a reason for your meeting." Tek paused. "And my suspected assassination would make the perfect cover."

"What if that never comes?" Komatra asked.

Tek shook his head. "It will—even if it needs a little push."

The officers gave a murmur of support.

"That is all for now," Tek said and rose from his seat.

The officers stood and saluted him before filing out of the room.

Tek turned to Haersen in the corner. "You joined us at an interesting time—getting to see history made. The Bakzen are forging a future path just as Tararia's era comes to an end."

Haersen slid from the chair and knelt in front of Tek. "It is a great honor to witness."

"Continue being useful and you'll get to see even more." Tek headed for the door. "Oh, and Haersen, take care of that." He gestured toward Felak's lifeless body on the floor.

"Yes, sir."

Laecy gathered her team around the holodisplay. She had the better part of the warship design completed, but there was no way she could finish it on her own. Even though her team of specialists was already strapped, Taelis' mandate was clear.

"So, what are we doing here?" Nolan asked.

"We've been tasked with scaling the neural interface technology from the IT-1 jets to a warship," Laecy replied.

Richards raised an eyebrow. "Seriously?"

Laecy brought up her incomplete design to show to the group. She'd pieced together the snippets of Wil's concept, tying in the individual systems as best she could. Mechanically, though, it was hardly space-worthy. "Right now, it has no life support, the structural bracing is a total mess, and I have no idea how we're going to integrate the telekinetic energy relays with the weapons and jump drive, given the placement of the Command Center."

Nolan's eyes widened. "It has telekinetic weapons systems?"

"That's the idea, anyway. And the neural interface can bypass the nav console so the pilot can jump the ship directly." It still seemed crazy to Laecy, but Wil's specs were always on point.

"Why isn't Wil working on this?" Richards asked.

"He's too busy training his officers to be bothered with ship designs anymore. Besides, this is a fun challenge for us!" Laecy said, trying to rally her team. *Taelis made it pretty clear we're on our own with this one.*

Richards scanned over the design. "Even if we can get everything linked up, there's no way we could construct a ship like this. Even with the expanded facilities at Prisarus, getting our hands on the materials for a craft of this scale..."

"Let's just say there's a contingency budget," Laecy said.

Nolan sighed. "How will—"

An alarm sounded in the hangar.

"What the...?" Richards ran out of the lab, and Laecy followed close behind.

Laecy searched the room for sign of an incident. There was no indication of anything in the quadrant near the engineering lab, so she ran toward the opposite side of the circular hangar.

The blast doors over one of the portals to space were open, leaving the room protected from the void by only a forcefield.

"Why is that open?" Laecy demanded.

"Emergency alert from the front lines. Incoming fleet with heavy damage," an engineering tech replied as he ran by.

"Shite."

Such incidents were at least a monthly occurrence, but it

never got any easier to witness the destructive power of the Bakzen.

As Laecy approached the door, the first of the incoming jets slipped through the forcefield. Its right wing was charred and smoking, filling the hangar with the stench of burning metal.

"Get the fire crew out here!" Laecy instructed.

Four crew members were already donning fire suits and had suppression canisters in hand.

The jet screeched to a halt. With a hiss, the pilot popped the top hatch and clamored out, falling to the ground.

One of the crew members in a fire suit ran forward to drag the pilot away from the jet while the others doused the smoldering sections on the wing.

Laecy dashed over to help the pilot. She released the seal on the helmet.

The pilot was a young woman with dark brown hair pulled into a bun and glowing brown eyes. An Agent, making her the leader of the squadron. "Are the others back?" she gasped.

"No, not yet, ma'am." Laecy helped the pilot to her feet.

"They were shooting at us with something I'd never seen before."

Another innovation. Just what we needed. "Any idea what it could have been?"

"I didn't get a good look," the pilot replied. "I called for a retreat as soon as I realized we were outnumbered."

A roar drew Laecy's attention back to the door. Another jet had just passed through the forcefield and others were lined up outside.

"What happened to your escort cruiser?" Laecy asked the pilot.

The Agent only shook her head in response.

Fok, not another one. "Get to Medical, ma'am. We've got it handled here."

"No, I need to know."

Laecy understood. She'd want to make sure all of her crew were accounted for, too.

Another jet passed through the door. It was singed like the first two, but something looked wrong about the tail end—covered in a gray substance that was almost indistinguishable from the hull metal aside from a slight protrusion.

Richards ran up behind her. "What's that?" he asked, pointing at the jet's tail.

"I was wondering the same thing," Laecy replied.

The substance on the tail shimmered slightly. Richards stepped forward to investigate.

The pilot came to stand next to Laecy. "That's what they were shoot—"

Suddenly, a red glow began to emanate from the substance, and within a second the jet exploded with a sickening crack. Laecy was thrown backwards.

Her vision blurred and ears ringing, Laecy tried to rise to her feet. The instant she put weight on her right arm, a bolt of pain shot through her. She collapsed back on the ground, clutching her elbow.

Laecy rolled to her back and tried to focus. Muffled shouts sounded around her. Heat scorched her face. She looked to the side, blinking.

The jet was a mangled mass of metal on the singed deck plates. Red blood was smeared amid the soot. Several bodies lay motionless on the floor.

Laecy struggled to her feet, using her left arm for support. As she rose, she saw that Richards was face-down on the floor three meters in front of her.

The ruins of the jet were in flames, casting billowing smoke into the air.

Two of the crew in fire suits were rushing toward the fire spraying the contents of their suppression canisters.

Laecy stumbled toward Richards shouting his name. Her

face twisted in horror was she neared his body. He wasn't breathing.

"Jack!" She knelt by his side and tried to flip him over with her good arm.

When he was on his side, his head lolled lifelessly to the side, his eyes open and vacant.

No! "Medic!" Laecy screamed over her shoulder, though she knew it was already too late. A piece of shrapnel in his chest nearly bisecting him. *Not him…*

"Stars! Denna, your arm!" the medic exclaimed as he ran up.

Laecy glanced down at her own wound. Her jumpsuit was stained dark red down her side and the sleeve was in tatters around her lacerated skin.

"That can wait. Richards—"

The medic took one look at the fallen engineer and shook his head.

"Fok." Laecy clutched her injured arm and rose to her feet, turning away. *I don't want to remember him like that. I can't…* With her vision finally clear, she took in the carnage around her.

Half a dozen crew writhed on the ground with serious injuries, and another was dead a few meters from Richards. The air was gray with smoke and stank of burned metal and flesh. Laecy's stomach turned over.

"Foking Bakzen," the Agent pilot said from behind Laecy. "I never should have led us back here. Shite."

If you hadn't, he'd still be alive! Laecy swallowed the bile rising from her stomach. No one could possibly know what the loss meant to her. But making it any more than a fallen friend wouldn't do service to his memory. She fought to maintain composure, fighting every instinct to drop to her knees and hold Richards one last time.

"What triggered the explosion?" Laecy stammered.

The pilot shook her head. "All the other jets that were hit detonated right away. I thought it was automatic. I don't know why this one waited to go off."

"It doesn't matter." *The dead can't be brought back. I never thought the war would come inside these walls...*

"We need to get you to Medical," the medic said to Laecy, pulling her from her thoughts.

"I'm fine. Get everyone else to safety."

"You're bleeding out," the medic stated. "Get to Medical." He ran to help one of the crew members laying on the floor clutching her bleeding leg.

Laecy looked down and realized that a pool of blood had formed beneath her injured arm. "Shite." Her head felt woozy.

"Let me cauterize that," the pilot offered. "You look like you're about to pass out."

"I—"

Before Laecy could finish her protest, the Agent had cupped her hands around the wound. Laecy felt a searing heat followed by numbness. She examined her arm and saw that it had been completely burned, but the bleeding had stopped.

"Old battlefield trick," the Agent explained. "I know it looks terrible now, but you needed a complete graft anyway."

"Thanks," Laecy muttered and stumbled toward the central elevator. With her nerves burned and bleeding quelled, she was finding it hard to acknowledge that the attack had just taken place. She would be healed in a matter of hours, but there was no bringing back her fallen friends. *Jack...* Some people were completely irreplaceable, and he was one of them. *And how many others?*

The end of the war couldn't come soon enough.

"They have something new," Taelis informed Banks over the viewscreen.

Banks gritted his teeth. *Another Bakzen innovation. We can't keep up.* "What is it?"

"A new kind of explosive charge," Taelis explained. He hung his head. "We had an attack here at H2."

"Is everyone okay?" Banks asked, but the answer was already clear from Taelis' grim expression.

"I don't have the final casualty reports yet, but it looks like the engineering team was hit pretty hard."

Banks let out a slow breath. "What about the new warship?"

"This attack may mean a setback in the design, but we have the materials now to proceed with the neural interface. We'll get it built."

I still don't like the idea of going behind Wil's back. I know why he scrapped the idea—I wouldn't want to wield that kind of power, either. "Maybe we should refocus our resources under the circumstances."

"No, this attack is precisely why we need the ship. And why we need Wil. We have to end this."

Banks nodded his understanding, even though he would never fully agree with the approach. "I'll keep him focused on training his officers."

"And I'll make sure he'll have the fleet he needs," Taelis replied. He swallowed, drooping slightly. "Watch your back. We're never safe, even at home."

"I know." *All too well.*

Taelis eyed him. "Any more word from the Aesir since that night?"

Banks shook his head. "But I have no doubt that they're watching us."

"Fok, all of our preparations could be for nothing if…"

Wil will pass their test. But will he still be on our side once he learns the truth? "We're going to see this through to the end, Erik. Don't lose hope."

The other High Commander nodded. "I never do."

‹ CHAPTER 16 ›

Calls to the High Commander's office always put Wil on guard. Either big news was coming or there was a problem. Hopefully not both.

His father was waiting in the guest chair across the desk from Banks.

Banks gestured Wil toward the other open guest chair. "Take a seat."

"We were discussing the training progress of the Junior Agents," Cris commented as Wil got situated. "Saera came up, of course."

Wil nodded. "She's progressing nicely."

"So much so," said Banks, "that it's time we prepare for graduation."

That seems premature. "She hasn't hit a telekinetic ability limit yet."

"That's what the CR exam is for. Are there any other shortcomings?" Banks asked.

Wil thought through their years of training together. "She has all the attributes we'd hope for in an Agent. I can't think of any typical skill where she's deficient."

Banks eyed him. "Yet you seen unsure about her graduating. What's giving you pause?"

"That's more about the prospect of her getting involved in the war," Wil countered.

"Still, there has to be something that would make her hesitate," Banks pressed.

"By that measure, even graduated Agents have issues," Wil pointed out.

"Fair," conceded Banks, "but what's her biggest hang-up? We should focus on that."

There is one thing. "That couldn't be addressed with a traditional internship. And trying to certainly wouldn't be worth missing those months of training with the Primus Elites."

"Maybe we should forego an internship," Cris suggested. "We have the authority."

"Wil, is there any alternate assignment that comes to mind?" asked Banks.

"Would you be able to cover Primus Elite training for a few days?" Wil asked his father.

Cris nodded. "Sure."

"Then I'll make the internship arrangements," Wil stated.

"You'll need an objective third-party observer," Banks reminded him.

I hate the idea of someone intruding on Saera's private life. "It'll have to be someone who's proven to be trustworthy."

"Scott?" Cris suggested.

"I'll abide it," Banks agreed. "Make the preparations, Wil. I look forward to your report."

The spatial awareness chamber felt like a second home after nearly two years of almost daily training. Michael floated at the center of the chamber along with the other Primus Elites.

They were chatting amongst themselves, waiting for Wil to return so they could resume the practice session.

Michael didn't like being left in the center of the chamber without an Agent. What minimal telekinetic abilities had manifested for him weren't enough to make it back to a wall. He was trapped. *Why aren't the others concerned about getting stuck here?*

He did recognize that he was more pessimistic than most in the group. Wil had commented on it, but in his usual fashion had made light of the personality quirk—saying that it was an important skill to anticipate and prepare for a worst case scenario. While that was true, it also meant that Michael worried, and with that came extra stress. He was envious of people like Ian who could live in the moment when everything was calm but immediately focus when necessary. Always being on guard was draining.

Michael's predisposition to anticipate a terrible outcome did him no favors the moment the portal to the spatial awareness chamber reopened. Wil emerged, followed by Saera.

He bit his lip. *It was only a matter of time before she began training with us.*

The others knew nothing of his past relationship with her, and it was best it stayed that way. However, it would be difficult to mask when the primary purpose of the training exercises was to achieve openness between each other's minds to facilitate faster telepathic communication. Wil had helped each of them learn how to compartmentalize private information that might cloud communications, and Michael's relationship with Saera was one of those items. But, it was always more difficult to bury shared experiences. Hopefully she was more adept at maintaining mental guards.

"Saera will be joining us for a few sessions each week," Wil announced. "She's been training with me as a Second on the side, but it's time we bring it full circle."

"So much for the boys club," Curtis quipped.

Ethan chuckled. "I guess we'll have to be on our best behavior."

Michael glared at them. *"Show some respect,"* he chastised telepathically. *Captains should set a better example.*

"I'm in Primus," Saera replied to the side conversation. "I've been training alongside men far raunchier than you since the beginning."

"And no," Wil cut in, "that wasn't meant as a challenge."

Ethan feigned disappointment, slumping his shoulders.

"Now," Wil continued, "we're going to try some new things. With the independent jump drive now in commission, I need to focus on simultaneous observation."

"Where do we come in?" Curtis asked.

"That's for us to figure out," replied Wil. "The entire point is for me to observe the events on both planes and relay orders. And that needs to be done faster and more efficiently than electronic systems allow. In fact, that's the whole point. We need a telepathic communication network, of sorts."

"So, a communication hub suspended in subspace?" Michael questioned.

"Not just in subspace—oscillating between the planes," Wil clarified. "At least, I think that's how it will work. Really, there's no guarantee any of this is even possible."

"I've practiced serving as a Second—a grounding point for Wil, like an anchor," Saera chimed in. "But we haven't pushed it very far."

Wil nodded. "And I'll need to extend myself a lot farther than we've attempted." He paused, glancing at Saera. "Michael, as the lead Captain, I'd like you to be the first to train as an additional Second."

There it is. "Okay, " Michael acknowledged.

Wil scanned down the line of his trainees. "I want all of you to know how to serve as a Second eventually, but we'll add one at a time until we've figured out a good system."

"Tell me what to do," Michael said.

Wil and Saera pushed off the wall toward the center of the room and slowed themselves in the middle of the Primus Elites.

Michael felt the air congeal around him as he was pulled

toward Wil. The other men were rearranged into a ring. He found himself approximately a meter from Wil and Saera with the three of them in a triangular configuration.

"Relax," Wil instructed.

Letting out a slow breath, Michael opened his mind.

A moment later, he sensed a presence in his consciousness, and then another.

"You already know me. Trust in that past," one of the voices said. Saera—he could feel the steady confidence of her power, calm and grounded.

"Focus on Saera," the other voice said. The energy from Wil was far stronger, but seemed distant.

"I thought I was training as your Second?" Michael questioned.

"You're the most advanced of the group, but I need to hold back around you for now," Wil replied. *"Unshielded exposure would overwhelm you."*

Michael wasn't in a hurry to test that theory. *"Okay."* He closed his eyes and focused on Saera's presence, as instructed. She drew him in, guiding him without words or vision. Yet, he knew what he was supposed to do. He aligned with her energy, backing her up as she reached out to Wil.

An electrified wave washed over Michael's consciousness as he felt Wil extending toward the dimensional veil. Subspace was beyond—out of reach to Michael, but within Wil's grasp.

Michael could feel Saera extending herself as Wil contacted the dimensional veil, tearing his way through. A surge of energy rippled through the tether between them as Wil reached subspace—but he paused, searching. Subspace lay between normal space and the rift, but both were clouded while fully in the subspace plane.

Frustration filled Michael's mind, emanating from Wil. The tie to Saera began to slip as she stretched further to keep the tether on Wil while he delved deeper into subspace in his quest to observe both the rift and normal space.

"*Wait!*" Michael pleaded, beginning to drift. His heart raced somewhere in the distance, away from himself. Dark emptiness enveloped him—alone, helpless.

In an instant, he felt the support of the two minds return to him. His panic subsided.

"*Now we have a sense of limits,*" Wil said. The presence of his mind vanished.

Michael opened his eyes.

Saera's eyes fluttered open next to him. She smiled. "Not bad for a first attempt."

"Not bad at all," Wil said. "I wonder how many we can chain together."

"I don't think I'm up for that," Saera replied. "The tether didn't feel entirely secure."

Michael shook his head. "It wasn't. I slipped."

"You weren't completely grounded," Wil told him. "Admittedly, I skipped over a few steps."

"Then how am I supposed to know what to do?" There was more bite to Michael's tone than he intended.

"You followed my lead," Saera responded. "That was the right thing to do. But you followed too far. We need to elongate the tether—with me following Wil and you keeping a tie here for us to follow back."

"And we can keep adding to that chain?" Ian cut in.

Wil nodded. "Potentially. Or, with multiple grounding points, the tether to me can be longer and shared. We'll have to work up to that, but I think that's ultimately what we need to strive for. I'm having to hold back because it's too much for one person to take on as a conduit—even for Saera with our bond. But if you can share it among multiple people, maybe I can be free enough to push."

"So we're stuck for now," Saera said, sullen.

"Not completely," Wil countered. "We still need to

strengthen the telepathic bonds within the group. Once those are set, it should be easier and more fluid to change the tethering structures."

Michael crossed his arms. *If I'm the most advanced and this doesn't feel secure, how is it going to be for the others?* "We need to start with something more basic."

"Like what?" Wil asked.

Michael uncrossed his arms and shrugged. "I don't know. Like a telepathic game of telephone—just something to make sure we're communicating clearly."

Wil looked confused.

"It's a children's game on Earth," Saera clarified. "Lining up and whispering a message in your neighbor's ear, and they repeat the message as best they can to their neighbor, and so on. Generally, by the time the message gets to the end of the line, the phrase has completely changed."

"Hmm." Wil paused in thought. "That's actually not a bad idea. Let's try."

It was strange to be able to walk in public together. Wil glanced to his right and saw that Saera kept watching the passersby like they were about to call her out for being with an Agent. "We'll get used to it."

"Hmm? Oh. Yeah." She sighed. "I thought it would be easier once we didn't have to hide anymore."

"It will be," he assured her. "It's just new. We have a lot of ingrained habits to override."

"Yes, we do."

At the entrance to the Agents' wing, Saera hesitated. "You can come over," Wil said.

She eyed him, skeptical. "Walking down the hall together is strange enough, but going in your front door?"

"You've come over lots of times."

"But always all stealthy-like."

Wil chuckled and put his arm around her. "Come on."

She tensed under his touch.

"So what if people see us? They know we're together."

Saera relaxed a little and followed his lead down to the Agents' wing. "I know. You're right."

As they approached Wil's quarters, Scott was walking in the opposite direction. He perked up with surprise when he saw Wil and Saera behaving so openly as a couple.

Wil ignored him and unlocked the door. He let Saera through the door first. When he glanced back at Scott as he passed, Scott smiled and held up his index finger—a universal sign of approval or job well done.

No doubt what that was referencing. Wil was quite familiar with the antics of Scott's youth, courtesy of his father.

Wil closed the door to the hall. "Alone at last."

"Back to the familiar." Saera put her arms around his neck and pulled him in for a kiss. "I don't know about you, but after all those telepathy exercises I'm looking forward to just being near one other mind for a while."

"I agree completely." Wil kissed her back, following her lead toward the couch.

"And after all that work today—I need a distraction." She laid back on the couch, pulling Wil with her.

He kissed down her neck as her back arched in response to his touch. "Is this a suitable distraction?"

"That's a good start."

They spent some time decompressing from the day, forgetting the burdens of the outside world. Those intimate moments were the one escape Wil afforded himself. And Saera always knew just what he needed to temporarily take his mind off his problems.

The distraction never lasted, but it was a reprieve.

Afterward, with some clarity restored, Wil reclined on the

couch. It didn't take long for his mind to wander back to the practice session earlier in the afternoon. He sat in silent reflection for a few minutes before turning to Saera. "How do you think things went with the group?"

She slipped her shirt back over her head. The break was over. "Better than I expected. They're strong for Initiates."

In some ways, they were too strong. Whatever effect being around Wil had had on Saera seemed to be repeating with them, if not as pronounced. "I don't think they'll be at that classification for much longer."

"At least you get to set the rules for their advancement." Saera returned to the couch next to Wil, fully dressed.

"It's such a tight timeline, it's not as rewarding as it should be." Wil reoriented toward her, the couch cushion cool against his bare back.

"You're doing great. They'll be fine officers."

"I know they will." He took in Saera's loving gaze—the patience and support. His men weren't the only ones he needed to take care of. "But a break would probably do us all good, before we get too far into a new training routine."

Saera's eyes widened. "You. Voluntarily taking a break?"

Wil smirked. "Just a short one. I was thinking maybe we should take a trip to Earth."

Her brow furrowed. "Why?"

"Well, we've been engaged for almost two years now, and I have yet to meet any of the family that raised you. It might be nice to have some introductions before the wedding," Wil said.

Saera let out a long breath. "I'm not sure that's a good idea."

"If not now, then when?"

"Is 'never' an option?" she asked.

Wil shook his head. "Sorry."

Saera moaned. "What did you have in mind?"

"I'd like to meet everyone, but a little sightseeing might be nice, too. I've never been down there."

"Well, it's March right now. That's not a great tourist season for northeastern Virginia."

"I'll use my imagination."

Saera eyed him. "And you're sure you want to meet my family?"

"As many as I can. I'm curious to see where you came from." He took her hands. "I know not all of it was good, but revisiting the past with a new perspective can be a good thing."

"All right. I guess I should give my dad a heads up," Saera said, making no effort to hide her reluctance. "When do you think we'll be there?"

Wil shrugged. "We can go as early as next week, if you're up for it. That should give me enough time to brush up on the English you taught me."

"Or you could use that cortical imprinting machine like anyone else."

"They won't let me anywhere near that device."

"Why not? Afraid you'll modify it to turn yourself into even more of a crazy genius than you already are?"

If only that was the biggest concern. "No. My neural structure is... different. Ever since I was shot."

"Oh, right." Saera frowned.

"Besides, it's kind of nice to learn the traditional way. And you're a great teacher." He grinned.

"If you count 'teaching' as you memorizing a few books and me correcting pronunciation," Saera quipped. "Okay, we may as well get the trip out of the way as soon as possible, then."

"That's no way to think about it!"

"Yeah, well you haven't met my family yet..."

Wil laughed. "Like the meeting with mine went great."

"It's different. I grew up with mine."

"It'll be fine." Wil squeezed her hands. "I'll be there with you."

"I'll let my dad know we're coming."

◆▸   ◆▸   ◆▸

"You're free to go," the doctor told Laecy. "The High Commander asked to see you."

Laecy rose from the exam table, cradling her bandaged arm. The biografting had repaired the damage already, but the bandage would protect the new skin as it toughened overnight.

She wasn't in remotely the right headspace for talking to Taelis. However, declining a meeting with the High Commander wasn't an option.

Laecy made her way to the top level of H2, taking her time. Her arm ached from the repair procedure and her heart was heavy with loss. The final death toll from the explosion was seven, including two of her immediate crew—Richards and Jaeron. Their brilliance and optimistic attitudes would leave a hole on her team.

Richard's death left her especially hollow, knowing their dreams of "one day" and "maybe" would never come to pass. No more was there a fanciful future of retiring together to the green pastures on Aderoth and living a quiet life free of the war and responsibilities. The place he held in her heart would always be more than just a colleague or friend despite never having the opportunity to explore what the relationship could become. All that she could do was honor his memory.

The High Commander's office door was flanked by guards, as usual. They nodded at Laecy as she approached, and one opened the door for her.

Inside, Taelis was gazing out the window at the back of the room. He turned to face Laecy when she entered. "How's your arm?" he asked.

"Good as new, sir. What did you want to see me about?"

Taelis stepped over to his desk. "The timing of the attack is unfortunate. I had just procured something I wanted to share with you."

I couldn't care less about anything he has to share. Maybe if I go to bed I can wake up from the nightmare of today. "What is it, sir?"

The High Commander unlocked a cabinet behind his desk and pulled out a hard plastic case. He set the case on his desk and flipped it open toward Laecy.

Her eyes widened. The case contained a smooth metal sphere with a crack down one side. It was metallic but had an iridescent quality that made it appear to almost glow. "Is that one of the testing spheres?"

Taelis nodded. "The one Wil cracked several years ago. We've been using it with the new graduates, but we were finally able to collect enough material to craft a replacement. Rather than repair this one, I thought it might be useful for the telekinetic relays in the new prototype warship."

"Yeah, I bet it's perfect. Trouble is, that was Richards' specialization, not mine." The hole in her heart tore with the mention of his name.

The High Commander looked down. "Yes, I heard. It's a deep loss for all of us."

That doesn't begin to cover it. Laecy looked past Taelis and out the window. The nearly empty space dock revealed how thin the TSS' resources had become, compounding the impact of the latest blow.

"Unfortunately, we don't have the luxury of mourning our losses," Taelis continued. "The mission hasn't changed. When can you be production-ready?"

Laecy stared at the High Commander with shock. "That's the last thing on my mind!"

"I know it's been a tough day—"

"I just lost two of my best engineers! They were my friends. My family. And you want us to pick up like nothing happened?"

"We lose people every day, Deena."

"Not here in Headquarters. Not like that."

"You want revenge? Finish the ship."

"I think Wil would want us to take some time to recover."

Taelis stared her down through his tinted glasses. "Don't tell him about this attack."

"Sir—"

"I know you've been in communication with Wil."

Do I deny that we chat? She thought better of it. "Why would you keep it from him?"

Taelis paced across the room. "Because if he knew the enemy had breached our walls, he'd be here tomorrow to enter the fight."

"Good! Let's end this."

"No. With where we are right now, we could drive the Bakzen back, but not eliminate them. Only a large-scale telekinetic weapon will be able to finish the war."

Laecy swallowed her anger. "The warship."

"If Wil and his Seconds can pool their power, we have a fighting chance."

Laecy bit her lower lip. "I don't know if I can make it work without Richards."

"Find a way."

Laecy nodded.

"We win the fight at any cost."

"Yes, sir."

Laecy trudged back to her quarters, slumped under the weight of her assignment. The loss of her friends was a bitter reality she was reluctant to admit, but she needed to accept that they were gone. It should have been easier to accept, having seen them die. So many had gone off to battle and never come home—that should have been far more difficult, but it wasn't. That was the way it had always been. To have seen the moment of their death, witnessed the instant they departed, she kept thinking about what could have been done differently. She could have ordered everyone away, or ejected the jet into space.

Those actions only made sense in hindsight, but she couldn't help replaying the minutes leading up to the tragedy. Countless others had passed in battle, but this loss within her home would be far more haunting.

Once in her cramped room, Laecy eased onto her bunk. She was thankful for the quiet and solitude.

She laid down on the bed and closed her eyes. Her arm needed rest to finish healing. Yet, her mind was still too active to let her sleep.

Laecy grabbed her tablet off of the wall and scanned over her inbox. Most of the messages were mundane business, but she spotted a message from Wil titled: "Check-in."

Does he know about what happened, despite Taelis wanting to keep it secret?"

She opened the message: "I'm going to be unavailable for a while, so I wanted to check in and see how you and the crew are doing. Everything okay?"

So he didn't know, or at least didn't want to come out and say it.

No! Laecy wanted to scream. *Everything is falling apart! I don't know how we're going to make it to the end of the month, let alone through the years ahead. When are you coming to save us for good?*

But she couldn't say any of those things. If TSS Command was keeping track of Wil's personal files, they would certainly have an eye on her correspondence with him.

With nowhere left to turn, she allowed herself to cry.

Under any other circumstances, she would consider it an act of weakness. But in that moment, she needed the release— anything to relieve the crippling vice crushing her from within. She sobbed into her pillow for everything—everyone—that she'd lost. She mourned the life that her friends would never be able to have, and her own alternate path that had never been and never would be. *The war is my life. I need to see it through.*

In time, her mind quieted and her sobs ceased. She dried her eyes and exhaled the final barbs of pain still clinging to her. There was no sense dwelling on the past.

She had a ship to design—a weapon that could help deliver an end to the suffering around her. She couldn't imagine a future for herself without the war, but ending the conflict could perhaps offer others a new chance at life.

Laecy typed and sent her reply to Wil: "Everything is just fine. Best wishes to you and your bride!" At least half the statement was true.

‹ CHAPTER 17 ›

"I wish you would have let me drive," Wil muttered, sulking in the passenger seat of the rental car.

Saera rolled her eyes. *Is he going to be like this the whole trip?* "There was no way I was letting you behind the wheel. You laughed out loud when you read the driver's manual."

"But twenty-five miles per hour!"

"Yeah, case in point. At least I took driver's ed."

"Hey, I have thousands of flight hours logged," Wil countered.

"And that has absolutely zero to do with driving on a residential street." Saera returned her attention to the road.

The streets were familiar from her youth, but she was now viewing her former community with new eyes. Seeing an advanced world like Tararia made the precarious state on Earth that much more apparent to her. Trash littering the shoulder, homeless huddled in bus shelters, smoke in the air—things she had been blind to as a resident but that now turned her stomach. She couldn't be sure, but it seemed like conditions had noticeably deteriorated in just the six years she'd been away.

"This is so surreal," she murmured.

"Even for me," Wil commented. "Earth is one of the only places in the galaxy where any random person wouldn't know me by name."

"That's true."

Wil shook his head as they passed by a sprawling strip mall decked with sale banners. "It's crazy to think that there's such a thorough departure from typical Taran life so close to Headquarters."

Saera smiled. "Imagine my surprise when I found out what was just out of sight off-world."

"To go from thinking of yourself as being one life among billions to knowing there are actually trillions."

"Do you even know the total Taran population?" Saera asked him.

"The official citizen count is somewhere around six trillion, last I heard. But, I wouldn't be at all surprised if there were a lot more planets like Earth beyond the fifteen-hundred or so recognized Taran worlds."

Saera turned off the main artery into a side street to bypass some traffic up ahead. "I can't even fathom that number."

"It's so spread out you'd never know it," Wil replied. He examined the stores in another shopping plaza. "Are your parents expecting us at a particular time?"

"Not really. Why?"

"We should get you a ring," Wil suggested. "One that you can actually wear. If you'd like."

Saera eyed the pair of jewelry stores to her right. "Okay."

She pulled into the driveway and parked between the two stores. One appeared to be a cost-conscious provider while the other was more high-end. "What's my budget?" she asked Wil.

"Whatever you want," he replied.

"You have to have some number in mind," she pressed.

"I guess we've never really talked in detail about finances, have we?"

She paused. "No, we haven't. Clearly your family is wealthy. And I figured you get some kind of salary from the TSS."

"I do. My parents and I take the minimum allowable—about 20,000 credits each year into a retirement account, of sorts."

"And what about the rest?" she asked.

Wil slumped back in his seat. "Well, you've seen the Sietinen estate."

"Yeah, it makes a statement."

Wil nodded slowly. "That's only part of it. I don't even know how to put it in a perspective that you could understand. I can hardly grasp it, myself."

Saera smirked. "Throw out a number."

Wil hesitated.

"Come on," Saera encouraged.

"I'm worth somewhere around four quadrillion."

Saera blinked, speechless. *Did he just* quad*rillion?*

Wil looked down. "Yeah… like I said."

"And that's your personal assets?" she finally managed.

"More or less. A lot of it is tied up in SiNavTech, so I'm not sure where to draw the line. However, I personally got 200 billion credits for that two-year exclusivity term licensing the independent jump drive to the Priesthood."

Saera eyed him. "How can you even say that with a straight face?"

Wil burst out laughing. "I know, it's absurd."

"So, what you're saying is that money is no object."

"Right. But, get what makes you comfortable. Something you feel like you could wear regularly."

She nodded. "Okay. Well, I was ready to go the low-cost route, but I see no reason not to check out what the fancy designers have to offer."

"Then high-end it is." Wil unbuckled his seatbelt. "Now, let's go pick something out," he said in English, with only the slightest hint of an accent.

"All right," Saera replied, reverting to her native language.

Selecting a suitable ring proved harder than expected, since the jeweler kept suggesting special order pieces. They looked through a dozen in-stock options that were in her size, ranging from simple solitaire settings to behemoths that took up half her finger. In the end, she settled on a delicate ring with a modestly sized round center stone and two round side-stones. The design supposedly represented past, present, and future, which seemed fitting.

With the new ring on her finger, Saera and Wil returned the car.

"Now to my parents' place?" Saera asked.

Wil hesitated. "I was thinking we should make another stop first."

"More shopping?"

"No. I'd like to pay Michael's father a visit."

Saera let out a slow breath. "I'd tried to forget about that connection."

"It's still not sitting right that a former TSS Agent somehow ended up on Earth with what I can only assume were orders to watch over you."

If that was the case, he did a pretty poor job of it. "Is he still in the same house?"

"I looked him up before we headed down here, and it seems he is."

Saera nodded. "I know the way." She paused. "Are you sure about this? We might not like what he has to say."

Wil smiled. "Since when has that stopped us?"

"Fair enough." Saera started the car and headed for her former community.

The commercial streets gave way to residential neighborhoods, varying in affluence. Her neighborhood was in the middle of the spectrum—kept up well, but no overly large or lavish homes. The older vintage of most of the residences gave character to the streets, and the mature trees evoked a homey sense of establishment.

The Andres' house was one street over from Saera's former block. She had spent plenty of afternoons playing on the front lawn, which was presently short and brown in its late-winter dormancy. Seeing the aged, forest green house reminded her of a simpler time in her youth, before responsibilities and burdensome thoughts of the future clouded her mind. But looking back on it, perhaps the future was always closer than she'd realized.

"What do we say to him?" Saera asked Wil.

"That will depend on how he reacts to an Agent showing up on his doorstep with his former charge."

Saera nodded and opened the car door. "He might not even be home."

Wil stepped out of the car. "He is. I feel it."

They walked up the concrete pathway to the front door under a narrow overhang. Wil located the doorbell and pressed it.

Saera's stomach knotted, knowing some of the only fond memories from her youth were about to be cast in new light.

Footsteps sounded behind the door and a deadbolt unlocked. The door cracked open.

"Oh shi—" The occupant tried to slam the door shut.

Wil quickly extended his hand and foot, augmented by telekinesis, to keep the door from closing. "Jonah Andres?"

The person inside pushed back against the door telekinetically, keeping it in the same cracked position. "What do you want?"

"I'm Saera Alexander," she stated. *That'll either help or make this more difficult.*

After a moment, the door swung open the rest of the way. Jonah Andres shared his son's pale blue eyes and medium brown hair, though his features were more rugged. He evaluated them, surrounded by a hum of electromagnetic energy. "So you made it to the TSS," he stated, focusing on Saera.

"Yes, and now I have some questions."

Jonah shifted his attention to Wil. "Why the Agent escort?"

"Not an escort, exactly," Wil replied. "May we come in?"

"I suspect I don't have a choice." Jonah stepped back into the entryway to allow them through the door, scrutinizing Wil. "You're young for an Agent. Did you just graduate?"

Wil examined the interior of the house, his gaze resting on some childhood photos of Michael hanging on the wall. "No, it's been almost five years. I was sixteen."

Jonah chuckled. "Right."

"How long has it been since you left the TSS?" Wil continued.

"About twenty-five years," Jonah replied. He headed for the adjacent living room.

Saera crossed her arms. *Just a few years before I was born. How did he end up here with me?*

Wil followed him. "Do you recall a trainee named Cris Sights?"

Jonah smiled. "Of course! Anyone who shot straight to Junior Agent is hard to forget."

"Well, I'm his son. Wil."

Jonah sunk into the beige microfiber couch facing a set of dark brown plush chairs. "Oh." He thought for a moment. "You really did graduate at sixteen, didn't you?"

Wil nodded and sat down across from him in one of the chairs. "But that's not why we're here. It seems our lives have intersected."

Probably more than the Priesthood ever intended. Saera took a deep breath, still lingering in the entryway. "Wil is Michael's trainer at the TSS."

Jonah perked up. "Really? I'm surprised someone on such an accelerated path would be assigned as an instructor."

"There's more to it than that," Wil countered. "What do you know of the Jotun division?"

From across the room, Saera sensed Jonah's mental assessment of Wil before it passed to her. She kept her mind guarded. *If he was sent here to spy on me, there's no knowing where his allegiance lays.*

Jonah's brow furrowed with frustration, having been unable to glean any insight to the deeper meaning of Wil's question. "I know it exists."

"And what about the rift?" Wil pressed.

"I never told anyone, okay?" Jonah's face flushed.

That's an interesting reaction. Saera rushed over to the living room and sat down in the chair next to Wil. "We're not accusing you of anything. We're just trying to figure out how an Agent ended up on Earth with an assignment to watch over a little girl."

Jonah's eyes widened.

Saera stared him down. "I know about my mother."

"What about her?" Jonah asked, on edge.

"That she was sent here to have a daughter with a specific man—my father. And having a former Agent living one block away is too big of a coincidence in any matter regarding the Priesthood."

Jonah gazed down at his hands folded in his lap. He swallowed. "You've had contact with your mother?"

Saera nodded. "Yes, we have something resembling a relationship now."

"And you're a Junior Agent, it looks like, so you've been through disclosure," Jonah continued.

He's trying to gauge how freely we can talk. "I know about the real war with the Bakzen in the rift," Saera cut in.

"It's common knowledge within the TSS now," Wil explained. "The secret was doing more harm than good."

Jonah scoffed. "At least they finally listened to reason."

"I took the disclosure upon myself," Wil clarified. "I wouldn't say TSS Command or the Priesthood were happy about it."

"And you're still alive?" Jonah breathed, incredulous.

"I get more leeway than most. We're not here about me, though," Wil said. "Why are you here on Earth, and what do you know about Saera and her mother?"

Jonah sighed. "That requires some context. I was in Primus Command, as you probably saw in my file. My role was a liaison between TSS Command and the different divisions. It was my responsibility to facilitate resource allocations."

"There isn't a position like that anymore, as far as I know," Wil stated. "Your file didn't list an assignment."

"That doesn't surprise me," Jonah said. "It was sort of an experimental role. One that didn't go well. I had spent two years in the Jotun Division, so I understood the toll of the war. Supplies were tight, morale was terrible, and we were on a clear path to defeat. In my vantage as liaison, I identified that the morale problem, at least, would be mitigated by full disclosure of the war within the TSS. The biggest issues stemmed from new Jotun recruits trying to wrap their heads around the war. It made them unpredictable and ineffective."

"That was my reasoning, as well," Wil said.

Jonah shook his head. "Well, when I brought up the idea of disclosure twenty-some years ago, Command shot it down. I pressed the issue, wanting to know why maintaining secrecy was so important. Essentially, the response was 'because the Priesthood said so.'"

"Naturally," Wil muttered. "There's something deeper than the war that I've been trying to uncover for years."

"Command may know, but I don't expect to ever get a straight answer," Jonah replied.

Wil scoffed. "It never ends."

And I'm part of that master plan. Saera leaned forward. "The Priesthood is creepy and manipulative—we know that already. Now how did you go from a TSS liaison to being retired here on Earth?"

"'Marooned' is more like it," Jonah groaned.

"They just dropped you here, or what?" prompted Wil.

"Well," Jonah continued, "after several conversations related to disclosing the war, I was told my services as liaison would no longer be required."

Wil raised an eyebrow. "By Banks?"

"It was a joint conversation with him and Taelis, though it was pretty clear the order came down from their superiors at the Priesthood," Jonah explained. "They said they had another assignment for me. I was to establish myself here on Earth, and in a few years I would need to help a woman start a life here."

"Mary Alexander?" Saera asked.

Jonah nodded. "So, the TSS dropped me off here with only a subspace radio for communications and enough money to buy a condo and start to blend in. I didn't understand why they sent me here—if they wanted me out of the way, throwing me out an airlock would have been much easier. Left with no other choice, I found a place to live and waited. Sure enough, three years later a woman showed up at my door. I knew right away that she had abilities, and she had the look of someone noble-born. She never talked much about her former life, but I got the impression she'd been forced into her assignment as much as I had."

Years of preparation, all to make sure Wil had his perfect partner. "Her orders were to locate my father and have a daughter with him."

"I figured as much," Jonah acknowledged. "My contact with her was limited once I helped her get her bearings. I was already living with Michael's mother by the time Mary arrived. We said she was an old college friend, or something. Then you were born, Saera, and I thought that would be the end of it. But when your mother disappeared and left you with your father, an acolyte from the Priesthood contacted me and said I was to watch over you—make sure you didn't hurt yourself if your abilities emerged at a young age. We moved here to be close to you, and it was easy to befriend your family since Michael was about the same age as you."

Saera crossed her arms. "That seems like a waste of an Agent."

"It does," Wil concurred. "Given how the Priesthood seems to handle those matters, I'd have expected you to get assigned a suicide run in the rift."

"I've had a lot of time to think about it," Jonah said. "The only reasoning that makes sense is efficiency of resources. They wanted me out of the way, but Agents are in too short of supply to completely discard. Since it would take an Agent to recognize the emergence of abilities, assigning me here was an opportunity to maintain oversight of you, Saera, while getting some use out of an Agent who was otherwise a problem. And of course, there was the added bonus of potentially getting another child with abilities out of the deal."

"And let me guess," Wil speculated, "for motivation—aside from the chance to live—there was a threat to your family if you didn't cooperate?"

Jonah nodded. "I'm an only child, but I had my parents and aunt's family back home on Corela to think about. Then I met my wife here on Earth... I'd never intended to have a child, but she wanted a family. As soon as Michael born, I was reminded of my commitment to the TSS and Priesthood. As long as I kept quiet, Michael would be admitted to the TSS when he came of age and would have the chance to explore his abilities. If I talked, we'd all be killed—or so they told me. It was an easy decision."

Saera's brow furrowed. "That couldn't have come from the TSS! Banks would never threaten an Agent like that." *Would he?*

"No, that was straight from the Priesthood. Most of the communications were an email or radio call, but sometimes I'd see one of the acolytes watching me from a distance." Jonah shrank inward. "They're probably listening to this conversation right now."

"You haven't said anything that violates the terms of your arrangement," Wil assured him. "The Priesthood will have to answer to me if any harm comes to you as a result."

Jonah studied him, struck by such a brazen statement. "Who are you?"

"I'm the person this was all about," Wil stated with a level of objective calmness only achievable after years of coming to terms. "The Cadicle—the Priesthood's tool to end their secret war. And Saera was created as my ideal partner."

Jonah sat in stunned silence for a minute, his blue eyes shifting between Wil and Saera. "I'd tried to think of an explanation, but I could never make all of the pieces fit. That…"

"It's crazy enough to be true," Wil said and took Saera's hand across the gap between the chairs.

The facts of our lives that change our perception but could never undermine what we feel for each other. "The more we look around, the more we realize how many people have been manipulated along with us," Saera said.

Jonah hung his head. "At least it was all for a purpose. I had started to think maybe it was just a bizarre punishment."

"I wouldn't count out that option. It feels that way to me sometimes, too," Wil admitted. "Still, I have no choice but to keep moving forward."

"Where does the group you're training come in?" Jonah asked.

"My officers," Wil replied. "To help me win the war."

"Michael… He's well?" Jonah asked.

Wil nodded. "He is. I'm fortunate to have him as my second-in-command."

Jonah smiled. "I was worried when he joined the TSS—knowing how it ended for me. But, I could never train him here. It's what he needed. I'm glad he's in good hands."

Saera squeezed Wil's hand. "He is. The group is the talk of the TSS."

Fatherly pride filled Jonah's eyes. "I hope I can see him again soon."

Wil paused. "You know, with the war common knowledge within the TSS now, I can likely reverse your assignment to Earth, if you want to go elsewhere."

"I don't feel like I'd belong anywhere else at this point," Jonah said with a shrug.

"Well, we can always use more instructors, if you'd like to return to Headquarters," Wil offered.

"I'll think about it," Jonah replied. "Maybe after it's no longer just about training soldiers for war."

"Okay." Wil rose. "Thank you for speaking with us."

Saera stood alongside Wil as Jonah got to his feet. *All those years he was just as trapped as me. He had no idea what was going on in my life, but because of him and Michael at least I wasn't completely alone.* "Thank you for trying to look out for me."

Jonah frowned. "I wish I could have done more after your mom left. Told you what was going on…"

"You did what you could, under the circumstances," Saera said, taking Wil's hand. *At least I'll never have to feel alone again.*

◄ CHAPTER 18 ►

Saera pulled off to the side of the street in front of her light blue, two-story house. The yard was still barren in the late-winter weather, but the hedge was trimmed and the porch looked freshly painted. *Home sweet home. Haven't we been over enough history for one day?*

She turned off the car. "We can still turn back."

"Nonsense. We're going in," Wil declared, unbuckling his seatbelt.

"Okay," conceded Saera. She dragged herself out of the car.

The mid-March air was still blustery, though the snow had melted from the ground. Saera shoved her hands in her pockets as she took in the home from her childhood. She eyed her old bedroom in the upper left with a shudder.

"Come on," Wil urged.

Saera swallowed and led the way up the concrete path to the broad front porch. It was just as she remembered, with the same empty planter boxes and faded welcome mat. She took a deep breath and knocked on the front door.

After a minute, she heard the click of a latch and the door swung open.

"Hi, dad."

Her father stared at her, his hazel eyes wide and his lips parted. The flecks of gray in his dark brown hair were gone, which certainly meant he'd started dyeing it. "Saera... I didn't believe you'd actually come." It was the same deep voice Saera remembered from her youth, always touched with an air of authority from his time in the military.

Saera forced down the lump in her throat. "It was time to come back for a visit." She reached for Wil's hand next to her. "This is my fiancé, Wil. And Wil, this is my dad, Steven."

"Hello," Wil greeted and extended his hand.

Her father shook Wil's hand, tense with discomfort. "How long have you been engaged?"

"A couple years," Saera replied. "It's a long story."

"I suspect there are several of those." Steven stepped back inside and opened the door wider. "Come in, we're letting all the heat out."

Saera followed him inside with Wil close behind. *So many memories... I've changed, but will it still be the same here?*

The entry was just like she'd last seen it, down to the red shoe bench at the foot of the stairs and freestanding coat rack topped with a hat her father never wore.

"Everyone's out at the moment," Steven explained. "We weren't sure what time you would be by, so mom and Ashley went grocery shopping for dinner. Daniel should be here later, along with Brianna and the baby."

"Wait, Bri had a baby?" That was terrifying news. From Saera's vantage, her older sister was one of the least nurturing people imaginable.

Her father nodded. "Eight months ago. A boy, Brandon."

Definitely not the same. "And Daniel?"

"He's been in and out of jobs since he dropped out of college." Steven shook his head with exasperation. "I wish he'd just enlist... he needs some structure."

Saera nodded. "That doesn't surprise me."

"Ashley is still here with us, of course. She's a freshman this year."

That was almost a crazier notion than Bri being a mother.

Last time Saera had seen her younger sister she was in elementary school. She shook free of the disorientation and noticed that her father was observing Wil with reserved guard.

"Where have you been, Saera?" Steven asked, not taking his eyes off Wil.

"A military academy," Saera replied. It was as close to the truth as she could come. Discussing the TSS with the uninitiated human population—even family—would only complicate matters.

Steven scoffed. "So you said before. What branch?"

"That's classified," Wil answered.

"Of course. A secret branch of the military that recruits young teenagers," Steven stated, the skepticism thick in his tone.

There's no way to explain. "It doesn't matter."

"Actually, I think it's pretty important," countered Steven. "You all but disappeared for six years."

Saera's eyes narrowed behind her tinted glasses. "You sent me away."

"To boarding school! That's hardly whatever cult you got wrapped up in."

"You think I'm in a cult?"

Her father crossed his arms. "You're wearing sunglasses indoors on a cloudy day. It's either a cult or drugs—or both."

"Well, it's neither." Saera held back a groan. *"I should have taken you up on that offer to get contacts,"* Saera telepathically said to Wil. Lenses to mute the glow to their eyes would have helped dodge some of the questions, at least.

"Just part of the uniform for your secret military program?" Steven continued.

Saera sighed loudly.

Her father shook his head. "Right." He glanced toward the living room. "Let's sit down. Do you want anything to drink?"

Very badly, but not the sort he's asking about. "Tea?"

"And for you, Wil?" Steven asked.

"Sure, same. Thank you," he replied.

Steven nodded. "Make yourselves comfortable. I'll be right in."

Saera trudged into the living room adjacent to the entry. The dark wood floor was covered in an ornate oriental rug positioned between two gray microfiber sofas. Saera selected the couch with the best vantage of the front door and patted the seat for Wil to sit next to her.

"This is nice," Wil commented.

"Nothing like your family home."

He shrugged. "This feels lived in. I like it."

Saera noted how she was suspiciously absent from the family portraits hung on the wall. Apparently it didn't take long to be written out of the family. *I can't even imagine what it would have been like over all these years if I'd stayed.*

A whistling kettle sounded in the other room. A minute later, Steven emerged from the kitchen carrying two mugs, which he handed to Wil and Saera.

"Nothing for yourself?" Saera asked as she took the mug. She swirled the teabag in the water with its string.

"Not right now." Steven sat down on the other couch facing them. He paused in thought. "I have so many questions, I don't know where to start."

"Some I won't be able to answer," Saera admitted. *The TSS, who Wil really is…*

"Well, are you both in the same secret program?" Steven asked.

"Yes," Wil replied. "I joined before Saera, so I graduated a few years ago. I was just finishing up training when we met."

Steven tilted his head. "You can't be much older than her."

"No, I'm not. I started young," Wil said.

"None of this makes any sense." Steven crossed his arms, brow furrowed. "What you're describing isn't how the military or government operate."

On Earth, anyway… Saera leaned forward. "Well, I'm just here for a day, so we can spend it arguing or communicate like civilized adults."

"How am I supposed to have a conversation with you if you won't tell me anything?" Steven asked.

"You're asking the wrong questions," Saera responded. "For starters, I found my mother."

Steven froze. "Mary?"

"She goes by a different name now, but yes."

"How did you find her?"

Saera scowled. "It was kind of an accident—" Footsteps sounded on the front porch, accompanied by voices and a jingle of keys in the lock. *I guess everyone's home.*

"Don't say anything about Mary," Steven cautioned as he rose.

"Of course not." Saera stood up but stayed by the couch. Next to her, Wil got to his feet and took her hand, giving it a supportive squeeze.

The front door swung open. Ashley was the first through—glued to her phone even as she walked. She barely glanced up as she stepped inside, so it took her a moment to acknowledge Saera. "Oh shit."

"Language!" Saera's stepmother, Linda, chastised as she followed her through the front door, a grocery bag in her hands. Then, her gaze rested on Saera. "Oh…"

"Hi," Saera greeted, shifting on her feet. Wil's touch offered a much needed sense of comfort and grounding.

"How are you?" Linda stammered, her face flushed.

Saera forced a smile. "Great."

"You're not alone," Ashley said, looking Wil over from head to foot and pausing on his hand holding Saera's. She brushed her dark brown bangs to the side.

"Wil is my fiancé," Saera explained.

Linda shifted the grocery bag to her hip and closed the door, locking the deadbolt. "Lots of catching up to do, it seems."

More footsteps sounded on the porch, followed by a knock on the door.

"That's probably Daniel," Linda said as he headed for the kitchen. "Will you let him in, Ashley?"

Ashley rolled her eyes and stomped back to unlock the door her mother had just closed. "Hey," she greeted her brother in an unenthused monotone.

A man in his mid-twenties stepped through, but he was accompanied by a slightly younger woman carrying a baby. It took Saera a moment to process that they were her siblings.

Daniel had gained weight since she last saw him, and he had none of the energetic spark that was once so core to his character.

Bri walking up behind him was fighting to keep a squirming child contained in her arms. The bags under her eyes indicated that the challenges weren't an isolated incident. However, her expression was one of amusement, not frustration. There was love in her eyes. The fair-haired child paused his writhing when he caught sight of Saera and Wil, seemingly captivated by them.

Ashley closed the door, then took the diaper bag from her sister's shoulder. "Bri's here!" she called toward the kitchen.

"Hi, honey!" Linda greeted from the kitchen.

Steven walked over to welcome his children, giving each a hug. "I should help your mother. Get settled." He rushed to the kitchen with barely a glance back toward Saera and Wil.

"What are we even doing here?" Saera asked Wil telepathically.

"Gaining perspective," Wil replied. He smiled at the new arrivals. "Hello. Nice to meet you."

"And you are…?" Bri inquired.

"Wil. Saera's fiancé."

Bri's eyes widened. "Huh."

"Didn't realize she was bringing anyone home with her,"

Daniel commented.

Wil nodded. "Well, the entire trip was on short notice."

"What now?" Bri asked. "Do we pick up like you were never gone?"

"No," Saera cut in. "We're just here for the day. I'm gathering some of my old things."

Daniel raised an eyebrow. "After all this time?"

"I've been busy." *Is the entire day going to be one unending interrogation?*

Ashley sauntered into the living room and plopped down on the couch across from Wil and Saera. "What's with the sunglasses?"

"Fashion statement," Wil replied.

The teenager narrowed her eyes. "Are you a model or something?"

"It's more like a uniform," Saera tried to explain.

"For…?" Ashley prompted.

Saera's mind raced to settle on an explanation that would settle the matter once and for all, but was granted a reprieve by her father returning to the room.

"Who wants appetizers?" he asked.

"Me!" Daniel answered first. "I'm starving."

Quieter murmurs of affirmation from the others followed. Steven disappeared again to retrieve the requested items.

Saera continued to think through an explanation for where she had been over the last six years. All of the scripts she'd imagined leading up to the meeting now sounded stupid in her head. *They'll never buy any of it.*

"So, you were saying about the sunglasses?" Ashley resumed.

"And where were you?" Daniel questioned.

Why am I even trying to get their approval? Saera smiled, relaxing for the first time since setting foot on her home planet. "I've been away learning to fly spaceships, and these sunglasses make me look badass so others know not to mess with me."

Her siblings paused in dumbfounded silence for a moment, then burst out laughing.

Saera smiled. "Yeah, yeah. Suffice it to say I've been around. Now, how about you introduce me to my nephew?"

While Saera cooed over baby Brandon with her sisters, Wil found himself waiting awkwardly along the wall of the living room near Daniel. He had long since finished his mug of tea, but he wasn't sure where to set down the empty cup so it remained in his hands.

Nervous energy emanated from Daniel. Wil wasn't sure if it was from being around him or a more general anxiety related to the family. *It must be tough being the oldest and yet having the least direction in life.*

Being away from the others was a prime opportunity for Wil to put the next stage of his plan into action. Reuniting with her family wouldn't get Saera what she really needed. Another hurt ran far deeper.

"Does Saera have any old acquaintances who might like to see her while she's back?" Wil asked, searching Daniel's mind. Normally, delving into the mind of anyone who wasn't a suspected enemy would have been against his code as an Agent, but it was necessary in this case.

Daniel's thoughts flitted through vague memories of some of Saera's former female friends, and a flash of Michael. Then, another memory floated to the surface—a friend of Daniel's who commented on Saera's absence. The memory would have been innocuous if Wil didn't already have a window into Saera's past.

"Or one of your friends?" Wil pressed, guiding Daniel to the memory with subtle mental cues in his subconscious.

"Lucas, maybe," Daniel mused in a trance state so subtle even a trained eye would have difficulty detecting.

"Does he still live around here? Maybe you should invite him," Wil suggested.

"Yeah, I guess I'll do that," Daniel agreed, unable to resist Wil's manipulation. He pulled out his phone and started typing a text message.

Wil released Daniel from the hold, feeling a pang of guilt for what was to come.

Saera beckoned to Wil from across the room with a nod of her head. She handed her nephew back to Bri and skillfully extracted herself from the conversation, gesturing for Wil to meet her by the entry.

"My parents said we could go up to my old room. There's some memorabilia in the closet I'd like to take back with us."

"Sure," Wil said.

She headed up the stairs and checked over her shoulder to make sure no relatives were nearby. "Brandon is cute, but... Please tell me you don't want kids right away."

Wil chuckled. "No worries there. I think I have a few other things to deal with before that."

Saera took in her old room. Little touches of her remained—a fairy figurine on the bookcase, some participation trophies from childhood activities, her plush horse resting on the chair in the corner—but it didn't feel like home. The bed was made up in a boring geometric gray and blue bedspread that was well suited to a guest room. Her former desk was configured as a compact home office adjacent to the door.

"It's so strange seeing all of this again," Saera murmured.

"I can only imagine," Wil said, coming up behind her. He placed a hand on the small of her back.

"I never wanted to see this room again."

Wil rubbed her back and stepped further into the room, examining the bookshelf. "Well, I'm glad I got this insight into where you're from."

"And what do you think of me now?"

"I appreciate you more every day," Wil replied.

"Such a diplomatic answer!"

Wil grinned. "It's true! But, seeing this does put things in perspective for me. It's pretty remarkable that you adjusted so quickly to the TSS."

"Maybe my mom had something to do with that."

"Possibly."

Wil picked up one of the books from the shelf in the wall. "I sometimes wonder what experiences we miss out on by being surrounded by high technology. I can honestly say I've never read a physical book."

"That *is* a loss."

Wil set the book back. "And I know I've missed out on a lot more."

"But you've also had a lot of opportunity," Saera said. "I would have given anything as a kid to be able to travel across the galaxy."

"Well, there are some days when I would have given anything to be anyone other than who I am."

Saera's chest constricted. "Sorry, I didn't mean—"

Wil shook his head and smiled. "Don't. That all changed when I met you. Being anyone else, you might not have come into my life. And that's something I wouldn't change, no matter what."

Saera melted. "And there's no one with whom I'd rather travel across the galaxy."

"Even into a war zone?" Wil pulled Saera toward him, placing his hands on her hips.

"Admittedly, that's not high on my tourist list."

"We'll find a way to make the most of it." Wil pulled her in for a kiss.

She leaned against him, but then remembered where they

were and pulled back. "Let me find that box."

Wil let her go. She sensed that he was aware of her tension, and he knew enough of her past to be aware that the room was wrapped up in some unpleasant memories.

Her father had said the box was somewhere up in the closest. Saera slid open the closet door, noting that the roller still caught in the same place as always. She scanned along the top shelf and spotted the box she was seeking. It was just beyond her grasp. After a quick check to make sure the bedroom door was closed, she telekinetically lifted the cardboard box into her hands.

The black pen scrawled on the side of the box marked it as "Saera's Stuff." She cracked open the interlocked top flaps and peeked inside. Just what she wanted.

"What's in it?" Wil asked.

"Some old items from my mom." Saera pulled out a framed picture of her with her mother. She couldn't have been more than three years old when the photograph was taken. "If I'd had this with me at Headquarters, you would have recognized who my mother was from the beginning."

"Maybe. But it would have been so out of context that I might not have noticed. Not to mention, I've never once visited your room."

Saera set down the picture. "That's true. Still, I can't help but wonder if things would have been different somehow."

"You're making up for lost time now," Wil assured her. "And we can put up as many pictures as you want."

Saera smiled. "Thanks."

The doorbell sounded through the wall.

Wil looked at Saera quizzically. "Expecting anyone else?"

"I didn't think so." Saera opened the bedroom door, hearing voices in the entryway. She turned around to grab the box.

"I've got it," Wil said, picking up the box for her. "I'll take this out if you want."

"Sure." Saera handed him the car keys and left the room.

The voices grew louder as she reached the end of the hall.

She glanced back at Wil and then descended the stairs.

Halfway down, she froze mid-step. There was no mistaking the man standing in the entryway talking with her brother. The person who had taken her innocence and cast her aside without a second thought. Lucas Moran.

Competing emotions instantly filled her mind—rage, hurt, fear. Her hand trembled as she reached for the banister to steady herself. *Why is he here?*

Saera shifted her weight and a floorboard creaked underfoot.

Lucas turned to identify the source of the sound. When he caught sight of Saera, he shook his head with disbelief. "You really are back."

Saera's breath caught in her throat, her heart beginning to race. Lucas still had that same self-confident smirk that he always sported when he'd paid her a nighttime visit—knowing that she'd eventually give in to his unwanted advances. And he'd leave with the same expression, satisfied that he got what he came for while she huddled in shame, feeling like there was nowhere to turn.

"It's crazy, right?" Daniel said.

Saera glared at her brother. "Did you invite him?"

Daniel turned up his hands dismissively. "Yeah, so? This is a reunion, after all."

"Yeah, Saera. That's no way to greet an old friend." Lucas gazed up at her, taking her in.

She tensed, sensing the lewd thoughts already filling his mind—blending his memory of her with updated visions of her present self. It filled her own mind, taking her back to that sense of helplessness. Her hand tightened on the handrail as she willed herself to move, to back away and hide. But the horrific visions had her pinned, overwhelming her senses as Lucas' eyes locked on her. Then, a gleeful sneer spread across his face as he saw that he still had control over her, even after years apart.

And then, Lucas' eyes flitted behind her at the sound of

descending footsteps.

Saera yanked free of Lucas' hypnotic hold over her, comforted by Wil's approaching presence—her safe place where no harm could come. She wasn't alone.

But Wil jogged down the stairs right past her, still carrying the memorabilia box. For a moment she thought maybe he was going to take Lucas on. Then, she realized that Wil had hardly glanced at the others standing in the entry. He was just… leaving.

"Where are you going?" The question sounded panicked even in her own mind.

"This is between the two of you," Wil replied, calm and level. "I need to make a quick phone call. Why don't you catch up. I'll drop this box in the car." He reached the bottom of the stairs and slipped out the front door before Saera could conjure words of protest.

"Who was that?" Lucas asked, his brow knit with confusion.

"My fiancé," Saera stammered, wishing the quaver wasn't in her voice.

Lucas huffed with surprise. "You're engaged, really?"

"Is that really so difficult to believe?" Saera shot back, her initial shock beginning to give way to pure anger.

"I dunno," Lucas shrugged. "I guess you didn't strike me as the type for settling down."

"A lot has changed since you last saw me." Saera took a calming breath. *I'm not that person anymore.*

"I can see that," Lucas reposed replied, still undressing her in his mind.

The thoughts churned Saera's stomach, fueling the loathing boiling within her. "You came here for a reunion? Let's chat." She stormed back up the stairs toward her room.

"All right," Lucas agreed, the smugness thick in his tone. "We'll be back," he called back to Daniel as he jogged up the stairs after her.

‹›   ‹›   ‹›

It took every modicum of restraint for Wil to keep himself from punching Lucas out as he walked past. The way he was looking at Saera—with such lustful desire to control and possess—was so contrary to his own way of thinking that he couldn't even understand the impulse. All he knew was it wasn't his place to intervene. *Saera needs to face him. She needs to show herself that she's the one with the power now.*

Wil hit the trunk release on the car key fob and dropped off the memorabilia box, then jogged around the side of the house. He needed to find a good vantage for Saera's impending confrontation with Lucas.

Facing the darkness in her past was the greatest obstacle Saera had left to overcome. It was the driving force behind the visit to Earth and something Saera needed to handle by herself. She was never weak or helpless, but she had felt that way in the past. Now, there was no arguing her power. Yet, he saw how she quaked in Lucas' presence. If she could break free of the mental barriers that made her question her inner strength, then she would be ready to be a full Agent.

There was no way to get a good line of sight into the second story window, but Wil could observe from a distance. He found a hollow in the bushes next to the house and dove in. He bundled his jacket around himself and sighed. Spying—especially on a loved one—felt wrong.

Wil cast aside the feeling and cleared his mind. He detached his consciousness from himself, seeking Saera's presence. Extending himself toward her, he hovered just out of view from her mind but able to listen in—to observe the encounter and assure that her demons were put to rest, and also to make sure that she wasn't in harm's way.

He waited for her revelation. *She can overcome these ties holding her back. She can cut free.*

◇〉   ◇〉   ◇〉

Saera stomped into her old bedroom, fury consuming her mind. *He needs to pay.*

Lucas swaggered through the door after her and she slammed the door shut. He playfully reached out for her. "Couldn't wait to get alone with—"

Before he could finish, Saera locked him in a telekinetic vice, lifting him off the ground. He gasped, unable to speak and barely able to breathe.

She removed her tinted glasses, her glowing green eyes locked on his terrified face. "Like I said, some things have changed."

"Your eyes—" he choked.

Tears stung Saera. "You may have been able to take advantage of me before, but not now. What you did was sick and wrong. You had no right, and I won't let you hurt anyone else."

He trembled in her telekinetic grasp. "Freak," he stammered through panting breaths.

She grinned with the promise of sweet vengeance. "You're lucky I've learned some restraint." She stabbed a telepathic spire into his mind, branching it into tendrils that burrowed to the depths of his subconscious. He was powerless to resist her.

With control of Lucas' mind, Saera dove beneath his fear and confusion, searching for the memories of what he had done to her. Never again would he be able to take pleasure in reliving the experience or have any sense of closeness with her. She wished she could take away those thoughts from all the others who had pained her, but he would have to do. A symbol for her wrong turns. He was the first—and if the past could not be fully undone, facing just this one person would grant her the chance to write a new beginning.

She found the memories and rended them clear from Lucas'

mind, not bothering to replace the experiences. He would just have a hole there, always feeling like he'd forgotten something but never knowing what.

Still, that wasn't enough. She could alter past perception, yet the future remained a blank slate. *I could make him never want to touch another woman, or feel pain any time he thinks of love.* Except, she couldn't bring herself to afflict him for life. What he had done as a teenager shouldn't define him forever going forward, even though his present self hardly seemed any better. The best course wasn't punishment, but rather a chance at redemption. To help shape him into the person he hadn't been able to become on his own.

She latched onto his subconscious, preparing to imprint a new moral code to guide him. "You will never force anyone to do anything against their will."

"I will never force anyone to do anything against their will," Lucas repeated, hanging limp in the air.

"And you will respect others for who they are, and never try to control or possess."

"I will always respect," Lucas said.

Saera nodded. "Now, you're going to leave this house and forget we ever had this little chat."

"I understand," Lucas murmured in his suggestible daze.

She removed the telepathic tendril's from Lucas' mind and brought him back down to his feet. She restored her tinted glasses.

He swayed, unsteady. After a moment, he looked at her with confusion. "What were we talking about?"

"You were just saying how much you miss your mom and how you are going to bring her some flowers."

Lucas' brow furrowed. "Oh." He reached for the door handle. "Wait, have I been in here before?"

Saera shook her head. "I don't think so."

"Huh." He opened the door and entered the hallway, still

unsteady on his feet. He supported himself with the bannister on his way down the stairs. Once on the ground floor, he called to Daniel, "I'm going to head out now."

Daniel walked over from the living room. "Already?"

"Yeah. I have somewhere else to be." Lucas opened the front door just as Wil was stepping up onto the porch. "Later." Lucas brushed past Wil and hurried to his car.

Daniel shrugged it off and went to grab another drink.

Wil came back inside the house and raised an eyebrow at Saera. "What happened?"

"Let's just say I laid down a new law," Saera replied with a coy smirk, her greatest weight finally lifted from her. "Now, it's time for dinner."

"Sounds great," Wil replied with a smile. "And, I was thinking maybe we should stay down here for an extra day or two."

"Don't say that where they might overhear!" Saera hissed.

"No, not here," Wil replied. *"Anywhere in the world—it'll practically take minutes to get anywhere in the shuttle. Any fantasies you wanted to live out?"*

Saera thought for a moment. *"I had always dreamed about visiting the Austrian Alps."*

Wil nodded. *"Okay, then that's what we'll do."*

"Are you sure? I know you have a lot going on right now."

"I don't think we'll get much of a honeymoon. We should take some time while we can, since we're already away."

Saera lit up with the prospect of the extra time together outside the TSS. *"Then I guess we're going to Austria. But first, dinner."*

"It's a date." Wil took her hand and examined her. *"You seem a lot more comfortable here all of a sudden."*

There was no doubt about it—she did feel different. A burden was lifted. *"I think I found that perspective I needed."*

‹ CHAPTER 19 ›

The low rumble of the shuttle's engine subsided as the view outside turned to starscape.

Saera relaxed back in her seat. "I'm glad to be going home."

Wil set the shuttle on an autopilot course to the TSS spaceport behind the moon. "Was the trip... healing?"

"Yes, it was." Saera crossed her arms. "I do finally feel some closure."

"Then why do you still seem upset?"

Because I wished I'd done so many things differently. "Reliving the past is difficult."

"Our histories led us here. And I couldn't be happier that the path led me to you."

A touching sentiment, but it wasn't quite enough to break Saera from her dark introspection. "With the Priesthood involved, I'm pretty sure that would have happened regardless."

"True. But bad experiences shape us as much—or more— than the good. Knowing what I'll need to face in a few years, I wouldn't trade getting kidnapped or shot for any happier memory."

Saera frowned. *Even in my worst times, my life was never in danger.* "I'm not sure how applicable my past traumas are to the war."

"Really?" Wil eyed her. "Didn't you learn something about yourself over the last couple days?"

"I have a thing for schnitzel?"

Wil laughed. "Before that."

Saera thought about it. "I'm stronger than any of them now. I'm in control."

"It's the same in the war," Wil replied. "We control our fate. We'll win as long as we believe in ourselves."

He makes it sound so easy. "Do you really feel that way?"

"I have to."

There wasn't any other choice, she realized. To have doubts would only undermine Wil's ability to achieve the best possible outcome. And she couldn't have doubts, either—about herself, or Wil, or anything they were trying to do.

They sat in silence for the rest of the brief shuttle ride, taking in the view of their home from afar. The moon seemed so quiet and peaceful—calling to her with the promise of a return to comfort and familiarity.

As soon as the shuttle docked alongside the other transport crafts at the spaceport, Saera unbuckled her harness and rose. She took Wil's hand when he was done powering down the flight systems. "Thank you."

"What for?"

"Taking me on that trip. It was just what I needed."

Wil pulled her in for a hug between the two pilot chairs. "I'm glad it was beneficial for you."

She nodded. "I feel… lighter."

"Despite all that schnitzel?" Wil grinned.

Saera pulled back from the hug, rolling her eyes. "It was really good!"

"I'll say! How many—"

"*Anyway*," she cut him off, "don't we have some sort of work to get back to now?"

Wil laughed. "Yes, we do." He stepped to the back of the shuttle to grab his travel backpack.

Saera picked up hers, as well. "I guess I'll get caught up on my email before dinner."

"First, we have a stop to make," Wil said as he opened the shuttle door. He led her to the transports down to the surface of the moon, and entered the central elevator back into Headquarters.

Saera was surprised to see that Wil selected Level 1 as the destination. There was no reason to stop by Medical. Maybe he needed to get something from his desk in his office along the Command wing—not that he used the space for much beyond one-on-one check-ins with his men. She pondered the potential reasons for the stop on the rest of the ride.

All possibilities were immediately thrown out when they exited the elevator and headed straight for the High Commander's office.

"I can head down to my quarters if you need to meet with Banks," Saera said.

"Join me," Wil replied.

"All right."

He opened the door to the High Commander's office for her. Inside, Banks and Cris were waiting.

What is this? Saera looked to Wil, questioning.

"Hi, Saera," Banks greeted. "Please, come in."

"Hello, sir." Saera took a hesitant step into the office. *Is this about me?*

Cris smiled. "Sorry for the ambush. Let us explain."

Wil closed the office door and went to stand by his father and Banks. "A few weeks ago, we determined that you were eligible for graduation—minus one last piece: your internship."

"Given the complexities of your position here within the TSS, we felt a different approach for your internship was in order," Cris explained.

"Wait…" *Is that what the trip was?*

Banks activated a holographic projection on his desk. It was predominantly text, and looked to be formatted like a mission brief. "Wil advised us that your greatest inhibitions were related to your past conflicts on Earth. So, we structured an internship around facing those issues."

Saera's mouth went dry. "Were you spying on me the whole time?"

"No," Wil hastily assured her. "It was a private matter for you to face yourself. I provided an objective report of events— just the minimum for documentation purposes—which Agent Wincowski verified. There's nothing about the nature of the conversations."

Saera crossed her arms. "I don't appreciate being misled."

"And I hated putting you in that position," Wil said. "But I couldn't have you go away for months. This seemed like the best solution." He continued telepathically, *They don't know about any of what you went through, I promise.*

Saera nodded. "So..."

"So," Cris continued, "the report indicates that you met the parameters to complete your internship. That means that you have fulfilled all of the requirements for graduation."

"Graduation?" *To an Agent? Already?*

Wil smiled. "That's right."

Graduating to Agent—so many things had been tied to that elusive "when." Saera was speechless.

"Congratulations," Banks told her with a nod like a proud father.

"I'm really graduating?"

Cris nodded. "Just a handful of final formalities, including the CR exam. We can make it official within two weeks."

"Thank you, sir," Saera murmured, still stunned.

"We'll let you go celebrate," Cris said. "I'll be in touch about the remaining administrative items."

"Thank you."

Wil bowed his head to his father and Banks and then headed for the door with Saera.

"I can't believe it," Saera said as soon as the office door was closed. "I thought it would be at least another year before graduation." *This is all happening so fast...*

Wil tilted his head. "I thought you'd be happier."

Saera took a deep breath. "It'll take some time to sink in. That's all."

Wil smiled. "You know what else it means?"

"Hmm?"

"We can finally get married."

Saera looked up at him. "It feels like that happened a long time ago."

"I know what you mean. But still…"

Saera smiled. "It'll be nice to make it official."

They walked in silence for a minute. "I'm sorry again about the whole internship thing," Wil said.

"Don't be. It was exactly what an internship should be." *Not what I would have chosen, but exactly what I needed.*

"So no hard feelings?"

Saera took Wil's hand. "Never."

"I feel old," Cris announced to his wife.

"No you're not," she replied. "Because that would make me old, too, and I'm not ready to think about myself that way."

"Our son is about to get married. How did that happen?"

Kate groaned. "Okay, now I *do* feel old."

"I know we were about the same age as them, but somehow it was different."

"It's this bomaxed life experience—always puts things in perspective," Kate replied. "We were naive babies then."

"But they aren't."

Kate nodded. "No. I'm not sure if they're lucky or not for knowing what they're getting into."

Cris placed his hands on his wife's waist. "I still would have married you, even knowing what I do now."

"Me too." She kissed him.

"I wonder if we'll be able to make it through an event on Tararia without a fight breaking out…"

Kate laughed. "Let's not start the crazy-talk just yet." She plopped down on the couch.

Cris reclined next to her. "I suppose we'll have to be on our best behavior."

"Yes, but we'll also have the chance to assess our contacts."

She did bring up a fair point. All of the friends and family across the network of Tararian nobility would be gathered in one place. "Except allegiance comes in many shades. We'll never know who might turn at the critical moment."

"We do have advantages when it comes to gauging such things," Kate pointed out.

"You're not suggesting spying inside our friends' minds, are you?" *Though it is tempting.*

"Just gleaning, like we so often do."

"It's a fine line. Maybe we should just go all-in and plant a command to follow our lead."

Kate sighed. "Obviously we can't do that."

But it would be so easy… Erase our problems. "They couldn't stop us."

"But they would find out. The Priesthood has its ways." Kate repositioned on the couch. "No, we need to do this properly, with old-fashioned persuasion. We need to make the others truly believe."

"Enduring change."

His wife nodded. "That's why we're playing the long game."

"That also gives the Priesthood time to prepare."

"Doesn't matter. We can't be stopped."

Cris smiled, always encouraged by Kate's enthusiasm. "Our families will never see it coming."

Kate grinned back. "They'll have to join us or get out of the way."

"Well, we'll see where we stand. I'm up for the challenge."

For once, Banks' check-in with the Priesthood brought purely good news. "Saera passed her internship. She'll graduate next month."

The Priest nodded. "Excellent, so their official union is forthcoming."

"Yes, this was the remaining hurdle. I haven't heard the date for the wedding—if one has been set—but within the next several months, I'm sure."

"Extra security that can't come soon enough. If anything happens to him, either because of the Aesir or during the war, we'll need the precedence set to turn to the Archive."

If he doesn't make it back from the Aesir's test, then we might not have a future at all. Banks suppressed the thought; Wil failing wasn't an option. "Saera is aware of her duty, but hopefully it doesn't come to that."

"The line must continue."

"And it will. But first, the war must end."

The Priest's eyes narrowed. "Do not forget our long-term objectives."

Never. But ours are not entirely the same. "The sense of duty within the Sietinen line is strong. You will have the heir you seek."

"I don't suppose we could convince them to have a child now," the Priest pondered.

"Not a chance," Banks replied right away. "They have enough to think about with the war ahead. And besides, it would be highly suspicious to suggest they divide their attention in any way."

"But if she—"

"He needs her," Banks cut in. "The moral support she offers is far more valuable than saving a couple of years on your timeline."

The Priest nodded. "Very well. But keep her safe."

That's one instruction I don't need. "Of course."

"Our best regards to the bride and groom." The Priest ended the transmission.

‹ CHAPTER 20 ›

Saera stood in the center testing chamber for her Course Rank exam, her chest tight with anticipation. Wil had assured her the test would be easy, but it was too important an event for her to not feel the pressure.

She gazed up at the window to the observation room and saw Wil watching alongside Banks. "I'm ready," she told them.

Banks nodded, and a buzzer sounded—starting a one-minute timer for the first phase of the exam. Saera would need to dispatch as many simulated enemies as possible within the time allotted.

Geometric holograms representing enemies appeared around her. She knocked aside the first wave of ten opponents with a series of airborne kicks.

Landing lightly on her feet, she centered her mind to generate a spatial distortion while the second wave of twenty materialized. Hovering on the edge of subspace, time appeared to halt. She lunged forward toward the next wave of opponents, kicking and punching them aside. Each opponent fractured as it was dealt a blow. When the last opponent vanished, she pulled back into a normal state.

Six seconds had elapsed on the exam clock. Saera was about to reinitiate a spatial distortion, but the third wave of opponents materialized more quickly than she anticipated. *Damn it.* She had no choice but to punch and kick her way through the third wave while the seconds on the clock ticked down.

The moment she vanquished the final opponent, she hurriedly reestablished the spatial distortion. The next wave was already forming—ready to engage her in a melee assault. However, within the spatial distortion, Saera was far faster than the enemy. They didn't stand a chance.

She returned to a normal state to trigger the fifth wave. But, she misjudged the timing—there was no way for her to establish a spatial distortion between every wave. With the new wave of fifty enemies closing in, she oriented to take on an opponent to her left. As she turned, something struck her from behind.

Almost losing her footing, Saera spun to attack the opponent behind her. She leaped into the air, simultaneously kicking both opponents. With a surge of energy, she flipped down the line of opponents surrounding her. The holographs shattered with each blow, precise hits taking out multiple opponents at the same time. But, the clock was against her. Three holograms remained when a harsh buzzer sounded. The remaining opponents dissolved and the lights restored to full illumination. Her minute was up.

"One-hundred-forty-seven," Banks announced over the intercom.

Saera nodded. It was a respectable showing—at least twice what a soon-to-be-Agent would be able to achieve without "stopping time." If only she could achieve the state as quickly as she'd like. Even still, being able to do it at all was a rarity. *At least I know where I can improve.*

"The next stage will begin momentarily," Banks stated over the speaker.

A low tone sounded as the lights dimmed again. Red holographic boxes—representing enemy targets—appeared around the room at varying heights, with some alone and others in groups. Blue boxes—representing friendly units—were interspersed among the red. Saera smiled to herself. Wil had been over similar training exercises with her countless times.

She quickly conjured a telekinetic spire and shot it toward the first dozen red boxes. The holograms exploded and vanished as each was hit. When the first set was eliminated, new boxes appeared and began to shift around the room, overlapping and changing heights as they swirled around Saera. She honed in on the red boxes, weaving her telekinetic spires around the blue obstacles.

The test picked up speed, and she threw out the spires two at a time to keep up. For each, she waited until she had a clear line of sight before sending the attack—taking advantage of the minute moments where she had an open shot. She adjusted her aim, turning and throwing spires. Soon, the blue boxes greatly outnumbered the red. Without breaking concentration, she dispatched the remaining red cubes. All one-hundred targets were eliminated.

A wave of excitement washed over Saera when the last red box exploded. She looked up at the timer and saw that just under two minutes had passed. By no means a record, but well within expected parameters.

"Good," Banks said over the intercom. "Are you ready for the next stage?"

"Yes," Saera affirmed. *I think.* Her stomach knotted. The next stage was the only part that had given Wil difficulty in his exam. He never said it outright, but she knew he was disappointed that he wasn't able to complete the maze without any missteps.

There was no time to dwell. The lights extinguished completely, leaving Saera in blackness. She closed her eyes, taking a slow breath to settle her heart rate.

An energy pulse called her attention to her right side—the starting point to an invisible maze. She sensed her way to the precise location through the darkness. A warm energy glow enveloped her as she reached the destination. She stretched out her arms straight forward. Tendrils curled around her forearms, fusing artificial wings up to her elbows. She tested the movement of the lightweight material, finding it easy to maneuver. However, she knew manipulating the wings wasn't enough on its own. She needed to sense their presence in space—make them a true extension of herself.

A wave of energy rippled through the room as the invisible maze activated in the darkness. Saera's skin tingled, sending a shiver down her back. She stood still, trying to sense the exact position of the maze walls. There would be just enough clearance for her to traverse the maze with her artificial wings stretched out to either side, keeping the wings perfectly level to travel through a channel that granted only three centimeters of variance in the vertical position. Her telekinetic senses would be pushed to their limits.

She stepped to the start of the maze, focusing on what she felt around herself. An electrical hum emanating from the walls filled her mind and she constructed a mental map of the maze. With her arms outstretched, she stepped forward and carefully kept the wings within the narrow channel along the walls at her shoulder height. The vertical clearance in the channel shrank with every bend in the maze, until soon the space for the wings to pass through was barely a centimeter in height.

Perspiration formed on Saera's brow, her arms aching from being outstretch for so long. She blocked out the pain and focused on the path ahead, unwilling to give up. The maze was clear in her mind—her course to the target at the edge of her consciousness.

The maze took a sharp turn to the right, and she quickly adjusted her stance to keep her arms outstretched in the right position.

She went around three more bends before she felt a new energy presence in the distance, drawing her in. She made her way toward it, careful to keep her arms outstretched despite the burn. The energy surrounded her in a warm glow.

A high chime sounded and the lights restored. Without warning, the artificial wings vanished into holographic dust around her arms. *Did I do it?*

The intercom clicked on. "You completed the maze."

Saera's heart leaped. Based on everything she'd heard, there was an extremely low completion rate—less than two percent. Even Wil hadn't succeeded. "Really?"

Wil crossed his arms, looking a little miffed next to Banks. Saera gave him a bashful grin and he softened.

"We'll proceed to the fourth stage whenever you're ready," the High Commander said.

"Okay." Saera shook out her arms and stretched her fingers. The burn began to subside. After a couple minutes, she returned her attention to the observation window. *Time for the Command test.* "I'm ready."

The lights in the testing chamber dimmed as a holographic starscape appeared. At the center of the starscape was a large planet, nearly touching the floor and ceiling. Two moons circled the planet, and a sun floated in the distance on the other side of the room. After five seconds, ships appeared in orbit of the central planet, each surrounded by a blue glow. Two seconds later, red dots appeared on the surface of the planet and in orbit, representing enemy assets of various sorts. Almost out of view around the curvature of the planet, a particularly large red dot glowed on the surface.

"Capture the enemy base," Banks said over the intercom.

Saera studied the planet. *Where—*

Missiles launched from the surface toward Saera's ships. Without a clear plan, she jumped into action, running to activate her units orbiting the planet. To buy time while she got her bearings, she raised the shields and initiated intermittent return fire that would provide cover without draining the weapon charges.

She took a step back to evaluate the planet. Rotating the view with her hands, she tried to get a better vantage of the large red spot in the southern hemisphere. Multiple units were clustered together in one menacing mass. At its center was a deep space cannon and a fortified compound filled with ground troops.

Saera ordered her carrier to wait behind the second moon, out sight from the deep space cannon and away from the immediate danger of close combat. She then turned her attention to configuring an attack force to take on the enemy cluster. The tight spacing was to her advantage, but all of the units were shielded. It would take a good portion of her firepower just to break through the outer shield, let alone the interior fortifications. *Guess I don't have a choice.*

Taking manual control of her ships in orbit, Saera redirected her fleet to the back side of the planet and opened fire with all vessels. The shields on the base below didn't budge. *I need more power. There has to be a trick.*

As she started to review her fleet manifest, Saera suddenly noticed a tiny red spot on the first moon. She returned her main fleet to an automated barrage and ran over to investigate.

The small dot seemed like nothing at first, but Saera zoomed in on the image. It was a small surface port with several shuttles docked along a concourse, connected to a domed shelter. Her brow furrowed, trying to make sense of the structure. It seemed familiar.

Five agonizing seconds passed as her ships in orbit of the planet were bombarded by enemy defensive fire.

Wait, that other compound on the planet isn't the base! The shelter on the moon was so familiar because it was a miniature version of the spaceport for TSS Headquarters, containing the elevator down into the moon. Almost defenseless aside from one central elevator shaft. One way in, one way out.

In an instant, Saera refocused her attack on the real target behind the moon. The units on the planet weren't able to mobilize as quickly as her ships already in orbit, giving her a narrow window of advantage for her attack.

The first blows to the moon base stunned the few enemy units guarding the exterior of the base, but the shields held. While in transit, one of Saera's ships exploded under the fire of the deep space cannon on the planet, but she was able to fan out her other ships to avoid damage from the resulting fireball that was quickly extinguished in the simulated vacuum.

Slowly, the shields on the moon base began to weaken. The enemy units from the planet were launching. She didn't have much time left before her forces would be pinned between two enemy fronts.

Saera directed the ships in for the final assault—bombarding the remaining shields. Five percent... Three percent... With an explosion, the shield collapsed.

All that remained was capturing the facility. Saera tapped on her carrier to deploy ground troops at the base. Zooming in on the ground unit controls, she activated a specialist to crack the security code on the elevator. A progress bar appeared while the crack was in progress, proceeding agonizingly slow. Troops from the planet were closing in. If they didn't get into the elevator in time—

The progress bar flashed "complete." Without hesitation, Saera directed her ground units into the elevator. The red glow on the base extinguished, replaced by blue.

Lights in the chamber returned to full brightness as the holograph dissolved. Saera breathed a sigh of relief. *Success!*

The intercom clicked on. "Well done," Banks said. "You had a fifteen percent casualty rating, only marginally above the fourteen percent estimated minimum for this scenario."

"Thank you, sir," Saera replied. Achieving the absolute minimum would have been ideal, but that was calculated based on efficiency gained through countless computer models. She knew the result was far better than usual under the circumstances.

Up in the window, Wil gave her a proud nod. She smiled up at him, filled with relief and pride. The main examination was over—she was about to become an Agent. Just one more measurement remained to determine her rank.

"Are you ready for the final test?" Banks asked.

Saera took a deep breath. Facing the testing sphere was daunting, though curiosity was keeping her nerves at bay. *What's my limit?* "Yes."

A tile in the floor slid to the side, revealing a golden sphere atop a pedestal that rose to waist height. Standing so close to it, anxiety set in. *Wil broke the sphere in his test.*

"Begin when you're ready," Banks said over the intercom.

Saera placed a hand on either side of the sphere. A cool static charge leaped between her fingertips and the shiny surface. She concentrated on the presence of the sphere, closing her eyes.

As she started to focus energy into the object, the sphere warmed between her hands, glowing with golden light. She reached, pushing herself further than she thought she could go. Somewhere ahead, there was a limit, but it wasn't yet in sight.

She extended herself further, gathering the energy within her grasp and funneling it into the sphere. Never before had she felt so free and exhilarated—no requirements of control, just an open conduit on the edge of a new level of existence.

And then, she felt it. A wall closing in on her. She wanted to push further—to continue exploring the unseen world that was just beyond her grasp. Yet, she couldn't get through. She was at her limit.

Sadness filled her. There was so much she would never know—everything that laid beyond the unseen barrier holding her back. The only way to go was down.

Wil watched Saera release her hold on the sphere, an aura of energy still around her. She dropped to her knees, tears rolling down her cheeks.

He took a step toward the door, wanting to go to her and offer comfort.

Banks held up his hand to stop him. "She'll be fine. It's normal to be drained after this part of the exam."

She's crying... He bit back a protest. "How did she score?"

Banks evaluated the final data from the testing sphere on the touchscreen monitor. "9.4," he read off. "That's more than half a point above her estimated potential."

And her estimate of 8.8 would have been impressive as it was. She's definitely going to stand out even more now. "I wonder how much her bond with me contributed to the higher rating," Wil pondered.

"A significant factor, no doubt," Banks replied. "Either way, it confirms her Command placement."

"Yes, it does."

Banks smiled. "Well, I'll let you two go celebrate."

"What about graduation?" Wil asked.

"We're mid-year. She can walk in four months with the others, if she wants to."

Wil nodded. "Let's file the results now and make it official. I'll put in the request for her new uniform."

"It should all be final by tomorrow. Let's hope your men have similarly impressive results."

"Hopefully." Wil left the observation room and jogged down the stairs to retrieve Saera from the testing chamber. She was still on her knees when he opened the door.

She glanced over her shoulder at him and started to rise.

"Are you okay?" he asked, rushing over to her.

"Yeah. I just feel kind of... empty now." She straightened, taking a wide, stable stance.

"I know what that's like. To taste the power and then need to turn away."

"It was so strange to hit a wall like that. I wanted to go further but just couldn't," Saera said.

Wil pulled her in for a hug. "Well, all things considered, your limit is well above the ceiling for most."

Saera looked up at him. "How'd I do?"

"9.4."

Her eyes widened. "That high?"

"It's the third-highest CR on record."

"Wow." Saera let out a slow breath.

"And you got top marks on all the other stages. Three and Four were especially impressive."

Saera grinned. "Thanks."

Wil took her hand, a swell of pride in his chest to have her as his partner. "Congratulations. You're an Agent now."

◄ CHAPTER 21 ►

"Do you prefer 'Effervescent Bloom' or 'Alatrician Violet'?" Saera asked Wil, looking up from the wedding catalog. Frankly, she couldn't identify a difference between the two hues.

"Whatever you prefer," Wil replied in the same way as he had for her barrage of previous questions.

Saera examined the color swatches again. "The Alatrician Violet, I guess."

"Great."

"Did you even look?" Saera asked.

Wil glanced up from his desk on the other side of the room. "They're practically the same shade. If that's what you had it narrowed down to, go with whichever."

"The accent color will set the tone for everything. I don't want it to clash."

"It's a garden. It'll be fine."

"But—"

"Saera, I really don't care. Pick whichever you want."

"What do you mean you 'don't care'? You have to have some opinion on the matter."

"I like the Alatrician Violet more, too."

Saera evaluated him. "Are you just saying that now to please me?"

"If I was, it doesn't seem to be working."

"Ah, okay. I see how it is."

Wil raised an eyebrow. "Are we seriously bickering over this?"

"Well, I can't read your mind." Saera caught herself. "Okay, I could, but—"

"Deep breath." Wil rose from his chair and came over to Saera. "I think you're obsessing over this a little too much."

Saera smoothed back her hair. "I told myself I wasn't going to turn into bridezilla."

Wil looked confused.

"Idiom. Anyway, there's some wedding planner on Tararia named Claude who keeps asking me all sorts of questions I don't know how to answer."

"So fire him," Wil suggested.

"I'm not sure that's an option."

Wil shrugged. "You can do whatever you want. Complete creative control over the day."

"I'm pretty sure your grandparents would disagree."

"That's their problem."

"Which would become ours," Saera pointed out.

Wil sighed. "I have no further suggestions, then. I've never planned a wedding before, either, so I'm not going to give you advice."

"But you can at least state your preference when I ask."

"I have."

Saera crossed her arms over her new black uniform. "Which have all just been replies agreeing with me."

"Maybe we have the same taste."

"Or maybe you don't want to say anything contrary to me."

"Given how you react even when I agree with you…" Wil countered.

Saera paused. "Okay, fair point." She pushed the projection of the catalog away. "I don't want to pick the wrong thing and ruin the day. We've waited for so long."

Wil softened. "Saera, whatever you decide will be fine. I

don't care about any of this. All I want is to spend whatever I have left of my life with you."

"I thought you wanted a big wedding."

"Stars no! I thought you did," Wil replied.

What the...? "When I asked, you said we'd have it at the Sietinen estate."

"You mean that question two minutes after I proposed? I didn't think that was binding. You started pulling all of this together and I figured that's what you wanted. You've been so patient with me over the years, I was willing to make any concession just to ensure you got at least one perfect day."

Saera flushed. "Oh." *Why didn't he say anything sooner?*

"Are you saying you don't want a wedding on Tararia?"

"Maybe. I don't know." Saera buried her face in her hands.

Wil pulled her hands back, grasping them gently in his. "What's wrong?"

"I got so wrapped up in these stupid details, I forgot to make it about us."

Wil gave her a sympathetic smile. "So let's scrap the whole thing."

"No! I still want a wedding."

"I just meant this giant show on Tararia. Let's bring it back to us."

Saera thought about it. "What would that be?"

"I don't know."

"Not helpful," Saera said with a glare.

Wil gave her a meek smile. "Well, we met here. Maybe something centered around the TSS would be more fitting."

"Yes, that's true."

"While most of Headquarters isn't exactly scenic, the spaceport isn't bad."

Saera considered the proposition. "The starscape would make for a nice backdrop."

"And maybe Banks could officiate."

"That would be more meaningful than someone we've never met before."

Wil nodded. "Exactly."

Saera searched his face. "Is that what you wanted all along?"

"It occurred to me, but I wanted to make sure you got your dream day."

"I think that would be it. Easy, low-key—this other thing just isn't us."

Wil smiled and gave her a kiss. "Then it's settled. Tell Claude he's out."

Saera grinned. "All right. But I do have one condition."

"What's that?"

"I still get to wear my dress."

Wil knocked on the High Commander's door and waited to be beckoned in. *Let's see how receptive he is to the change in plan.*

Five seconds passed and the door clicked open.

"What can I do for you?" Banks asked as Wil stepped inside.

Wil closed the door. "I wanted to speak with you about a private matter."

"Sure, anything."

"Well," Wil began as he took a seat across from Banks at his desk, "Saera and I talked, and the formal wedding on Tararia just doesn't feel right."

Banks nodded thoughtfully. "You don't have many personal ties there."

"And those we do have are… strained. Saera's been driving herself crazy trying to plan for an event we don't even want."

"I understand. Did you have something else in mind?"

"We thought about having it here, in the spaceport."

Banks's eyebrows raised with surprise. "I hadn't even considered that as an option for you."

"Our entire life together has revolved around the TSS. It makes the most sense."

The High Commander nodded. "It does. Whatever you'd like for the event, name it."

"Would you be willing to officiate?" Wil asked.

Banks' face lit up. "Wil… I'd be honored."

Wil smiled back. "Thank you."

Banks leaned back in his chair. "It'll be nice to have a happy occasion like this for a change."

"And an opportunity for those who mean the most in our lives to take part in the event."

"Indeed."

"I assume the Primus Elites and some of Saera's Junior Agent friends can have the day off?" Wil asked.

The High Commander smiled. "Of course."

"All right. We can work out the details later. Since we have your approval to conduct the wedding here, I guess I should go tell my parents the Tararia event is off."

"Good luck with that."

Wil sighed. "Yeah… not quite sure how they're going to take it."

"I wish you the best either way."

"Thanks." Wil rose.

Banks stood to see him out. "I'll be awaiting instructions regarding the ceremony script, and anything else."

Ugh, so many details. No wonder Saera was losing it. "We'll let you know. Thank you, sir."

After leaving Banks' office, Wil sent a message to his parents asking to meet at their quarters. He jogged down the stairs and headed back toward the Agents' residential wing. His parents were just arriving at their door as Wil approached.

"Is everything okay?" his father asked as he palmed open the lock.

"Yes, just wanted to discuss something with you." Wil

followed them inside.

"What?" Kate asked.

"Why don't you sit down," Wil suggested, gesturing toward the couch.

Cris and Kate glanced at each other as they complied.

"So, about the wedding," Wil began, "we don't want to have it on Tararia."

Kate's eyes widened behind her tinted glasses. "What do you mean?"

"We've barely spent any time on the planet. We'd rather have it here—with our friends and TSS family," Wil explained.

"Can't say I blame you," Cris muttered.

"But there's an expectation—" Kate started to protest.

Cris raised an eyebrow. "Since when is pleasing our families on Tararia a motivating factor?"

"True. But what about having everyone together so we could talk?" Kate questioned.

Cris sighed. "That's a good point."

Wil eyed them. "Did I miss something?"

"You know that long-term plan of ours—involving a certain change on Tararia?" Cris asked.

Overthrowing the Priesthood, of course. "What of it?"

"Well, the wedding would be a prime opportunity to do some mingling and see where everyone stands."

"Count votes?" Wil clarified.

His father nodded. "Essentially."

Wil let out a long breath. "I didn't think a change of venue would have those kind of ripple effects."

"Are you completely against having it on Tararia?" asked Kate.

"I'd say it's more of a strong preference not to," Wil replied, thinking through the possibilities. "But maybe the change to TSS Headquarters would actually work to your advantage."

Kate perked up. "How so?"

"I'd wager that almost no one on Tararia has ever been to a TSS facility, right?" Wil posited. His parents nodded. "So, why not show them what we're really about here? It's one thing to tell them about our power, but quite another to show it."

Cris frowned. "I'm not sure intimidation is the best way to go about this."

"Not intimidation," Wil countered. "Just insight into an underrepresented population."

Cris shook his head. "Speaking from experience, most people are unnerved to be outnumbered in a room with telekinetics. I don't think we'd win many friends."

"No, think about it," Kate cut in. "It's not about winning favor. We just need to show them that there's a whole population that's been relegated to the outside. Perfectly normal, sociable people that have been made outcasts."

"Show them that perhaps their supposedly impartial overseers are not as fair and just as everyone has been led to believe," Wil added.

"Plant the seeds of doubt," Cris mused.

Wil nodded. "It might be too premature to count your votes, but it would help lay the groundwork."

Cris smiled. "Well, I guess we have some wedding invitations to send."

<>   <>   <>

Michael entered the study room with caution. It wasn't like Wil to call private meetings outside of his office.

He peeked in the door and saw Wil playing on his handheld.

Wil looked up and set down the device. "Hey. Sorry for the weird meeting place. I thought my office would be too formal."

Michael entered the rest of the way and closed the door. "No problem."

"This isn't about training or the TSS," Wil continued. "I know I've been your commander officially, but you've become a true friend to me and I value your council. And you've been a great friend to Saera, too. We talked, and we'd like you to be a part of our upcoming wedding. I think 'Best Man' is what you called it back home?"

Michael smiled. "Yeah, that's it." He let out a sharp breath. "I didn't realize the wedding was happening already."

"Well, Saera graduated, and that was the main holdup. It was going to be next year on Tararia, but we decided to do a more personalized event here at Headquarters."

"Makes sense."

Wil bit his bottom lip. "I understand if you don't want to be a part of it."

Because part of me wishes that I was the one marrying her. "No, I'd be happy to stand with you."

"Great," Wil beamed.

"You know, I'll always care about her, but it was never like what you two have. I'm genuinely happy she found you."

Wil nodded. "Thank you, that means a lot." He hesitated. "I hope you'd be there for her if anything happened to me."

The statement caught Michael off-guard. "Sure. Of course." *He said that almost like he expects something to happen.*

"All right, then," Wil said as he rose. "We don't have all the event details worked out, but I'll let you know. It should be pretty straightforward."

Michael stood, as well. "Looking forward to it."

◄ CHAPTER 22 ►

The time had come to make a move.

Haersen was gathered in Tek's office along with the other officers involved in the plot to overthrow the Imperial Director. Months had passed since the plans were laid. Everyone was antsy for action.

Tek folded his hands on the desktop and addressed the group. "In his usual fashion of incompetence, the Imperial Director has failed to take my threats against him seriously. Given his failure in the most recent attack on TSS Headquarters, it's time to get more aggressive."

"How?" Komatra asked.

"By making a threat he can't ignore," Tek replied. He met the glowing red eyes of each of his officers. "Once this begins, events will unfold quickly. We'll need to take out the Imperial Director and gain control of each office immediately."

"We're ready to act," Komatra assured him.

Tek nodded. "We must force his hand—to take me out preemptively. Once he thinks I am subdued, Komatra, Gerek, and Iko, will enter the Imperial Director's office with Haersen. I'll follow once the path is cleared. The rest of you will need to secure the military command complex."

"What do we do with anyone who resists?" Colonel Takara questioned.

"Eliminate them," Tek replied without hesitation.

"It's a large complex to take with only four of us," Dekon ventured.

"We have made preparations in advance," Tek said. "We have found that others are receptive to a leadership change."

The officers murmured their understanding.

"Now," Tek turned to Haersen, "let's knock on the Imperial Director's door."

Haersen took a deep breath and pulled out his handheld. He sent a simple message to the Imperial Director's personal account—an address supplied by Tek in one of their preparation meetings over recent months: "Sir, Tek is making his move."

"Done," Haersen reported when the message was sent. He returned the handheld to his pocket.

Tek smiled. "That should spur him to action."

It was unsettling to think about soldiers coming to eliminate Tek, but everyone in the room was prepared to defend their new leader. There was no way the Imperial Director could anticipate so many co-conspirators—the officers could deal with anything sent their way.

The entire point of the plan was for the Imperial Director to think Tek's betrayal was isolated—that he could get ahead of the situation. Since the Imperial Director hadn't previously taken action, perhaps he had maintained hopes that Tek would change his ways. After all, the Bakzen had made a significant investment in Tek and it would be a shame to throw that all away. But, respect for Bakzen leadership was paramount from the administrative office's viewpoint. Unfortunately, military control was the way of the future.

Haersen stood in silence along with the officers. They were pressed along the side of the room and the wall shared with the door, out of immediate sight from anyone entering the room. Tek paced by his desk in anticipation.

Half an hour passed with no conversation or communication from the administrative office.

"Will they come, sir?" Haersen finally asked, unable to bear the silence any longer.

Tek crossed his arms. "I'm surprised they aren't here already."

No sooner had he spoken then the door burst open. Half a dozen guards poured in, aiming pulse rifles at Tek.

"On your knees!" one exclaimed.

The Bakzen officers leaped into action, securing the guards in telekinetic shackles. The guards hung suspended in midair at the center of the room.

Tek approached the helpless soldiers, looking each in the eyes as he walked down the line. "You have a choice to make now. Join me or die."

"We're here on orders from the Imperial Director," one soldier stammered.

"He won't hold that position for much longer. Will you die for him, or be a part of the future?" Tek asked.

"I'll join you," another guard said.

"But our orders!" one of the other guards protested.

Tek snapped the neck of the protester, startling the others to silence.

"Have you succeeded in your mission of eliminating me?" Tek asked the first guard who'd spoken.

He paused for a moment. "Yes, sir."

Haersen felt Tek assessing the guard's mind—judging if he was telling the truth. He pulled back, seemingly satisfied.

"Make your report to the Imperial Director," Tek ordered.

The soldier nodded. The Bakzen officers released the telekinetic holds on him enough for the soldier to retrieve his handheld from a pocket on the front of his jumpsuit. "Sir, this is Karn reporting in," he said into the device.

"Is it done?" the Imperial Director asked.

"Tek is dead, sir," the soldier reported.

"Was there anyone with him?" the Imperial Director asked.

"No, sir, he was alone."

"Good. Incinerate his body," the Imperial Director instructed. "I will handle the communication to his former officers." The call ended.

"Now to pledge your loyalty to the Imperial Director," Tek instructed Komatra, Gerek, and Iko. "He won't be able to read all of you at the same time. Once he begins to evaluate the first, the rest of you must subdue him. Go now. I'll come as soon as you're in position."

Komatra beckoned for Haersen to follow. The four men rushed to the central elevator and descended to the maglev station.

They entered one of the cars headed to the administrative complex.

"You'll need to pose as a prisoner," Komatra told Haersen as soon as the door closed. "You're known as Tek's advisor. Even though you alerted the Imperial Director to Tek's supposed plan, none of us should trust you, because of your association with him."

"I'll do anything you need of me," Haersen replied. He was far too invested to offer any resistance. After how quickly others had been dispatched, he didn't want to take any chances.

They rode in silence for the remainder of the transport to the administrative building. It's gleaming light-gray walls were cast in red from the setting sunlight—a fitting image for the events about to transpire.

The officers formed a triangle around Haersen, with Komatra in front and Gerek and Iko walking abreast behind.

Komatra led the way to the front desk and scanned his ID chip on the reader. His clearance was unquestioned and required no explanation for entering the lower levels of the building.

They set a straight course to the elevator. Komatra selected the tenth—and top—floor of the building. The reader turned yellow, indicating conditional clearance. "I'll lead," he told the others.

When the elevator doors opened at their destination, Komatra strode toward the secondary security checkpoint. "We're here to see the Imperial Director."

"We're in lockdown," the guard replied. "What is your business?"

"We have in custody the advisor to former General Tek."

"It can wait until the lockdown is lifted," the guard replied.

"Let the Imperial Director decide that," Komatra shot back. "Tell him I'm here." He waved his wrist over the scanner on the desktop.

The guard examined the credentials. "Yes, Colonel, I'll alert him." He entered a message on the console at his station. After several moments, he nodded to Komatra. "Very well. The Imperial Director will see you."

"Thank you." Komatra snapped the guard's neck with the telepathic whip—leaving the pathway open for Tek to pass by without notice.

Haersen's stomach turned over with the sudden act of brutality, but he recognized its necessity.

Komatra set off down the hall with Haersen and the others in tow. The entry to the office was immediately past the security checkpoint. He opened the door.

The Imperial Director sat behind his desk. He evaluated the party with mild surprise, pausing on Haersen. "Why have you come here?"

Something about the Imperial Director's energy signature felt strange. Haersen glanced at Komatra to see if he noticed it, as well, but the young officer was focused purely on the mission at hand.

"We are aware of Tek's recent death," Komatra stated as he stepped into the room. "We came across his 'advisor,' here," he prodded Haersen forward. "He has pledged his continued allegiance to the Bakzen."

Haersen dropped to his knees. "Sir, I tried to reason with Tek, but he insisted that coming for you was the only way."

The Imperial Director shook his head. "Allegiance? You revealed Tek's plan to me. After he took you in, you were still willing to undermine him? You can't be trusted."

"Sir, my actions have all been in the service of the Bakzeni Empire," Haersen countered. He just needed to stall for long enough.

"You're an outsider. Why should we continue to indulge his fancy?" the Imperial Director asked.

Haersen gazed up at him with all the confidence he could muster. "Because of what I can demonstrate. This gene therapy has already transformed me. If it can increase my abilities, it will show a path for the Taran population."

"A complement to the plans we have already set in motion," the Imperial Director mused.

"Yes. And I'm so close to being able to show you," Haersen urged.

"Perhaps." The Imperial Director rose from his desk. He waved Haersen aside, turning his attention to the officers. "And what of the rest of you?"

"We are loyal to the Bakzeni Empire," Komatra stated, his mental guards firmly set.

There was no way Komatra's mental guards wouldn't rouse suspicion, but it was the distraction Haersen needed. He took the opportunity to slip his handheld from his pocket and send the awaited message to Tek: "Now."

The Imperial Director's eyes narrowed, but he seemed willing to overlook the mental wall. "Komatra, you will assume General Tek's former position."

"Yes, sir. I am honored," Komatra acknowledged. He glanced over at Haersen.

"It's sent," Haersen told him. The position of General was a

position Komatra would no doubt assume under Tek's leadership, anyway, Haersen figured.

The Imperial Director focused on the next in line. "And Gerek—"

Tek appeared in the open doorway. Without hesitation, he fired a pulse gun blast into the Imperial Director's chest.

An electronic ripple passed over the Imperial Director as the blast dissipated around him. "How stupid do you think I am?"

Tek, Haersen, and the officers were thrown to the ground in a telekinetic vice. Haersen fought against the restraints, but the control was too powerful. There was no way the Imperial Director was acting alone.

A moment later, ten officers appeared in the doorway and filed into the room. Two focused on each of the prisoners.

Haersen was completely pinned by the two officers—each captor individually stronger than himself. There was no way to break free. That wasn't part of the plan.

"You made it even easier than I anticipated, coming for me like this," the Imperial Director stated. "Tek, I'm disappointed."

Tek glared up at his commander. "Your time is over."

The Imperial Director loomed over them, his body shield flickering as it recalibrated. "Not yet."

Tek leaped to his feet, free from his telekinetic vice, to the Imperial Director's horror. "We've come for you."

Four of the guards cried out in surprise as the others turned on them. They collapsed to their knees, gripping their heads. The cries subsided as a trickle of blood flowed from their eyes and noses.

The invisible bonds holding Haersen released. He scrambled to his feet to find that the remaining six guards supposedly working with the Imperial Director had redirected their attention to the former commander. Tek's newest insiders.

"Our supporters are everywhere now," Tek told the Bakzen leader. "You should have made a move earlier when you had the chance."

The Imperial Director evaluated his former supporters now penning him in. He snarled at Tek, "You know how to make a compelling argument. It's a pity you're so wrong."

"Wrong? I'm a visionary." Tek sent a telekinetic lash toward the old Bakzen leader, crackling the air with electromagnetic energy.

The Imperial Director dodged the blow, wrapping a telekinetic whip of his own around Tek's torso and throwing him against the right wall. The wall cracked under the impact, raining dust and chunks of concrete.

Tek slid to the floor, clutching his shoulder that had borne the brunt of the impact. He shook it off, sending out another invisible snare from his position on the floor—this time catching the Imperial Director by his ankles. He whipped the old Bakzen against the far wall, shattering a viewscreen in a flash of sparks.

Both men rose to their feet struggling to subdue the other in a telekinetic vice. Bred from the same genetic line, their strength was evenly matched—making it a battle of wills.

Tek's officers stood by, unable to intervene without questioning Tek's position as a leader. His victory needed to stand on its own.

The two commanders strained under the pressure, perspiration on their brows and knees shaking from exertion. Tek was the first to slip.

The Imperial Director threw him against the window. The glass crunched as Tek was forced against it. "We never should have brought you into being."

A crack spread out from the impact site, cross-crossing the window. Tek was suspended in midair at the center of the window, framed by the setting sun. Long shadows lined the ground ten stories below.

Tek sneered back at the Imperial Director. "And you should

have retired."

He threw the Imperial Director back against his desk. The desk flipped over, partially pinning the old Bakzen.

Tek landed on his feet, strong as ever. He telekinetically rended one of the legs from the upturned desk and drew it into his hand. "It's over." He hurled the desk leg into the Imperial Director's chest, piercing him clean through just below the heart.

The elderly Bakzen fell backwards, blood pouring from the gaping wound. He gasped, sputtering a laugh of surprise. "I underestimated you."

"You're old and weak," Tek said, coming to stand over him. "The Bakzen can't wait any longer. I will give us the future we deserve."

The Imperial Director fought for breath, his teeth stained with blood. "You can't lead us."

"This was my birthright," Tek declared. "Born of the imperial line and raised to be the Bakzen's deliverance to freedom."

"Not like this," the Imperial Director murmured with his dying breaths.

Tek shook his head with disgust. He stomped on the Imperial Director's skull until it was crushed, eliminating any chance of recovering his consciousness.

Haersen quavered from nerves and excitement. It had been bloodier than planned, but they'd done it. He inched away from the fallen guards near his feet.

Stepping over the Imperial Director's body, Tek brushed off his uniform and approached the chair that had surprisingly remained in place throughout the fight—the seat of power he had pursued for so long. He ran his finger along its upper edge. It was finally his, and now Haersen and all others who had supported him would reap the benefits.

Haersen smiled. He wouldn't have to grovel any longer.

Tek looked over his officers and nodded—the thrill of victory in his eyes. He pulled out his handheld and activated a planetwide broadcast.

"I am assuming control of the Bakzeni Empire," Tek announced. "I will be the new Imperial Director, overseeing both military and administrative operations. I will deliver us victory in the war. Join me."

◄ CHAPTER 23 ►

The plan of attack was laid. Cris rubbed his hands together, ready for battle. "After I talk with my parents while you're with Kaiden, we'll rendezvous near your parents and go tackle Vincent Talsari together."

Kate sighed. "Cris, dear, this is a wedding not a war. I think we can play it by ear and be just fine."

"It was your idea to investigate today. I'm just trying to be prepared."

"And we are perfectly equipped to discuss this and other matters without further preparation," his wife assured him.

I guess we shouldn't come on too strong if we're going to successfully show outsiders that the TSS and its people aren't so different from them—that the Priesthood was wrong to disparage us. Cris let out a slow breath. "I'll try to relax."

"Good." Kate straightened a slightly askew ribbon on Cris' dress uniform. "Now, go make sure our son is taken care of while I begin greeting our guests." She gave him a kiss.

"I'll meet you out there soon. If you want to start with Kaiden—"

Kate flashed a prim smile. "There'll be plenty of time for business after the ceremony." She shooed Cris away. Fatherly duties were far more important than politics.

"It doesn't even seem real." Wil performed the final check of his TSS dress uniform in the mirror. "We've already been together for so long that this formality seems like it should have happened already."

Michael nodded, making the final adjustments to his own dark-blue TSS uniform—a slightly premature color advancement, but well deserved and a better fit with the rest of the color scheme for the event. "So think of how much better you'll feel afterward."

Part of me still feels guilty for dragging Saera into this life. "She'll have some security."

"...And each other," Michael prompted.

Wil smiled. "And we'll have each other."

A knock sounded at the door and it slid opened. "How's everything going in here?" Cris asked.

"All set," Wil replied.

His father looked him over, evaluating. "Need anything?"

Wil shook his head. "I don't think so."

Cris grinned. "Then let's get this party going."

Wil and Michael followed Cris from the suite on the Vanquish that had been serving as his dressing room up at the TSS spaceport above the moon. Friends and some hired help had been busy transforming the port into a ceremony space and reception venue, complete with decorations, seating, and dining facilities. *I wonder how everything came out.*

Two minutes later, he had his answer.

"Wow." Wil took in the entrance to the transformed spaceport.

One concourse had been sectioned off for the wedding. The outer portion of the wing was filled with tables to accommodate the reception dinner. Each table was covered with a white tablecloth, topped with an elaborate vase of flowers in a spectrum of purple and blue. Fiber optics woven throughout the vases and foliage added a twinkling sparkle that played off the starscape visible through the curved ceiling above.

Further down the concourse, at the entrance to the rotunda, three hundred chairs were arranged in rows facing the expansive starscape beyond. The holographic map that was normally suspended in the center of the room was deactivated, replaced by streamers of flowing white fabric draped in elegant arches from floor to ceiling. Flowers lined the center aisle, and additional planters atop silver pedestals framed the back center of the rotunda beneath an arch of fabric. Another pedestal table at the center of the arch was topped with a silver chalice for the ceremony.

"This is amazing," Wil breathed.

"I don't even recognize it," Michael said behind him.

Cris nodded. "I was pretty surprised myself. I hope Saera likes it."

"She'll love it," Wil replied. "No doubt."

Banks walked over from the left wall of the rotunda where he'd been chatting with Scott, who was attending as a guest. "Hi, Wil. How are you feeling?"

"Great!" Wil exclaimed. "Have the guests arrived?"

The High Commander nodded. "We've been holding them in the concourse set aside for the civilian attendees. We wanted to make sure everything met with your approval before we brought them in."

"Looks good to me," Wil affirmed.

"Excellent. We'll get everyone seated, then," Banks replied. "Did you want to go over the ceremony script again?"

Wil shook his head. "I think I've got it."

Banks flashed him a broad grin. "All right. It's time for a wedding!"

Saera couldn't take her eyes off the reflection of herself in the mirror. Her wedding dress was even more stunning in its final form than it had appeared in the holographic model—crystal and silver embroidery along the precise pleats that hugged her perfectly. She was afraid to move, lest it somehow harm the garment.

"Are you ready?" Elise asked. Her own purple dress brushed the ground with a light fabric that billowed as she moved, paired with a form-fitting bodice that connected to straps cris-crossing her back.

"I guess I am." *I can't believe I'm getting married today.*

The door cracked open and Marina peeked inside. "Oh, Saera, you're beautiful."

Saera blushed beneath her makeup. "Thanks, mom."

"Are you nervous?" Marina asked.

"Not really. More excited."

Marina checked Saera's gown one last time. "Good. Everyone's in place, so we'll proceed whenever you want."

Saera took a deep breath. "Okay, let's do this."

Wil scanned the concourse leading up to the aisle, waiting for Saera to come into view. His heart pounded in his ears and his stomach fluttered with excitement. *We're about to get married. She'll be my wife…*

Guests shifted in their seats, anxious for the event to get underway. Old acquaintances whispered to each other while they waited for the bride's arrival.

Cris and Kate were seated in the front row, the hint of tears in their exposed glowing eyes. Wil glanced over his left shoulder at Michael, who gave him a supportive smile.

Wil took a deep breath. *This is just a formality. She's always been my life partner.* He returned his attention to the concourse.

He felt Saera approaching before he saw her—emanating joy and a sense of fulfillment. He reached out to her, sharing his own elation and excitement. Their bond called them together across the remaining distance. He craved to be back with her, thinking it impossible that he could love her or desire her even more. And then, she stepped into view—more beautiful and radiant than a fantastical dream.

Everything went still. Their eyes locked and they smiled at each other. Their years together had been leading up to that moment, and there was nowhere else they'd rather be.

Saera walked slowly down the aisle with a bouquet of flowers to match the other decorations, her confidence making her even more stunning. Guests murmured with awe as they took her in. She kept her eyes locked on Wil's, except for the occasional glance down to check her footing.

When Saera reached the end of the aisle she handed her bouquet to Elise and turned to face Wil. Elise quickly ducked down to arrange the train of Saera's dress, then stepped back to the side.

A pace back from Wil and Saera, Banks stood at the center of the arch behind the pedestal waiting to officiate. He glanced at Wil and Saera, and they nodded to indicate they were ready to begin the ceremony, consisting of elements from both of their native cultures.

The High Commander gazed out at the audience. "We are gathered here today to celebrate one of life's greatest moments, and to cherish the words which shall unite Williame Sietinen-Vaenetri and Saera Alexri in marriage. Marriage is the promise between two people who love each other, and who trust in that love, who honor one another as individuals, and who wish to spend the rest of their lives together.

"This ceremony will not create a relationship that does not already exist between them. It is a symbol of how far they have come in their years together. It is a symbol of the promises they will make to each other to continue growing stronger as individuals and as partners, no matter what challenges or successes they encounter together in the coming years. Today, their lives, which began on separate paths, will be joined as one."

Wil and Saera took each other's hands, trembling slightly with anticipation.

"Though we are far from the home of our people," Banks continued, "the essence of that ancestry is a part of us all no matter where we may travel. To solidify Wil and Saera's bonds to their people and to each other, they will drink the headwaters of the Bethral Mountains."

Banks picked up a dual-spout chalice from the pedestal, angled such that they each could sip when the cup was tipped forward. The clear water filled the bottom of the silver vessel—just enough for a swallow each. He handed the chalice to Wil and Saera, who took it in their hands together.

Taking a step closer to each other, they tilted the chalice forward and drank. The cold water sent a chill down Wil's throat as he swallowed. With the chalice emptied, they handed it back to Banks.

The High Commander placed the chalice back on the pedestal. "You have demonstrated your connection to Tararia's past, and now you will seal your place with its future."

Cris rose from his seat in the front row, carrying a small tablet in a leather case embossed with the Sietinen Dynasty crest. "As heir to the Sietinen Dynasty, I declare you and your future children my successors. Do you accept this responsibility?"

"I do," Wil murmured simultaneously with Saera.

Cris held up the tablet, projecting two beams of purple light underneath—one tuned to the frequency of the High Dynasties, and the other to that of the Lower Dynasties. Wil pulled up his left sleeve to expose his Mark under the appropriate beam, and Saera turned over her wrist to show hers. The screen on the tablet lit up with the serpent crest of Sietinen and the broadleaf tree of Alexri.

"Your commitment has been recorded and ratified," Cris

stated. "The Dynasties of Sietinen and Alexri are now joined."

Wil and Saera took each other's hands again as Cris returned to his seat.

Invisible to all but the Agents in the audience, Banks then wove a telekinetic ribbon around Wil's and Saera's hands, reflecting the bond that would always bind them.

When the telekinetic lacing was in place, he looked to Wil. "Do you take Saera to be your wife, your partner in life, and your one true love? Will you cherish your union, trust and respect her through good times and bad, regardless of the obstacles you may face together? Will you give your hand, your heart, and your love, from this day forward in service to each other and to Tararia?"

Wil nodded, looking into Saera's eyes. "I do."

Banks turned to Saera and repeated the lines for taking Wil as her husband.

Saera beamed. "I do!"

The High Commander released the telekinetic binding from around their hands, leaving their skin tingling. "May I have the rings?" he asked Michael.

Michael retrieved the rings from his pocket and dropped them in Banks' outstretched hand. Banks then handed Wil the ring for Saera.

"Wil, please place this ring on Saera's finger and repeat after me: Saera, I give you this ring, as a daily reminder of my love for you, no matter what we may face."

Wil slipped the wedding band onto her finger in front of the engagement ring. "Saera, I give you this ring, as a daily reminder of my love for you, no matter what we may face."

"Saera, please place this ring on Wil's finger and repeat after me: Wil, I give you this ring, as a daily reminder of my love for you, no matter what we may face."

Saera slid the wedding band onto Wil's finger. "Wil, I give you this ring, as a daily reminder of my love for you, no matter what we may face."

Banks smiled. "You have made your marriage vows to one another, witnessed by your friends and family. You have sealed your vows to uphold your duties to Tararia. So now, by the power vested in me, I pronounce you husband and wife. You may kiss!"

Wil pulled Saera in for a kiss as the audience erupted in applause and cheers.

They separated from the kiss, grinning at each other as they savored the moment.

Saera took her bouquet back from Elise and they strode back down the aisle hand-in-hand. The Primus Elites, seated toward the back of the audience, whistled and clapped louder as Wil and Saera passed by.

"We're married!" Saera exclaimed as soon as they were in the dining area out of earshot from the guests. She stared down at the additional band on her finger.

"I know! I can hardly believe it." Wil's new ring felt strange on his finger.

"I had finally gotten used to saying 'fiancé.' Now it'll be 'husband.'"

"And 'wife.' Wow."

Their eyes met and they laughed.

Conversation filled the concourse as guests began to rise from their chairs.

"They'll be expecting us to play hosts, I suppose," Wil said with a nod toward the approaching group.

"We'll get some time just for us later." Saera pulled him in for one more kiss. "Now, let's go show everyone what the TSS is all about."

◂ CHAPTER 24 ▸

Cocktail hour was well underway by the time Cris was able to grab a drink for himself. And after a talk with his parents, a drink was very much in order.

"What'll it be?" asked the bartender, a shorter man with a wholesome face and graying hair.

"What would you recommend for taking the edge off without messing with my head too much?"

"Your best bet is probably pomoliquor," the bartender replied, "but it can sneak up on you."

"That, please." Really, Cris would have accepted anything, but he at least recognized that liquor by name.

"Something troubling you?" The bartender handed Cris a miniature fluted glass filled with a deep red liquid.

"Only the fate of Taran civilization." Cris took the drink from him.

The bartender frowned, seemingly unsure if the statement was a joke or not.

Cris brushed it off with a smile and sipped his drink—hints of dark fruit with just the right amount of bite. "Thanks for this." He saluted the bartender with the glass. *Now to find Kate.*

He spotted his wife across the room still engaged in conversation with her brother, Kaiden.

Cris took a gulp of the drink, draining the glass to half-full. He put on his best smile and walked over to them. "Hello! Not talking too much business, I hope?" *Except that's exactly what we want to do.*

Kate smiled coyly. "Only catching up. Kaiden was just commenting on all the familiar faces in attendance."

"That's not surprising. Everyone's a relative if you go back far enough," Cris pointed out.

Kate nodded. "If you really think about it, just a handful of the people in this room control more of the most critical infrastructure for all of Taran society. SiNavTech and VComm have complete authority over transportation and telecommunications—"

"Well, the Priesthood always has final authority over what's said," Cris interjected.

Kaiden didn't flinch with the statement. In fact, he gave the hint of a nod.

He passed the first test. "Add in the connection to Talsari for TalEx's ore mining operations and MPS' power generation headed by Monsari, everything except for food and home-goods is covered."

"We control the future, when it comes down to it," Kate emphasized. "We have the power to shape Taran society."

"Not without a moral compass to guide us," Kaiden cautioned.

Cris raised an eyebrow. "Like the Priesthood?"

Kaiden shifted on his feet. "Or some entity."

So he's not in their pocket. "I sometimes wonder if having one organization with absolute authority is best for the people. I mean, you've seen some of the TSS now, Kaiden. Is this what the Priesthood led you to believe about us?"

"I can't say it is, no," he replied.

Cris went in for the kill. "It makes you wonder what else might be miscommunicated by always running through the same filter. As the communications hub for Tarans, I'd think that would be bad business for VComm to be party to disseminating unreliable information."

Kaiden's brow furrowed. The statement had caught him off-guard, but it was dead-on and he knew it. "We always strive to be as open and unbiased as possible."

"Of course," Kate said with exaggerated sincerity. "As is our duty to our people. And we would be remiss if we didn't remain flexible and adaptive as new information and circumstances come to light."

"Yes, as we must," Kaiden agreed.

"But that's enough heavy talk!" Kate cut in.

"Yes, here we've gone and talked business after all!" Cris exclaimed. "Forgive us."

Kate bowed her head to her brother. "Please, go enjoy yourself."

Kaiden smiled. "It's been a pleasure." He wandered back into the crowd.

"I'd say that went well," Cris said to Kate.

"I'm confident we'll have his support when the time comes," she concurred. *"And I was able to pull your maternal grandmother aside before I talked with Kaiden. It sounds like Talsari is becoming a bit disillusioned with the Priesthood, as well."*

"So that's three."

"Let's see if we can secure a fourth." She barely stopped for a breath before positioning for the next conversation. "It's been so long since we've seen your paternal grandparents."

Following her cue, Cris zeroed in on the next target—his cousin Sal, heir to Monsari. He was more than twenty years Cris' senior and had seemingly acquired a constant scowl from too many years reviewing financial tables for his family's company. "Sal has already taken over day-to-day operations for MPS. I've heard rumors that his father is going to retire soon."

Kate examined him. *"So it's Sal's vote we have to win."*

"Precisely. I've met him maybe four times in our lives."

"Have any sense of his loyalties?"

"None whatsoever."

"Let's find out." Kate led the charge. "Sal, hello!" she greeted. "I don't think we've talked much since Cris' and my wedding, which means it's been entirely too long. How are you?"

Sal was startled by the sudden engagement, nearly spilling his drink on himself. "Hello, uh… Kate. Nice to see you. "

"Thank you for taking the trip out here. What do you think of the TSS from the inside?"

"It's a bit cold." Sal wouldn't meet their eyes.

"Well, space, you know," Cris interjected. "Why they insisted on all this glass is beyond me."

"The view," Kate replied.

"Yes, the view," Sal stated without any effort to sound entertained.

"So, aside from the less than balmy temperature, are you finding your stay comfortable?" Cris prompted.

"Pleasant enough," Sal replied. "Though I could do without some of the company." He glared with distaste at a group of Agents on the other side of the room.

"You do realize we're Agents, too?" Cris asked.

"Like I said." Sal took a sip of his drink and sauntered away.

"That little—" Kate started, fuming in her mind.

"Yes, that could have gone a lot better." Cris rubbed Kate's back to set her at ease.

Kate took a deep breath. *"Who knows? He might be swayed in the future, but we won't be able to rely on the same sentiments as we can with the others."*

"No," Cris agreed with regret.

As they tried to spot others worth a quick conversation, Cris noticed Wil approaching.

"How are you faring?" his son asked.

"Happy and joyful," Kate said for cover.

"We feel confident in three of the six," Cris replied, catching

onto the hidden meaning.

"That's a decent start." Wil placed his hand on Cris' arm. "Why don't you take some time to enjoy the party?"

"Isn't that what I'm supposed to be telling you?" Cris shot back.

"We should probably listen to our own advice, then," Kate admitted.

Wil smiled. "See?" He searched around for Saera and waved to her across the room. "Besides, it's almost time for dinner."

Cris took Kate's hand. "Very well. The rest can wait."

After an hour and a half of appetizers and drinks, Michael's stomach rumbled its request for a proper dinner. He broke from his conversation with Ian and Kalin to eye the dining tables in the distance. "When are they going to feed us?"

"There's a whole buffet right there," Ian replied with a gesture toward the exquisite display of cheese and fruit several meters away.

Michael scowled. "I've already had enough grapes."

"Forget the main course—I'm anxious for dessert," Kalin chimed in.

Ian rolled his eyes. "Chocolate is all you think about."

Kalin grinned. "Well yeah, when it's in fountain form!"

"I have to agree with him on that point," Michael concurred, turning his attention to the tiered chocolate fountain between the open area for the cocktail hour and the dining tables.

"Who am I kidding? I can't wait, either," Ian yielded. "I bet we could sneak over there and—"

"Please take your seats in the dining room," an unfamiliar male voice announced over the intercom, halting Ian's scheming.

"They read our minds!" Kalin joked.

Michael smiled. "All in an attempt to prevent an uprising.

Hungry people are a force to be reckoned with."

Ian nodded gravely. "A truer statement was never spoken."

Ushers gently directed the guests down the concourse to the dining area.

When Michael and his friends approached the tables, he noticed a holographic seating chart suspended in the walkway. "Where did they put us?" he pondered out loud.

After studying the chart for a moment, Ian let out a huff. "You get to be all fancy while we're stuck in the back with the commoners." He used each of his hands to point to the respective positions on the chart.

"Head table!" Michael exclaimed.

"Have fun with that." Ian clapped him on the back, then headed with Kalin toward a table in the back row where the other Primus Elites were gathering.

Left on his own, Michael stepped cautiously toward the head table along the wall of the corridor. Seven chairs behind the table were decorated with an elegant bow of purple fabric. Wil and Saera were taking their seats at the center, with Marina and Elise to Saera's left, and Cris and Kate to Wil's right. Wil waved Michael over and gestured to the seat to his right at the end of the table.

Kate gave Michael a warm smile as he approached. "Looks like we'll be neighbors for the festivities," she said as she took her seat.

"I wasn't expecting to be up here with you," Michael replied and sat down, feeling exposed in his new position. A fresh glass of sparkling wine was waiting next to the silver place settings.

"The role in the ceremony carries through the evening," Kate stated. "While there's no way of knowing if you'd have more time out there with your friends than up here, I will say that at least we get served first."

Michael's stomach made another quiet plea. "That's reason enough for me."

Cris remained standing behind his chair on the other side of Kate, surveying the audience. When everyone was seated, he raised his hand to silence the crowd. "Thank you all for coming! Before dinner is served, I wanted to take a moment to acknowledge this special occasion. It's more than a wedding— which would have been reason to celebrate on its own. But more than that, today has started to bridge a longstanding gap between our people. For all of you to be here within the walls of the TSS would have been unthinkable only years before. We appreciate you demonstrating such an open mind and setting aside past differences."

The Tararian nobles at the front tables, including Cris' parents, stirred uncomfortably in their chairs.

They may be here, but I'm not sure how accepted we really are, Michael thought as he watched them squirm.

"I've had the honor of watching Wil and Saera come into their own, and to find strength in each other," Cris continued. "As a parent, I couldn't have asked for more than to see my son so happy. I know firsthand how important it is to have a partner with which to share my life. And with Wil and Saera, I have no doubt that they have an exceptionally bright future. Together, anything is possible." He pulled out his chair, preparing to sit. "But, there is more to their relationship than my singular vantage. I think we need to hear from their friends, too."

Michael's face instantly flushed. *That means me, doesn't it?* He glanced up from his empty plate to see Cris looking straight at him. He tried to shrink into his chair.

"Come on, Michael," Cris urged, beckoning Michel to stand as he sat down himself.

Reluctantly, Michael rose to his feet. *What am I supposed to say? I should have prepared something.*

Three hundred sets of eyes focused on him, sending an anxious flutter through his chest. He cleared his throat. "I've known Saera for most of my life, and the last three years with

Wil have felt like a whole other lifetime."

A chuckle rippled through the audience.

Michael hadn't meant it as a joke, but the audience's positive reception bolstered his confidence. "If there's anything that I've learned in my time here, it's that the TSS is a family. When I look at Wil and Saera, I see the greatest manifestation of that bond: love. Love for each other, and love for those around them. They are proof of how much stronger we are together than alone. I wish Wil and Saera the best in their lives together—as a couple and as part of the greater TSS family. May their love always be an inspiration!" He raised his glass. *Even if it's just a distant aspiration for someone like me.*

The members of the audience raised their own glasses in cheers.

Michael returned to his seat and gulped the sparkling wine.

"Nicely done," Cris said in his mind. *"Sorry to put you on the spot."*

"I should have expected it," Michael replied.

"Elise, would you like to say a few words, as well?" Cris asked.

The Maid of Honor pushed back her chair and stood, looking every bit as nervous as Michael had felt moments before.

"It's fine," Michael assured her.

Elise flashed him a quick smile down the table and turned her attention to the audience. "All right, I'm not much of a big group speaker," Elise began. "In fact, Saera and I first became friends because we were the quiet ones.

"I'll always remember the first day when I met Saera and she said she was from Earth. If you had asked me then if I thought she'd ever end up marrying the Sietinen heir, I would have laughed. But knowing her the way I do now, I couldn't imagine any other outcome. Never have I met a more intelligent, caring, and dedicated person," her voice cracked as she started to tear up. "I'm so very thankful to call her my friend. And I'm so glad she and Wil found each other despite the odds, because I can't imagine a more deserving couple." She raised her glass in a quick salute before ducking back to her seat.

Cris rose again and smiled out at the audience. "Thank you for the kind words. Now, I'm sure you're all anxious for dinner, so we won't make you wait any longer. While we eat, I hope you'll enjoy some entertainment courtesy of the TSS."

Michael came to attention as a hum of electromagnetic energy filled the air. Eight Agents had taken positions around the perimeter of the room, each with an orb of colored water suspended above their hands. The water orbs in pairs of teal, purple, deep blue, and silver rose out of the Agents' hands, circling above the heads of the audience in the center of the room.

Some of the Tararian nobles placed their hands above their heads to shield from water drops, but there was no need—the Agents skillfully kept the orbs in a perfect sphere without the slightest splash.

After two revolutions in the colored procession, the orbs each suddenly broke apart into into a dozen smaller forms. Silver glitter from atop the tables levitated to join with the water, and the main lights dimmed, replaced with colored laser lights in the same hues as the water. The Agents orchestrated a beautiful dance of water, glitter, and light—creating intricate forms of stars and spirals that swelled and swirled throughout the room.

Even the most wary members of the audience were soon smiling with delight as they watched the show, completely captivated.

Michael was so mesmerized by the show, himself, that he barely noticed when a plate of food was placed before him. The savory aroma pulled him from his reverie. He sliced off a piece from the generous steak main course and took a bite—by far the most tender and succulent he'd ever tasted. The sides of potatoes and green beans were equally delectable.

"Wow," he murmured, taking another bite of steak.

"Beats the regular TSS fare, doesn't it?" Kate commented to his left.

"I'll say."

He quickly devoured the remaining food on his plate.

The water and light show continued for the duration of the meal, casting rippling shadows over the walls as the display glittered overhead. When the final plates were emptied, the water split back into the original orbs and returned to the Agents, who placed it in transport containers at their feet.

Cris initiated applause, which was soon joined by every member in the audience—though a handful of nobles seemed reluctant to admit their enjoyment. The Agents bowed and silently slipped toward the exit.

"I hope you liked that display," Cris stated. "Now please, help yourselves to dessert and more drinks. Have a wonderful rest of your evening!"

Guests left their seats, returning to mingling with family and business associates as they enjoyed the dessert buffet.

"Back to it," Kate said with a smile to Michael, and walked hand-in-hand with Cris toward a group of nobles with Wil and Saera in tow.

Moving to the perimeter of the hall, Michael watched the bride and groom from a distance. The love that flowed between them was only a distant dream to have one day for himself.

"I know how it feels," a voice said to his side.

Michael turned to see High Commander Banks approach to his right. "What do you mean, sir?"

"To be the outsider looking in." Banks glanced at Kate with Cris. He smiled at Michael and wandered back toward the main festivities. "Have fun at the party."

I guess some of us need to make sure others stay on course, no matter the sacrifice. Michael decided to help himself to another round of dessert. Even if love was still out of reach, at least he could enjoy the chocolate fountain.

Mingling was hard work. Wil spotted an empty table and pulled Saera aside for a momentary reprieve from the post-dinner festivities. "I thought today was supposed to be about us?"

Saera laughed. "What gave you that idea? Weddings are for the family."

Wil let out a long breath. "At least it was on our terms."

"It's been a beautiful day, Wil. I couldn't be happier." Saera took his hand.

"I'm glad."

On the other side of the room, Wil spotted his parents still making the rounds with relatives.

"Something wrong?" Saera asked.

"No, you're right. Weddings are about the family."

Saera followed his gaze to Cris and Kate. "What are they talking about?"

"They're trying to impress on the guests that those of us in the TSS are just like anyone else and the Priesthood had no place to marginalize us."

"That's true…"

"But we're *not* like everyone else," Wil countered. "Abilities are a rarity, and no one without them can be expected to understand that power."

"So you think they're wasting their time trying to convince people otherwise?" Saera asked.

"No, broaching these topics *is* necessary. I just wish the venue was different."

Saera squeezed his hand. "I don't mind. I get to call you my husband now. If political dealings on our wedding day come with the territory, so be it."

Somehow she always knew what to say to set him at ease. "I'm so lucky to have you."

Saera scrunched up her nose. "And don't you ever forget it!"

He leaned in to kiss her and she slipped into his embrace. As he pulled back, he noticed his grandparents approaching. Quiet moments together were always too short lived. *"Back to it,"* he said to Saera and he stood. He smiled at his grandfather. "Are you having a good time?"

Reinen's brow was furrowed.

Alana responded on her husband's behalf, "It's wonderful."

"Yes," muttered Reinen. "But I'm confused about something."

"I'll answer if I can," Wil replied.

"Everyone within the TSS I've met talks about you like you're a legend. Why?"

How do I dodge this one? "Is it bad to be popular?"

Reinen shook his head. "It's more than that."

"Well, I'm in a pretty senior position for my age," Wil explained in an attempt to deflect from the real issue.

"It's almost like there's some plan for you that everyone knows about," Reinen mused.

Because there is? "I'm not sure what to say—"

"Wil is something of a celebrity around here," Cris cut in as he jogged up to rescue Wil. Kate was close behind him. "He did figure out the independent jump drive, after all."

Reinen frowned. "You're keeping something from me. You always have been."

Wil met his father's eyes. "Maybe we should just tell them. If you want to rally support, you won't get very far if you insist on keeping secrets."

Cris looked down, and Kate gave him a quick hug around his waist.

"Come on," Kate said to Saera, pulling away from Cris.

"Let's go get another drink and find your friends."

Wil and Cris were left alone at the back side of the rotunda with Reinen and Alana. No one else was nearby, but it was still out in the open.

"If we're going to do that, should we perhaps go somewhere more private?" Cris suggested.

"Why?" Wil questioned. "Everyone in the TSS already knows. The point is to get it out in the open."

"What do they know?" Reinen questioned, eyes narrow.

"About my role in defeating our enemy in the war." *One that could destroy your lives if I don't succeed.*

His grandparents were stunned to silence. Alana was the first to gather herself. "Cris, didn't you once mention a war? But you brushed it off then," Alana said. "Is there really a conflict we don't know about?"

Cris exhaled through grit teeth. "Are you sure about this, Wil?"

"I can't take all the secrecy anymore," Wil replied, knowing his father would understand. *I just hope this is the right move.* He focused on Reinen. "There is a war brewing with a race called the Bakzen. They are building their forces in a dimensional rift, preparing for an assault on the Taran people."

Reinen's face twisted with appalled disbelief. "That's ridiculous."

"In just a few years, I will be asked to lead the TSS forces against the Bakzen. To be successful, I need Seconds who can help me achieve my potential, and Saera is one of those people. That is why it was so important that we be together."

Reinen squinted. "Why have we never heard of this war?"

"For whatever reason, the higher powers have decided to keep it a closely guarded secret. That mandate has come down from the Priesthood." *And there's still so much more they won't tell us.*

"This all seems farfetched," Reinen dismissed.

Wil stood his ground. "Well, it's very real for me. Seven years ago when I came to Tararia, I wasn't recovering from a 'training accident.' I had been shot by a traitor working with the Bakzen, after I had been abducted by the Bakzen and rescued."

Reinen scowled. "If that's the case, why didn't you tell us the truth then?"

"Because we didn't know if we could trust you," Cris replied. "Frankly, we still don't. But resources within the TSS are tight enough that we could really use the support from SiNavTech to help us prepare for the final moves against the Bakzen. A front that Wil will lead."

Alana gazed at her son and grandson, her confusion morphing into horror. "If what you say is true, we have been very shortsighted indeed."

Reinen, stunned, stared at his wife. "You accept this?"

"I accept that there are things I do not know," Alana replied. "That includes the inner dealings of the TSS."

Wil nodded. "Very few know what we face. Still, I wish circumstances were different—that we could speak openly of the danger and rally support to win this fight. Instead, there's just been a trail of lies with broken relationships in its wake. It's led us here. But while our destination may be set, we can still control how we treat one another going forward."

Reinen growled with frustration, but his eyes were darting back and forth in thought. "I don't see how any part of this 'war' is possible…"

He's so wrapped up in his own world he doesn't want to acknowledge what's right in front of him. Just a little more... "You don't have to believe it, but it is *my* reality. And I can't help being at the center of the conflict."

Reinen shook his head and took a shaky breath. "You're asking me to change my entire way of thinking."

"I'm only asking you to open your mind so that we can find common ground." Wil paused. "We need to come together as a family. I would like to have you as an ally."

Reinen thought for a long moment and looked to his wife.

Tears welled in Alana's eyes. "Why would they lie to us, Rey? If we can't trust our own family, then who?"

Reinen swallowed. "Have you really been preparing to go to war this whole time?"

Cris nodded. "It's a grim reality, but it's one we can't ignore. Some might look down on the TSS, but we're the ones fighting to make sure they can keep those comfortable lives of luxury on the inner Taran worlds."

Reinen took a deep breath. "You shouldn't have to face it alone." He paused. "What do you need?"

Wil's heart leaped. *He actually wants to help us?*

Cris' eyebrows raised with surprise. "For starters, we need you to respect us," he replied. "We need people to stop seeing the TSS—and especially its Agents—as outsiders. Our abilities may set us apart, but they're not something to hide."

"Changing the public consciousness takes time," Reinen said.

Wil nodded. "All the more reason to start now." *Maybe by the time we're ready, they'll be able to see that the Priesthood isn't what it seems.*

"Let us work out those details, Wil. This has been enough depressing talk for one day," Cris cut in. "Your honeymoon comes first."

"Yes, that's right," Reinen agreed, clearing his throat.

I wish we had the time to spare for that. "We already took some time off recently."

Cris raised an eyebrow. "Those two days on Earth? No. The TSS can wait two weeks more for you—you need a proper vacation. I'll make sure the Primus Elites keep up on their training while you're away."

Wil was about to protest, but that time with Saera would mean too much—a gift he couldn't refuse. "And I'm guessing you already made some arrangements?"

His father beamed. "Of course."

"Is our island villa on Alushia, acceptable?" Reinen asked.

For the finest luxury and service money could buy, "acceptable" was a considerable understatement. "It's perfect. Saera will love it."

His father clapped him on the shoulder. "Now go find your bride. There's a shuttle prepped for you. See you in two weeks."

Wil said goodbye to his grandparents and went to look for his bride.

The spaceport had cleared out, with only a handful of guests still talking amongst themselves. Filled with a warm glow of contentment, Wil scanned over the happy faces. *I'd say today was a success.*

He found Saera chatting with her friends near the former dining area. He waved to her and jogged over. "Apparently we get a honeymoon after all."

Saera lit up. "Really?"

"Really." He held out his hand. "We're all packed and ready to go."

Saera glanced at her friends and took Wil's hand. "I guess we're heading out, then."

"Have fun," Elise told them.

Saera grinned. "We will."

Cris surveyed the remains of the party. "Are you sure an airlock didn't open at some point?" he asked Scott.

His friend smirked. "The carnage is just the sign of an event done right."

Cris worked his way around the room, taking mental inventory of the leftover supplies. Most of the food could be incorporated into the meal plan for the following day, but nearly half the alcohol cases behind the bar were still unopened. "We have way too much liquor left over."

"I find it impossible to consider that as a bad thing," Scott replied. "So many options…"

"Let's just stash it away," Cris suggested. "Hopefully we'll have more occasions to celebrate soon."

"An excellent point," Scott agreed. "I'll make sure all of this finds a good home. Now, go see off the rest of your guests."

Cris smiled. "Thank you." He started walking back toward the corridor hub. "And yes, you're welcome to take a couple of bottles as payment for your troubles."

"You read my mind."

With Scott handling the leftovers, Cris strolled through the nearly emptied port to make sure there were no straggling party guests. Most of the corridors were empty or occupied by only TSS guests. However, at the end of his inspection he spotted his parents walking toward the concourse reserved for visiting civilian vessels.

"Heading out?" Cris asked as he approached. *I'm surprised they didn't stop to say goodbye.*

"There you are," Reinen said. "We looked around but couldn't find you."

"Sorry, I've been helping with the cleanup. Thank you for coming." He paused, then added, "And for hearing us out."

Reinen nodded. "It's been quite a day. Very illuminating, indeed."

"I know much of what we revealed is difficult to believe," Cris continued. "It was a leap of faith telling you, but we've been divided for too long. We'll never get anywhere unless Tarans work together."

"I know." Then, in a burst of emotion Cris had never seen from his father, Reinen embraced him. "I'm so sorry for not listening to you before."

Cris awkwardly patted his father's back. "I wasn't always a very good listener, either."

Reinen pulled back, searching Cris' face. "We went astray so long ago. It took me years to recognize that you ran away because I'd never given you a reason to stay. Every time you've been back since then, I've wanted to pull you aside and tell you how I finally understood what you meant when you asked me if I worried about you—it was your way of saying you were unhappy, and I didn't listen. But I never had the courage. You are a far stronger man than I, Cris. I want you to know that despite our differences, I'm proud of you."

Alana hugged him from the side. "We both are."

"We have always loved you," Reinen said. "I'm sorry it took this long to say."

Cris almost choked, reliving years of pain and tension. He swallowed the lump in his throat. "That's all I ever wanted to hear from you." *One proclamation can't undo all the past years, but maybe there is hope for the future.*

His parents pulled back from the hug, and Reinen placed his hand on Cris' shoulder. "Let us know what you need to help you in your fight. We'll try to support you as best we can."

"Thank you," Cris acknowledged. "We will."

He showed his parents to their ship, for once parting ways with hugs. It would take some getting used to, but he was willing to put in the work.

After they departed, Cris wandered back toward the reception area hoping to find Kate. The last of the decorations had been put away, removing any evidence that the rotunda had been anything other than a functioning spaceport. Kate was nowhere to be seen, but he found Banks gazing out at the stars.

"Nice job officiating today," Cris commented.

Banks cracked a smile. "I didn't know I had it in me."

"Post-retirement side-job?" Cris quipped.

"You assume I'll ever retire."

"Distant dreams for anyone in TSS Command, I know…

"Maybe not," Banks said with a wistful sigh. "The next

generation will have to take over eventually."

Cris nodded. "The best we can hope for is to turn over a system worthy of inheritance."

"Does what we have now count?" Banks asked, suddenly serious.

The question caught Cris off-guard. "Of course." *Most of it, anyway.*

"Be honest—between old friends."

But a friend who reports to the Priesthood. "Any system needs some tweaking now and then."

"And who gets to decide those changes? "

Cris shook his head. "I'm still trying to figure that out."

Banks nodded, thoughtful. "For what it's worth, I think it should be a reluctant leader—not driven by self-interest, but a desire to fulfill the common good."

"Idealistic thinking."

"But find a way to balance idealism and practicality, and things might just change for the better."

"We'll have a chance to rebuild after the war, when the time is right," Cris assured him. "And we'll make it the best it can be."

Haersen stepped into the rebuilt office of the Imperial Director. It was now the most significant location in the Bakzeni Empire—the seat of power for both civil administration and military force. He would likely be the only Taran to ever enter the room, and for that he was honored.

Tek was gazing out the window. It was rare to see him indulging in luxuries like a view, but his new position him granted those moments of reflection.

"All of the bases have reported in," Haersen announced. "Your authority is acknowledged and unquestioned by all remaining senior officers."

"Final casualties?" Tek questioned.

"3,572," Haersen replied, "87 of which were officers."

Tek scoffed. "It still surprises me that the drones have strong enough opinions worth dying for."

"Imprinting is imperfect."

"Indeed. The flexibility of loyalty is difficult to express." Tek turned his gaze out the window once more. "Soon all of those worlds out there will be ours."

"We are well on our way to achieving that goal."

"Have the new drones been deployed to the edge of the rift?" Tek asked.

Haersen smiled. "Well, the casualty number I quoted wasn't entirely accurate. Komatra realized we could subdue the drones that remained loyal to the previous command structure. They will make the perfect tools to begin forming the new pathways."

Tek nodded. "Excellent thinking."

"The Tarans will never see us coming."

PART 3: REVELATIONS

◄ CHAPTER 25 ►

A chill ran down Wil's spine. Whispers filled his mind, beckoning. He looked around the dark room, but saw nothing out of place. *What was that?* "Did you…?"

His men were watching him from around the edge of the freefall chamber. Their eyes glowed softly against the artificial starscape.

"Are you okay?" asked Michael, who was floating just to his left.

Wil shrugged it off. "Yes. Sorry, I thought I heard something." He returned his attention to the training session.

The Primus Elite trainees had all progressed to Junior Agents, far stronger than anyone had anticipated. Wil had been working with them every day for just under five years, and that training was nearly complete. The daily exercises had made them a tight-knit group, and his Captains were trusted advisors and knew how to carry out his orders with precision.

"You're just losing it from spending too much time in subspace," Ian joked.

It's probably true. Wil had spent the last year focusing on spatial dislocation with his men. His four Captains and five of the other trainees had already mastered hovering on the brink of subspace in the maneuver affectionately known as "stopping time," but Wil's own training had taken it a step further. He was still struggling with simultaneous observation—perceiving tactical movements on the two habitable dimensional planes so he could anticipate where and when a Bakzen ship would jump to the other plane. To do so, Wil effectively needed to oscillate between the planes, passing back and forth so quickly that he would be in both almost at once.

He knew the theory behind what he must do, but he was struggling with the execution. Though he kept trying, he couldn't seem to hold both places in his mind at the same time. He was growing increasingly more anxious over the impasse, because he knew that simultaneous observation was his entire purpose in the war. If he couldn't do it, then Tarans would remain at a major disadvantage in any battle against the Bakzen.

"Come on, let's run through it again," Wil said. *We need to keep trying. Even if it is driving me crazy.*

Michael and Ian took their positions to either side of Wil at the center of the freefall chamber. Around the perimeter, the men regrouped into their core team of specialists. Each man held a tablet that was serving as an analog for the controls of a vessel. The purpose of the exercise was to hone the timing of telepathic orders coming from Wil and his Captains, reducing the lag between commands and action. They had been making progress, but Wil kept pushing them for even greater response times. *Milliseconds could make the difference, we don't know.*

Wil surveyed the room. Everyone appeared to be in position. *"Fleet?"* asked Wil telepathically.

"Fleet check," replied Michael. He was Wil's second-in-command responsible for relaying Wil's orders to the battleships with the help of his team.

"Tactical?"

"Tactical check," replied Ian, the team lead for special tactical assaults.

"Pilots?"

"Primus team check," replied Ethan, the lead for the Primus Elite pilot specialists.

"Pilot command check," replied Curtis, who was responsible for relaying commands to the precision strike groups in the larger TSS fleet.

The telepathic communications were almost instantaneous, in theory, but in a real battle scenario his men would need to interpret field data, and that would cause delays. The tighter they could get their own communications, the faster they would be when it mattered most.

Wil took slow, even breaths as he became the hub of the telepathic network. He slipped into a relaxed state of consciousness, hovering on the brink of subspace. It wasn't the state of simultaneous observation he ultimately needed to achieve, but it was as close as he could hold for any meaningful duration.

He doled out commands, and his men responded. He tried to keep the commands varied and seemingly random so they couldn't fall into a comfortable rhythm of familiarity. Likewise, inventing new scenarios kept Wil fresh. As they worked, the tablets recorded all the inputs, which they would review after the session to identify the places where they still needed the most work.

Wil was completely focused on giving orders when whispers again intruded into his mind. This time, however, the echoes formed words. *"We're coming."*

Wil pulled his consciousness back to the physical plane, his heart racing. The voice was familiar. *Is it them?*

His men were looking at him expectantly, waiting for him to complete his telepathic orders. In particular, Michael and Ian seemed almost alarmed that he had cut off the instructions so abruptly.

Wil took a deep breath. He had spent years touching subspace in such a manner, but never before had he felt a sentient presence. But a mysterious consciousness seeking him out—that was all too similar to his brief touch with the Aesir after the Headquarters break-in more than two years prior. *Am I just losing my mind or is it real? Maybe I need a break.* "Okay, that should be enough data collection for this session. Team leads, please run an analysis and get me a report before our check-in this afternoon. We'll discuss next steps then. Dismissed."

The Captains exchanged glances and the other men started heading toward the only door in the chamber. The practice session was scheduled to run for another hour, and such sessions were almost never cut short.

Wil noticed his Captains staying behind. "Go on," he told them, "you have work to do."

The Captains looked at each other again and nodded to Wil. They were far too trained and familiar with Wil's normal behavior to believe everything was fine, but they also respected his instructions, however irregular.

Wil took a few minutes to settle his nerves before exiting the freefall chamber. He found Michael waiting for him in the hall. Since the wedding two years before, he had remained a close friend to Wil and Saera, and with Michael working as a Second alongside Saera, Wil had been able to push himself further than with any other combination.

"What was going on with you today?" Michael asked. As Wil's second-in-command, it wasn't uncommon for him to be the voice of the group—and to be rather blunt when he did so.

"There was some weird energy in subspace today. I don't think it's anything to worry about." *Let's hope that's all it was. If they are coming for me now...*

Michael's mouth was drawn with concern. "Are you sure you're doing okay?"

"Yeah, just a little tired. I'll be fine."

"You've been wearing yourself pretty thin lately," Michael continued.

"I have to," Wil countered. "I'm running out of time to learn simultaneous observation."

"Burning yourself out won't do any good."

Am I heading toward burnout? But it's been this way my whole life—why is now any different? "It's hard for me to keep an objective perspective on my own state."

"So I hope you'll take our concern to heart." Michael paused for a moment. "Saera asked me to keep an eye on you in practice. Even she's worried about you."

That's not surprising. Saera had become even more protective of Wil since they had married, but he knew that was her way of looking out for him as the demands of his duty to the TSS threatened to take him from her. "Thank you, but I'm fine. Really."

Michael nodded. "Okay." It was clear from his tone that the matter wasn't resolved, but was willing to let Wil have some space for the time being.

He really does know me well. "I'm going to hole up in a study room down here and get some spec reviews done. I'll see you this afternoon."

"See you then."

Wil exhaled, trying to release the tension that had been building in his chest. *Now for some quiet time.*

Banks rubbed his eyes wearily. It wasn't even lunchtime yet and it already felt like it had been a long day. *That's never a good sign.*

He sighed and brought up his e-mail. As usual, there were tedious reports from Agents about various missions, a few progress write-ups on Junior Agents nearing graduation, and far too much other mundane business. He browsed through the message list and marked a few items for later follow-up. He was trying to invent an excuse to take an early lunch when the touchscreen on his desktop suddenly shuddered—going blank before returning with a pixelated flash. *What was that?* It looked like a hiccup in the Mainframe, but that seemed highly unlikely.

Banks studied the screen. It appeared to be functionally normally again. *I should let the Communications team know just in case—*

The viewscreen on the wall of his office illuminated in a pixelated flash, like what had passed over the desktop. The desktop again shuddered, and both screens went black. White text simultaneously appeared on the two screens: "Bring us the Cadicle."

Stars no! Banks leaped to his feet. He snatched his handheld from the charging pad on his desktop. Trying to control the shaking of his hands, he called Wil's handheld. Banks paced across his office as he waited for Wil to pick up. The agonizing moments dragged on.

Wil finally answered. "Yes, sir?"

"Where are you?"

"Down on Level 11. Why?"

"Wil, the Aesir are here for you."

"Now?" He didn't sound completely surprised.

"There was a message. I haven't received any notice of a ship's arrival yet, but I'm sure you don't have much time. If you want to say any goodbyes—"

Wil hung up before Banks finished his sentence.

Banks took an unsteady breath. *I can only hope he's prepared for whatever test they have for him. There's no escape.*

An alarm chirped. "Proximity alert. Unauthorized ship," CACI announced.

Bomax. Already? "Where?"

"The primary vessel has docked at the TSS port, and a shuttle has landed at the terminal on the surface," CACI replied.

How could they move so quickly? "Allow them to take the elevator to this level. Lock down the rest of Headquarters." However, after how easily the Aesir had overridden the security systems before, he doubted the lockdown would do any good.

Banks rushed down the long hallway to the central elevator lobby. As he waited for the Aesir, his heart pounded in his ears. *What are they going to do with him?* He paced to pass the time, trying to settle his nerves.

Without warning, the elevator door opened and the lights in the lobby simultaneously cut out. Only a single emergency light above the elevator remained lit. Banks froze. *They have control of the Mainframe again. We're helpless.*

In the dim light, Banks recognized the three figures as Oracles, though he had never seen one in person. There were two men and one woman, though few distinguishing features of gender were visible through their dark robes. They peered into the lobby.

"Where is the Cadicle?" the male Oracle in the center demanded. "You cannot keep him from us."

Can I really just hand him over? "Please, don't take him. If he doesn't survive…"

The Oracle glared, his eyes glowing white orbs. "If he does not survive, then he is not who you think."

"He's still so young—"

"If he is not ready to see now, then he never will be," the Oracle replied.

The three Oracles closed their eyes for a moment. "We have found him." The controls lit up on the elevator. "Go to him with us," the Oracle commanded. "We must speak with you."

Banks felt someone in his mind, but he was unable to keep them out. He was compelled to comply.

Wil ran down the hall toward the Primus classrooms. *I need to get to Saera while I still can.*

He arrived at his wife's classroom, finding that the door was locked. *Banks must have instituted a lockdown.* He palmed open the door. At the front of the class, Saera was trying to sooth her students. She looked at Wil with surprise when he appeared in the doorway.

"Saera, come here," Wil said.

"Everything's going to be fine, hold on," Saera said to the class. She jogged over to meet Wil in the hallway. "What's—?"

"The Aesir are here to take me." *It was only a matter of time.*

"Wil…" Saera threw her arms around him. Though no one knew much about the Aesir, Wil had said enough for her to know what the visit meant.

Wil hugged her back. "I couldn't leave without seeing you one more time, in the event…"

Saera pulled back and took a deep breath. "You can handle whatever test they have for you."

"I'll try."

The lights in the hall cut out.

Saera gasped. "What's happening?" Saera inched closer to Wil.

"The Aesir must be on their way into Headquarters."

Wil embraced his wife in the complete blackness. After a few moments, some emergency lights flickered on. He swallowed. *That must be my cue.* "I have to go. I love you always."

Saera pulled him in for a kiss. "I love you, too. Be careful."

Wil pulled away from Saera and strode resolutely down the hall. As he passed through the corridor, the overhead lights illuminated to form a path to the elevator lobby.

The lobby was empty. A single light was illuminated above one elevator, though the doors were closed. Wil took a deep breath. *Try to believe in yourself.*

As Wil approached the elevator, the doors opened. Three figures stepped out, and Wil saw Banks standing at the back of the elevator, staring at the floor.

The three strangers were robed in black with the iridescent fabric draping to the floor, contrasting with their pale skin—

translucent flesh that had never felt the unfiltered light of a real sun. Their eyes were faint blue, almost white, but they glowed in the dim light. They seemed to see right through Wil, looking at his very core. Wil struggled to retain composure as the figures studied him with unblinking eyes.

"Cadicle," the center figure said, a slim man. "The Aesir have felt your presence ripple the fabric of existence. We must see if you are worthy of such power."

"I am ready to be tested," Wil replied, trying to sound confident. *The Aesir! What happens if they don't deem me worthy?*

Banks stepped out of the elevator, looking distracted. "We await your return to Headquarters," he said to Wil. *"Be careful,"* he added telepathically.

"Yes, sir." *I hope I will see this home again.*

"Come with us, Cadicle," said the robed figure on the right, a woman.

Wil stepped onto the elevator, feeling the intense presence of the three Aesir. The air hummed with their power. *Never have I felt another like them. Is this what it's like for others to be around me?*

Banks stood motionless, processing the cryptic information the Oracle had disclosed in the elevator. With his mind racing, he gazed at the closed door through which Wil had just departed. *"What was lost can still be rebuilt. A descendant of Dainetris is alive, but she cannot be saved. A son, under the proper care, might prosper."*

Banks didn't know what to think. *Is it possible one of the Dainetris Dynasty survived after their fall?* It was conceivable. Only the Aesir and the Priesthood would be privileged to such knowledge. If it was true, such a living heir could change the face of Tararian politics—a return of the seventh High Dynasty. *Of all people, they entrust this information to me?*

‹ CHAPTER 26 ›

The Aesir ship was docked at the end of the port fixed above the moon's surface. Though similar in size to a mid-class TSS cruiser, its form was ethereal by comparison. The hull swept backward in rounded ridges, meeting in a conical protrusion at the back end of the ship, which Wil imagined was the jump drive.

He was led up the gangway into the ship. Inside, the halls were elegant arched passageways with soft blue lights set in recesses that gave the impression of glowing crystals. The design was alien in many regards, but Wil found something about the ship comforting. After a few moments, he realized that the pleasant feeling came from the vibration of the ship, as if it were resonating on the same frequency as his own body. It made him feel more at home than he had in any other place.

Wil was escorted down the hall and ushered into an airy conference room. The far wall was glass, and a clear, circular table occupied the center of the room. The same eerie lights from the hallway were inset in the ceiling above the conference table, branching down like a chandelier.

Several robed Aesir were standing by the window, and they encircled the table when Wil entered the room. They had the same translucent skin and pale, glowing eyes of his escorts.

Wil removed his tinted glasses and placed them in his jacket pocket. The expressions on the faces of the Aesir didn't change, but Wil felt like they were pleased with the action. He waited in front of the table for one of his hosts to take charge. As they stood watching each other, Wil felt a vibration through the floor—preparations for a spatial jump. Within moments, the view outside the window changed from a starscape to shifting blues and greens. The Aesir all closed their eyes for a moment as the ship eased into subspace, and when they opened their eyes they seemed more relaxed.

"We have waited so long for this moment, Cadicle," said one of the Aesir on the far side of the table. "We are the highest order of Oracles among the Aesir, and we have been tasked with evaluating your worthiness of the title Tarans have bestowed upon you."

"I am honored to be in your presence," Wil said and bowed to them. *How will they evaluate me?*

"We have awaited the Cadicle since before we ventured into the stars so many years ago. For generations we have willed true balance to return, and now we have reason to hope that day will finally come," the Oracle continued.

What is he talking about? "I will play my part as best I can."

"I am Daehl," said the Oracle. "I have been selected as the representative for the Aesir."

"Pleased to meet you. You can call me 'Wil.'"

"If you truly are the Cadicle, no other name is necessary," Daehl replied.

Clearly, 'Cadicle' means more to them than to anyone on Tararia. "As you wish."

The ship dropped out of subspace.

"We have arrived," said Daehl.

Wil gazed out the window. There was a black pit marring the starscape—not a black hole gravity well, but more like a tear in reality. He was inexplicably drawn to the void. "Where are we?"

Daehl's face remained expressionless. "The nexus. Can't you feel it?"

Wil did feel it, though he couldn't place exactly what it was. The pull toward the void grew stronger the longer he looked at it—his sense of self drifting away. He yanked himself back. "What is it?"

"It is a window to everything that was and everything that can be," Daehl said as he came around the table toward Wil. "Come, it is time."

Daehl led Wil and the other Oracles into the hall and down the corridor. At the end of the hall, they passed through a set of double doors that slid open when Daehl held up his hand. The room was fully glass—a bubble positioned below the cone that likely contained the jump drive. The void loomed outside to the right of the room.

The Aesir lined up on the left facing the void. Wil walked to the middle of the glass enclosure.

"All Oracles must learn to read the energy patterns woven into the fundamentals of our existence," Daehl said. "To be named among us, you too must perform this rite."

Is that my test? Wil glanced at the void. "What will I see?"

"In time, you will be able to read all that is there to be known. But at first, you will see a truth that will forever change you. The truth will be revealed based on what is in your innermost self—what you need to see most. It is different for everyone. Some cannot bear what they see and are driven mad. Others simply lose themselves in the void and their consciousness never returns to their body."

No wonder this test is feared. Wil looked at the void again with renewed seriousness.

"Proceed whenever you are ready," instructed Daehl.

What am I supposed to do? Wil's heart pounded in his ears, his mind jumbled with thoughts of his life back home. *I need to succeed here. For my family. For the TSS. For Tararia.*

Trying to refocus, he began the process of spatial dislocation—that seemed like the most appropriate action. Still weighed down by trepidation, he found it difficult to achieve the state hovering on the brink of subspace. He wanted to hang onto himself, where he had some sense of control. To let go from the physical world was not freeing as it had once been, but was rather a step toward a dangerous unknown in the presence of the void.

He forced himself to let go, despite his internal cries to turn back. As he pierced the dimensional veil, he balked. The sweet call of the rift wasn't there—no glow of energy to fuel him or give him a sense of direction. He was drifting.

Without thinking, he retraced the path back to himself while he still knew where to go.

He gasped as he returned to normal space, drinking in the air and energy around him. The familiar—the tangible.

The Aesir watched him with sadness in their eyes, though their impassive expressions remained otherwise unchanged.

They think I've failed. He couldn't give up. Wil took a deep breath and closed his eyes. *I have to let go—I need to trust. I am one with the pattern. I can't lose myself, because it is part of me.* The fear and doubts melted away, replaced by a commitment to fulfill his purpose for being. He opened his eyes again and gazed into the void.

At first, he drifted in its emptiness. He was a single speck in an infinite sea of blackness. Alone, lost. He looked around himself and found nothing. Desperate to feel connected, he searched—not with panic this time, but driven by a profound need to find grounding.

The emptiness sprawled before him, open and infinite. Then, a pattern started to emerge. The blackness became a web. Initially, it was jumbled, chaotic. But as he continued to stare at the silvery tendrils branching through the limitless beyond, he saw a new kind of order. What was once an empty void came alive as a woven tapestry.

He was bound to the tendrils, as though he could reach out

and tug the snaking forms to send a ripple through the fabric of the energy field underlying reality. The tendrils shifted and twisted around one another, with no beginning and no end. Wil delved further into his place within the energy network, tracing the tendrils that held the strongest ties to himself. But couldn't see where the tendrils led. He let go from his sense of self just enough to gain a better vantage. As he drifted outward, he saw branches spanning the Taran worlds—tightly woven tendrils through the fabric, amid holes and fainter connections. It was as if the lines of an ancient, uniform grid had been pulled and stretched to strengthen the corridors of communications and transit between the dominant worlds. Some corridors between the epicenters of activity were new, while others were so old that they were almost indistinguishable from the very foundation of the fabric.

The more he explored his place in the vast network, he felt pulled in two directions. The first was to Tararia, the home of his parents and countless generations of ancestors before. The other was out into a part of space he couldn't place at first, but then he knew—the Bakzen. Yet, there was something mitigating the opposite pulls, maintaining tentative balance within his own existence even as it changed the shape of the larger network. He searched, grasping for the answer in the depths of the void. And then, the key emerged. The opposing forces on Wil—to his homeland and his enemy—were balanced through a connection between the Bakzen and Tararia. They were three points of a triad within the network.

Looking closer, Wil saw that the fabric around Bakzen Territory was twisted and deformed. Whereas the corridors between other worlds were woven by freely flowing tendrils that bent from the ancient uniform grid, the tendrils to Bakzen space were pulled taught—leaving holes in spaces where it seemed that the natural grid should flow. The tendrils were being rearranged before his eyes, being torn away. As each tendril was yanked from its proper place, a shudder ran down the surrounding tendrils, straining the connections. The fabric was fraying.

Wil's eyes shot open. *What does it mean?* He turned around to face the Aesir.

Now they were watching him with fascination. "What did you see?" Daehl asked.

"I saw a cosmic energy field," Wil replied. "But I'm not sure what to make of it."

"If you know the question, you already know the answer."

"I'm not sure I do. What is the connection between the Bakzen and Tararia? Some kind of common history?" *Do I exist to maintain the balance between them? It looked like the pattern was trying to right itself—make order out of new chaos that has upset ancient ways.*

"You already know," Daehl said.

A common ancestry... "Are the Bakzen of Taran descent?"

"It is more than that. Did you not see the age of the connection?"

True. It was linked to new tears in the fabric—not anything born of systematic progression. "If they aren't a natural divergent race, then... they were made." *So, Tarans made the Bakzen?*

Daehl nodded. "You do indeed have the gift of sight." The Aesir bowed their heads to Wil.

Is that possible? "It doesn't make any sense. Why would Tarans manufacture such an enemy?"

Daehl raised his gaze to look Wil in the eye. "Now you are asking the wrong question."

Wil thought for a moment. "What turned the Bakzen into our enemy?"

"That is the right question. But the answer is something you must find on your own. The Aesir left Tararia to escape the path that led to the Bakzen. You must seek truth from those still bound to Tararia and the Bakzen's creators."

Who are their creators?

"You already know," the Aesir Oracles answered in unison inside his mind, reading his deepest thoughts through his safeguards.

The Priesthood?

"Our brethren. Too blinded by impatience to see the consequences of their actions."

Wil shook his head, his brow furrowing. "What was the Priesthood trying to accomplish?"

"Your High Commander knows," Daehl said.

Has such a truth been kept from me all these years…?

Daehl nodded. "They worry that you will not do what needs to be done."

"What, defeat the Bakzen?" *Even if I don't want to.*

The Aesir voices once again echoed in his mind, *"You must. The Bakzen should never have come to be."*

"But they *were* created." *You can't unmake what is already alive.*

"They do not belong," stated Daehl. "Their existence is an anomaly. So long as they remain, there will not be balance in the greater pattern. You saw how they are ripping it apart. They have such power, yet they use it to tear rifts in the fabric of reality. Driven by hate, they will stop at nothing. They will destroy us all."

Wil took a deep breath. "So I must do what the Priesthood commands? Eliminate the Bakzen to rectify their creators' mistakes."

"And to restore Tarans to the true path." Daehl looked at him levelly. "It must be you to do it."

It is what I was born to do, apparently.

"You misunderstand. It must be you, because you are what the Bakzen should have been. Through you, their legacy can live on as it was meant to be."

Wil's eyes narrowed. "What do you mean?"

Daehl looked down. "We have already said too much. We are but observers."

"No, please," pleaded Wil. "If I must do this, then I need to know why."

"You need only know this: you must fulfill your destiny. Only then can Tarans move forward."

"I can't see my own future path in the pattern." *Only what ties me to the Bakzen and my people.*

"You will see it once you are ready," Daehl assured. He looked around at the other Oracles, who nodded solemnly. "You are what we have been waiting for since we left Tararia a thousand years ago. You, Cadicle, are the Enlightened One who can take Tarans from their infancy and realize the full potential of what is held within. You are the first of what Tarans can become. The Bakzen must die so that we can begin to truly live."

"What of the Aesir? Will you continue to watch from afar as the Taran future is rewritten?"

The Oracles shook their heads. "Not rewritten," Daehl said. "It is a return to what should have been all along. There is no longer a place for us on Tararia. Eventually, others may join us here. You will always have a home with us, if you wish it."

"My ties to others are too strong to become one of the Aesir."

Daehl nodded. "It is an open offer. But for now, you must go back to complete what the Priesthood started."

The door to the office flew open, startling Banks.

Wil barged in. "Banks, we need to talk. Now."

That isn't the return home I envisioned. What happened out there? Banks stood up behind his desk. "Wil, I'm glad they got you home so quickly. It's only been a few hours—"

"Why didn't you tell me?" Wil's eyes narrowed behind his tinted glasses, accusing. He slammed the door closed.

"Tell you what?"

"About the Bakzen."

Stars! Banks held up his hand to silence Wil. "There's nothing to discuss," he said as cover while he hurriedly used his desktop to activate a communications shield to keep the conversation private from potential Priesthood ears and eyes. "The room is secure. Now, what about them?"

"That Tarans made them. That we made them and now we're trying to wipe them out of existence!"

"Wil, there's a lot more to it than that—"

"There have been enough excuses and justifications. I want the straight truth for once." Even with the dampeners in Headquarters, there was still a telekinetic hum in the air as Wil struggled to maintain composure.

Banks looked down. *Our greatest secret.* "Yes, Taran scientists made the Bakzen."

"What the fok is going on? How did we end up at war with each other?" The hurt was written on Wil's face.

He won't back down now. Banks' chest tightened. *We have tried to prevent him knowing for his whole life, and now he finds out just before we need him most in the war. So that was the Aesir's plan...* "We kept the truth from you because it's easier to think of the Bakzen as an alien enemy. Knowing they were once close to us makes what we must do that much more difficult."

Wil shook his head. "Is that why the entire war has been kept secret? Because it would eventually trace back to that truth?"

"That's part of it," Banks confirmed. "But the creation of the Bakzen is only a fraction of the history the Priesthood is hiding."

Wil looked on, expectant.

Banks sat back down. "It all traces back to the Taran revolution a thousand years ago," he explained. "Back then, the Priesthood was a religious order, dealing primarily in philosophical and metaphysical pursuits. However, the organization became divided. One branch was more drawn to spiritual growth, the other to science. At the core of both ideologies was the foretelling of the Cadicle—one who would be a prototype for a new generation of Tarans that would be one step closer to true ascension and enlightenment. The more spiritual branch—who became the Aesir—believed that the Cadicle would emerge in due time, when Tarans were ready to ascend into a higher state of being. The other branch—who became the Priesthood we know today—sought to bring about the coming of the Cadicle through deliberate scientific intervention."

Wil sat down in one of chairs on the other side of Banks' desk. "What kind of intervention?"

"Dissection of the Taran genetic code. The Priesthood became convinced that the answer to ascension must be buried somewhere in the genome, so they began manipulating the DNA sequences related to telekinetic and telepathic abilities to find a combination that strengthened those traits. Eventually, they did. But, the physical form of Tarans struggled to command the power unlocked by those enhanced abilities. They needed a vessel with which to imbue the abilities."

"The Bakzen."

Banks nodded. "Yes."

"What went so wrong?" Wil asked.

Everything. Banks took a deep breath. *Telling him all of this might get us both killed if the Priesthood finds out.* "The Priesthood forced evolution too strongly. It was not enough to create the Bakzen—they also wanted to take the existing population into a new era. The Aesir opposed this course, warning that such direct manipulation of Taran evolution would not be sustainable, but the Priesthood insisted on forging ahead. The Priesthood's scientists synthesized a biological nanoagent to adjust the genetic code of every living person within the known Taran worlds. When the Aesir learned of the plan, they departed Tararia before they were 'infected.' That split marked the beginning of the Taran Revolution."

"An era of cultural advancement and rapid colonization," Wil said.

That's what the history records state, anyway. "And nearly 350 years passed in this new age of prosperity. The Taran people had embraced their heightened abilities, and meanwhile, the Priesthood had cultivated the Bakzen subspecies to be our guardians. The Bakzen were an icon of perfection—cloned from a master copy to ensure the proper transmittal of the traits, and sterile to make sure it stayed that way. But then, everything changed. Without warning, after the twelfth generation of children born to Taran descendants who had received the nanoagent, the telekinetic abilities suddenly disappeared.

"There was public outcry, and the Priesthood desperately tried to find a solution. But they couldn't figure out what happened. At first, they called it a fluke, but the abilities remained absent in subsequent generations. Outcry turned to dejection, and eventually to apathy. Just when telekinetic and telepathic feats were a distant memory for all but the Bakzen— who had by that point been relegated to the outskirts of society—the eighth generation after the loss once again expressed abilities. Those abilities grew stronger for the next two generations, before dwindling. By the thirteenth generation, the abilities were absent again. That cycle of twelve generations, with only the last five expressing any ability, has repeated ever since."

Wil contemplated for a moment. "I knew I was Tenth Generation, but I thought abilities had always been on a cycle like that."

"Most do." *The Priesthood has rewritten history so most wouldn't know any better.*

"And if people found out—or remembered—that everyone used to have abilities and the Priesthood tampered with their existence…"

Banks inclined his head. "Revolts, civil war—there's no knowing how people may react. But, it's certain the Priesthood would fall, and self-preservation has become their singular driver. So the Bakzen, the war, and our common history has remained hidden."

Wil grimaced. "They change the entire course of history for our race and just pretend like nothing happened?"

"Essentially."

"So there's no solution to the Generation issue?" Wil asked.

"Well," Banks continued, "with the complete genetic map across all the generations at their disposal, the Priesthood was finally able to identify the anomaly causing the Twelve-Generation Cycle. Unfortunately, they found that the mutation was so embedded in the root of the genetic code that no nanoagent was capable of making the repair. The only way full abilities could be restored was through natural evolution— essentially, selective breeding. A report summarizing these findings somehow got leaked to the general public, and there was another uprising when everyone realized what the Priesthood had done. In an act of desperation to save their institution, the Priesthood decided to make the Bakzen the scapegoats."

Wil frowned, a crease deepening between his eyebrows. "How so?"

Through unconscionable selfishness. "What was the best way to get people to forget why they were upset? To make those lost abilities into an evil. And who best embodied all those abilities? The Bakzen. The Priesthood launched what became a propaganda campaign to set a new cultural norm, where telekinetic abilities were something to be looked down upon."

Wil nodded, thoughtful. "My father has mentioned that things were different when he was younger, compared to how it is now."

The Priesthood has yet again changed the public consciousness to suit their needs. "Yes, there was another shift in recent years—beginning shortly before you were born. But several hundred years ago, the public denouncement was at its peak."

"So the Bakzen were ultimately driven away?"

Banks hung his head and let out a pained breath. "Oh, it was far more than that. After a few generations of telekinesis being a thing of shame and people hiding any abilities they may have, the public sentiment reached critical mass. People called for the forced removal of the Bakzen. And the Priesthood had a swift way of dealing with the Bakzen issue: they simply outlawed cloning of full bodies. Of course, anything like an organ or limb was acceptable, as we do today, but nothing that could house a sentient mind. This law essentially disallowed the only reproductive means of the Bakzen."

"No wonder they hate us." Wil looked sick.

They have every right to. We started the conflict. "Up to that point, the Bakzen had been generous and accommodating. But, when their very existence was threatened, they stood up for themselves. When the political powers on Tararia sought to enforce the new anti-cloning laws, the Bakzen fled from the inner Taran colonies and found a new homeworld for themselves."

"So, then, how did the war get started? I was told the Bakzen attacked an unarmed freighter." The crease between Wil's eyebrows continued to deepen.

Even I haven't been able to find the truth about the beginning of the war. "I would tell you if I knew, Wil," Banks said. "My best guess? That freighter was carrying a biological weapon meant to exterminate the Bakzen. And the diplomats that were supposedly murdered in cold blood? I suspect that they were dispatched to once again enforce the anti-cloning laws, and the Bakzen were sending a powerful 'leave us alone' message."

Wil looked horrified. "How can you go along with all of this? I—"

"What choice do we have? This all happened hundreds of years ago. Hatred for Tarans has been engineered into the Bakzen ever since then. Whatever common ground our peoples once shared, that was phased out long before our lifetimes."

"That doesn't make it right!"

"No, but we have to think of ourselves."

Wil hung his head. "It was thinking of ourselves that led to this atrocity."

"I don't deny that."

"Yet, you are one of the insiders."

I only accepted this assignment because it was the one way I could infiltrate the Priesthood. Banks looked Wil in the eye. "I serve the TSS."

"Which reports to the Priesthood."

"Yes, but not all roles have clear distinctions." Banks folded his hands on the desktop. "Wil, I'm even older than your father. I grew up in a time where anyone with telekinetic gifts was an outcast. I was fortunate to be accepted as an Agent trainee with the TSS, and early in my career I discovered the seldom-acknowledged fact that the TSS reports to the Priesthood. I thought that by serving the TSS I could make things better for others like me." *Except the higher up I got, the more I realized that the Priesthood wasn't in it for the people. But, there's still hope.* His years of service were made worthwhile by having had the chance to mold Cris from a young age—from back when he was still just a rebellious High Dynasty heir who had already spoken out against the Priesthood. That opportunity to help shape the thinking of someone with real influence was a chance to enact true change.

"And what have you accomplished?" Wil asked, snapping Banks out of his reflection.

"It's not all about the present." *Seeing what you and your father are positioned to offer—we have a shot.* "But we do need to focus on the war right now. What it comes down to is the modern Bakzen aren't the same Bakzen that Tarans created all those centuries ago. Now they're merciless killers, and not one left among them would negotiate a peaceful end to the conflict. Our history of fighting is far too long, and they have changed their genetic makeup to be purely creatures of war."

"And so Tarans needed their own engineered killer." Wil looked down. "Me."

"You are so much more than that, Wil. Despite what we are asking you to do, you are also the salvation for us all—our hope for a new beginning after all this horror."

"That sounds like something the Aesir said," Wil murmured.

"What did they say?"

"They told me that I was the 'first of what Tarans can become.'"

"Yes." *You can be our savior in more way than one.* "I was getting to that… All of the careful orchestration that led to your creation also means that your genetic line holds the key to repairing the anomaly that causes the Twelve-Generation Cycle."

"It does?" Wil perked up ever so slightly.

"The Priesthood was exacting with their methods. The High Dynasties, having the strongest genetic lines and the un-tampered samples in the Genetic Archive, were used to start the process. It took hundreds of years, but eventually those lines were refined—leading to your parents, and then you. Those same traits that make you able to stand up to the Bakzen are also the gaps in the genetic code that were damaged through the Priesthood's manipulation. We need a Generation Thirteen, bypassing the reset of abilities that happens after the Twelfth Generation. Your great-grandchildren should have the code to enable a patch for the rest of the population."

"Which is why you needed to find—or create—a perfect genetic match for me. Saera."

"Yes." *But I'm so glad you have her, for far different reasons.*

"However, I don't think the genetic manipulation is confined to just the Dynasties. I suspect some of the Priests are the results of experimentation themselves."

Wil bit his lip. "What do you mean?"

"I believe the Priesthood might engage in the very cloning practices they outlawed—it is the most secure way to ensure information stays within the organization."

Wil sat in thought for a moment. "Who else knows about all of this?"

"Beyond select members of the Priesthood and the Aesir, just Taelis and myself as High Commanders."

"No one else?"

Banks looked down. *No one left alive, as far as I'd known...*

"What is it?" Wil asked.

"This is dangerous information, Wil. You can't underestimate the ramifications of such knowledge."

"Clearly."

"Just be careful," Banks cautioned. "The Priesthood can't suspect a breach. They will protect these secrets by any means necessary."

Wil evaluated him. "What are you talking around?"

Banks swallowed. "There is something that not even Taelis knows, and even fewer members of the Priesthood. I think that the Dainetris Dynasty learned of the Priesthood's actions all those years ago and that is what brought about their fall."

"The documentation around that fall has always struck me as suspicious."

"The Priesthood was quite thorough with their rewriting of history. Only their position of supreme oversight for all Taran scientific information and cultural knowledge enabled them to attempt such a colossal cover-up. But physical records—those are more difficult to search out and destroy. The propaganda campaigns after the revolution took care of much of that data cleanup, but it's possible the Dainetris had a vault that some unsuspecting descendant opened a hundred years ago and learned the truth."

"And so they were silenced."

"Perhaps. I have no evidence to support the theory." *But it would seem that the Aesir feel there is something related to Dainetris worth recovering.*

Wil sat back in his chair, grating his teeth.

"I know this is a lot to take in."

Wil let out a laugh that was closer to a cry. "This one day has changed almost everything I thought I knew."

Banks frowned. "I truly wish that there had been another way. But this revelation doesn't change what we need from you now."

"I know. Even the Aesir are convinced the Bakzen need to be eliminated."

Is that so? "Thank you, Wil. We put so much weight on you, and you continue to bear it."

"Don't thank me yet. I still can't perform simultaneous observation."

Something tells me that you will be able to now, since meeting the Aesir. "It will come in time. You'll get there."

Wil rose. "Forgive me if I can't look at you for a while. I understand why you did what you did, but that doesn't excuse you from lying to me for my whole life. That'll take some time to get over."

"And forgive me for continuing to push you, even when I know you already hate me."

"Banks, I could never hate you. Not when you kept these things from me as a little kid, when there was no way I could understand how history can change and the present isn't always what it seems. You did me a kindness. None of this is either of our faults. We just have our roles to play. But right now, you're the messenger. Play dead for awhile."

‹ CHAPTER 27 ›

How could they keep the truth from me? Wil felt even more adrift than when he had first stared into the void only hours before. *I thought that learning of the Bakzen war in the rift was the extent of the secrets, but this… it casts everything in new light, and yet it can't change anything.*

Wil trudged into the quarters he shared with Saera. His wife was waiting for him on the couch in the main room.

She stood when he walked in. "Wil, I heard you got back a while ago. Where have you been?"

What can I say to her? Wil closed the door and looked down. "I'm sorry for not coming to see you earlier. I had to talk to Banks. I… learned some things that needed to be discussed."

Saera came to Wil. "I'm glad you're back safely."

"Physically, anyway." His mental state was another matter.

"What did the Aesir do to you?" She searched his face.

Wil shook his head. "No, it's not that." *They only helped me see what's been right in front of me all this time.* "There's so much…" He couldn't find the words.

Saera put her arms around him, holding his head to her shoulder. "I'm here for you. Anything you need."

Wil took a minute to gather his thoughts. "This war… We've been set up from the very beginning."

"What do you mean?" She held him at arm's length, looking

him in the eye.

If anyone else can handle the truth, it's her. But it wasn't safe to talk out loud without the security system in Banks' office. *"The Bakzen were manufactured by Tarans. Rather, by the Priesthood,"* he told her telepathically.

Saera took a sharp breath, her eyes wide. *"Manufactured?"*

"The Priesthood intended them to be a forced evolution of the Taran race." An affront to the natural pattern that the Aesir have been so careful to respect. Wil ran his fingers through his hair. *"But when things didn't go according to plan, the Priesthood drove them away. They made them into the enemy."*

"Wil…" Saera took his hand.

We're the clean-up crew. He swallowed. *"Me—us—our place in all this. It's about much more than the war. The Priesthood also attempted gene therapy in the general populace, and that manipulation resulted in the loss of telekinetic abilities for all but a few. We're the remnants. The denouncement of telekinesis, the outlaw of cloning, the war with the Bakzen—it's all the Priesthood trying to cover up their past."*

Saera shook her head, struggling to comprehend. *"How did you learn that?"*

Wil let out a pained laugh. *"That's the worst part. Banks has known all along. But it was all so clear once I met the Aesir. I just didn't have the right vantage to see it."*

Saera exhaled slowly. *"Maybe that's for the best."* Then out loud she asked, "Would you have gotten this far if you had known all along?"

"Probably not. But should I have? Should I even move forward now?" *Could I walk away, even if I wanted to?*

"Did you learn anything that changes the present?"

"I've gained a whole new perspective."

His wife stroked his hand. "But does it change the facts?"

"Everything stems from a false history—"

"But what about the hard facts of the present?" Saera pressed.

My reality has certainly changed, but I suppose this information doesn't alter present circumstances. "Not materially."

"Diplomacy has failed with the Bakzen," Saera stated. "Regardless of how things came to be this way, they have made themselves the enemy. It may not be the moral right, but their defeat is the only way for you to keep the Taran people safe."

"I wish I could be as objective as you."

Saera rubbed Wil's back. "You're a good man in your heart, Wil, no matter what actions you may need to take. I believe in you."

"And I believe in my abilities. But I don't believe in the validity of the task that's been set before me." *Yet, the Aesir insist this is the way things must be.*

"You haven't been asked to pass judgment."

"You sound just like Banks."

Saera paused. "What did the Aesir say?"

Wil hung his head. "They said the Bakzen need to be destroyed."

"Well, then—"

"I know. I just wish it didn't have to be me to do it." *Even though the Aesir also said it had to be me.*

"Whatever happens, it's on all of us."

"But me most of all."

Saera took his hand. "Believe what you want. Personally, I'd rather focus on the lives that we're *saving* through our actions."

Maybe I'll be able to see it that way in time, but I can't yet. Wil nodded.

Saera hugged him. "I love you no matter what, Wil."

"Thank you. At least one of us will."

"It's not just me. You have an amazing team that will support you through anything."

"I'm so afraid I'll let everyone down. That I won't be able to do what's necessary when the time comes."

Saera looked him in the eye. "You can do it."

The words were little consolation, but Wil latched on. *I can do it. I have to.*

The moment had finally come—the test for all Haersen had worked toward all his years in allegiance to the Bakzen.

He savored the energy flowing through him, his skin tingling and his core on fire. When he yearned for more, the power came to him. A barrier was there, but so much farther away than it had ever been before. He pressed further, stretching, until he could take no more.

As he pulled back, a smile spread across his face. He had done it. The limits of his past were finally broken. His eyes glowed with red luminescence—showing all the power he now possessed. His transformation was complete.

Tek nodded with satisfaction—a rarity in their years together. "So it worked."

Haersen's transformation had changed his appearance to nearly match that of his Bakzen comrades, but, more importantly, it had also changed the abilities he had always sought to grow. After years of waiting and hoping, he had been able to break through the limitations on his abilities that were once holding him back. More than a personal accomplishment, it meant that Tek's plan was coming to fruition.

"The former Tarans will be more than just weak slaves," Tek said, satisfaction bringing a smile to his face. "They can be enhanced, just as you have been."

"A new race for the future."

Tek nodded. "Indeed."

"It's all thanks to you." Haersen's eyes stung with tears of gratitude, but he didn't let it show. He was stronger than that now.

"I'm only doing what should have been done long ago."

"They'll thank you, once they know the gifts you can give them." Haersen knew that other Tarans wouldn't understand the Bakzen ways at first, but they would in time. Tek was the leader they needed—they all needed. Regardless of the previous Imperial Director's doubts, Tek had proven that Taran transformation was possible. Above all else, it would ensure a Bakzen victory in the war. His first two years as Imperial Director would set the tone for a new era.

"Once the TSS is out of our way, we can shape our new home."

Broadening the rift—making a place where abilities had no limits. Haersen brimmed with anticipation. "What's our next move?"

"Now we go for Tararia."

ACKNOWLEDGEMENTS

This was a milestone book for me. It's not only the longest of the novels in the series so far, but it's also getting to the core of the story I set out the write. The foundation is laid and my characters are free to grow in their world. I'm so excited that you have come along on this journey with me as a reader.

Thank you to all of my friends and family who have supported me with this crazy project. I would especially like to thank my friend Annie for her advice and encouragement. She's kept me grounded and focused, which has been invaluable.

Special thanks to my beta reading team for helping to elevate the novel: Eric, Katy, Jakeb, Bryan, Cassie, John, and Kurt. Thank you also to my mom for her tireless support, and to my amazing husband for standing by me while I pursue my dreams.

GLOSSARY

Aesir - A mysterious group of people known to be of Taran descent that live on the outskirts of explored space, engaging in metaphysical pursuits.

Agent - A class of officer within the TSS reserved for those with telekinetic and telepathic gifts. There are three levels of Agent based on level of ability: Primus, Sacon and Trion.

Baellas - A corporation run by the Baellas Dynasty, producing housewares, clothing, furniture, and other textiles for use across the Taran civilization. Additional specialty lines managed by other smaller corporations are licensed to Baellas for distribution.

Bakzen - A militaristic race living beyond the outer colonies. All Bakzen are clones, with individuals differentiated by war scars. Officers are highly intelligent and possess extensive telekinetic abilities. Drones are conditioned to follow orders but still possess moderate telekinetic capabilities.

Cadicle - The definition of individual perfection in the Priesthood's founding ideology, with emergence of the Cadicle heralding the start to the next stage of evolution for the Taran race.

Course Rank (CR) - The official measurement of an Agent's ability level, taken at the end of their training immediately before graduation from Junior Agent to Agent. The Course Rank Test is a multi-phase examination, including direct focusing of telekinetic energy into a testing sphere. The magnitude of energy focused during the exercise is the primary factor dictating the Agent's CR.

Dainetris Dynasty - Formerly a seventh High Dynasty, the Dainetris Dynasty was responsible for ship manufacturing before its fall from power.

Earth - A planet occupied by Humans, a divergent race of Tarans. Considered a "lost colony," Earth is not recognized as part of the Taran government.

High Commander - The officer responsible for the administration of the TSS. Always an Agent from the Primus class.

High Dynasties - Six families on Tararia that control the corporations critical to the functioning of Taran society. The "Big Six" each have a designated Region on Tararia, which is the seat of their power. The Dynasties in aggregate form an oligarchical government for the Taran colonies. In descending order of recognized influence, the Dynasties are: Sietinen, Vaenetri, Makaris, Monsari, Talsari, and Baellas.

Independent Jump Drive - A jump drive that does not rely on the SiNavTech beacon network for navigation, instead using a mathematical formula to calculate jump positions through normal space and the Rift.

Initiate - The second stage of the TSS training program for Agents. A trainee will typically remain at the Initiate stage for two or three years.

Jump Drive - The engine system for travel through

subspace. Conventional jump drives require an interface with the SiNavTech navigation system and subspace navigation beacons.

Junior Agent - The third stage of the TSS training program for Agents. A trainee will typically remain at the Junior Agent stage for three to five years.

Lead Agent - The highest ranking Agent and second in command to the High Commander. The Lead Agent is responsible for overseeing the Agent training program and frequently serves as a liaison for TSS business with Taran colonies.

Lower Dynasties - There are 247 recognized Lower Dynasties in Taran society. Many of these families have a presence on Tararia, but some are residents of the other inner colonies.

Makaris Corp - A corporation run by the Makaris High Dynasty responsible for the distribution of food, water filters, and other necessary supplies to Taran colonies without diverse natural resources.

Monsari Power Solutions (MPS) - A corporation run by the Monsari Dynasty, responsible for power generation systems for the Taran worlds, including geothermal generators, portable generators, and reactors to power spacecrafts.

Rift - A habitable pocket between normal space and subspace.

Sacon - The middle tier of TSS Agents. Typically, Sacon Agents will score a CR between 6 and 7.9.

SiNavTech - A corporation run by the Sietinen High Dynasty, which controls and maintains the subspace navigation network used by Taran civilians and the TSS.

Starstone – An extremely rare gem. Only ten such gem veins know anywhere in the galaxy, and each of the six High Dynasties has claim to one. Only enough material for one set of wedding rings is produced by each vein every generation. Starstones emit a luminescent resonance when positioned near other stones cut from the same vein.

TalEx - A corporation run by the Talsari Dynasty, managing mining operations and ore processing across Taran territories.

Tarans - The general term for all individuals with genetic relation to Tararian ancestry. Several divergent races are recognized by their planet or system.

Tararia - The home planet for the Taran race and seat of the central government.

Tararian Selective Service (TSS) - A military organization with two divisions: (1) Agent Class, and (2) Militia Class. Agents possess telekinetic and telepathic abilities; the TSS is the only place where individuals with such gifts can gain official training. The Militia class offers a formal training program for those without telekinetic abilities, providing tactical and administrative support to Agents. The Headquarters is located inside the moon of the planet Earth. Additional Militia training facilities are located throughout the Taran colonies.

Trainee - The generic term for a student of the TSS, and also the term for first year Agent students (when capitalized Trainee).

Students are not fully "initiated" into the TSS until their second year.

Trion - The lowest tier of TSS Agents. Typically, Trion Agents will score a CR below 5.9.

Priesthood of the Cadicle - A formerly theological institution responsible for oversight of all governmental affairs and the flow of information throughout the Taran colonies. The Priesthood has jurisdiction over even the High Dynasties and provides a tiebreaking vote on new initiatives proposed by the High Dynasty oligarchy.

Primus - The highest of three Agent classes within the TSS, reserved for those with the strongest telekinetic abilities. Typically, Primus Agents will score a CR above 8.

Primus Elite - A new classification of Agent above Primus signifying an exceptional level of ability.

VComm – A telecommunications corporation owned and operated by the Vaenetri Dynasty.

ABOUT THE AUTHOR

Amy has always loved science fiction—books, movies, shows and games. After devouring some of the classics like Dune and Ender's Game in her tween years, she began writing short stories.

In the ensuing years, Amy attended the Vancouver School of Arts and Academics in Vancouver, Wash., where she studied creative writing. She eventually became a Psychology major at Portland State University, but also pursued a minor in Professional Writing. After graduating, she stumbled into a career as a proposal manager.

Amy currently lives in Portland, Oregon. When she's not writing, she enjoys travel, wine tasting, binge-watching TV series and playing epic strategy board games.

Made in the USA
Charleston, SC
07 March 2016